Also by John Ellsworth

THADDEUS MURFEE SERIES

The Defendants
Beyond a Reasonable Death
Attorney at Large
Chase, the Bad Baby
Defending Turquoise
The Mental Case
Unspeakable Prayers
The Girl Who Wrote The New York Times Bestseller (April 2015)
The Trial Lawyer

SISTERS IN LAW SERIES

Frat Party: Sisters In Law (June 2015)
Hellfire: Sisters In Law (July 2015)

DEFENDING TURQUOISE

A Novel

JOHN ELLSWORTH

For Turquoise, for the Dine

ONE

In Flagstaff the flow of Mexican drugs never faltered. In late December a suitcase arrived by train, bound for Boston. A Mexican national named Hermano Sanchez had stuck the claim ticket in his Stetson hatband. It connected him to enough marijuana to supply homecoming at a small college.

The suitcase rattled along the Amtrak conveyor belt while Queenie alerted and tracked along. Drug Task Force agent Avram Goloff hit PAUSE. The conveyor lurched to a stop, Queenie went on point, and the suitcase was jimmied.

DTF agents matched the contents in the luggage to the mahogany face in the waiting room, first bench, first Stetson. He had planted himself the closest he could get to the baggage window. On delivery, that suitcase would net him $1,000 and he wasn't about to let it get away.

Hermano Sanchez was desperate for the money. It was needed back home to save his family from the cartels. Instead, he was ID'd where he sat nervously picking at a backhand scab while he waited for the luggage to emerge. DTF clamped him with handcuffs and hauled him away in the back of a black SUV.

Sanchez's initial reaction was shock. He had been unprepared for the ubiquitous presence of American law enforcement. No one had told him they would be everywhere. No one had told him it would be like this at all.

He was a stooped, thin little man with close-set eyes that crossed and uncrossed in a glance, stubby teeth, and hands hardened from years of digging trenches in the caliche of northern Mexico. On his head perched a straw Stetson knockoff from Taiwan, unfit for the swirling snow of Flagstaff winters.

The next morning Sanchez appeared before Judge H. Ivan Trautman. Trautman was a man infatuated with religion who bore precious little patience for sinners. He had single-handedly populated an entire wing of the Winslow Prison with *narcotraficantes*. He feverishly hated each and every one and refused to include them when he prayed his prayer list.

Waist- and ankle-chained, Sanchez shuffled up to the podium. The interpreter reported that Sanchez was penniless.

Charged with a crime for which he was facing twenty-five years without parole, Sanchez was entitled to a free lawyer.

Judge Trautman asked the clerk for the next name up on the list of attorneys accepting criminal appointments.

That would be Thaddeus Murfee, said the clerk.

Judge Trautman scowled. Were it not for the rotation, the judge would have preferred any lawyer to Thaddeus Murfee. But he was stuck this time.

The case was trailed on the docket while the bailiff called Attorney Murfee to court. It was a short walk for Murfee. His office was just across the street in the Bank of America building.

On that icy December morning the young, dark-haired lawyer, wearing a Brooks Brothers three-piece, glossy shoes, starched white shirt, and foulard necktie made the slippery trek across Aspen Street. Upstairs, in the attorneys' conference room off Judge Trautman's court, Thaddeus sat opposite Sanchez. The room was sweltering, thanks to the thumping radiator pipes. The air reeked of stale coffee from the abandoned Starbucks cups littering the table.

The interpreter, a female grad student at NAU in Romance languages, made it a threesome.

Introductions were made and Thaddeus gave Sanchez a friendly smile.

"The court has appointed me to defend you. Do you understand?"

Sanchez listened to the interpreter and then nodded. "*Sí, tú eres mi abogado.*" You are my lawyer.

"And I want to help you. The judge has set your bail at fifteen thousand dollars. That means you will need fifteen hundred dollars to bail out. Can you put your hands on that much cash?"

He might as well have asked if Sanchez would mind flying to the moon and back.

His dark eyes glistening, the little Mexican shook his head. "I don't have any money at all," the interpreter relayed. "They gave me ten dollars for food when I left. Nothing since."

"The men who hired you to bring the drugs——will they help you with money for bail?"

"They will say they never knew me."

"Figures. Well, I can tell you up front, Judge Trautman won't let you out without cash bail. He doesn't release on your signature, nothing like that."

The little Mexican's eyes filled with tears. "Maria," he said through the interpreter, "I must get back to her with money to move her away! I can't be kept here!"

"Ask him about Maria, tell me her situation," Thaddeus told the interpreter. She translated and Sanchez responded with a rambling tale about *narcotraficantes, prostitución infantil,* and *dólares.* The upshot was that all normal commerce in the border town of Nogales had disappeared. All that was left were impoverished Mexicans, set to prey upon one another by the cartels. No one was safe there, not even the children, who were forced to join gangs or be raped. Sanchez's daughter, Maria, was nine and she had already been threatened with sexual assault if she didn't participate in drug trafficking. Sanchez had stepped in and brought the marijuana up from Mexico in an effort to obtain $1,000 and move his family deeper into the Mexican interior, away from the cartels. Only then could his family exist in safety. He had served as proxy for Maria, who otherwise would have been forced to smuggle drugs across the border on foot.

Thaddeus nodded and reached over and squeezed the little man's shoulder. It wasn't the first time he had heard such a story. Truth be told, it was commonplace. Starving Mexicans forced by drug lords to smuggle; high-risk ventures that more often than not ended in arrest. Whatever happened on the other end to the destitute Mexican families was of no concern to the American courts. Thaddeus knew this and wanted to help. He watched the little Mexican's eyes cross and uncross and he knew the man's life was hopeless, that he would likely never see Maria and his family again. Not in this lifetime.

Then Thaddeus surprised himself. "Tell him that someone is going to make his bail. Tell him to come across the street to my office when they let him out this afternoon."

The interpreter hesitated. She had interpreted thousands of cases and knew it was unethical for a lawyer to expend personal funds for a client's bail. She had never delivered such a message to a defendant. But in the end it wasn't her call. She was only the messenger. So she passed along the information and immediately Sanchez's face brightened. His eyes regained some luster and he sat upright for the first time since arriving on American soil. Someone was actually going to extend a hand!

Sanchez nodded and promised to appear when released.

Handshakes followed and Thaddeus opened the door and told the deputy they had finished. The deputy took Sanchez by the waist chain and escorted him out.

"Are you sure about this?" the court reporter asked Thaddeus when they were alone.

"What can I say?" said Thaddeus. "It's one time too many hearing the same tale. Sooner or later, someone has to actually do something to help."

"I'm sworn to secrecy," the court reporter said.

"Everything you heard here is strictly confidential," he agreed.

"I know, I know. It's nothing I would ever repeat anyway. I feel horrible for these people."

"That makes two of us," Thaddeus said, and gathered his briefcase and topcoat.

Judge Trautman was waiting. "Well?" he asked Thaddeus when he reappeared in the courtroom.

"No conflicts, Your Honor. I accept the assignment."

"How very thoughtful of you," the judge said with all the sarcasm he could muster.

"About bail—"

"Fifteen thousand, Mr. Murfee, so save your breath. No reduction. Your man needs ten percent to lose the orange jumpsuit."

"I wasn't going to ask for reduction, Your Honor. I was going to ask if he could be released to my custody. I'll take responsibility for him."

The judge cocked his head. "I see. You must have discovered some way you're related to Mr. Sanchez? That's why you're treating him like family? But the answer is no. You've been in trouble in here yourself and there's no way I would release a prisoner into your custody. Is your own probation even up?"

"One month to go."

"Get back to your office and focus on something else. We're in recess. The clerk will give you an arraignment date."

Thaddeus began buttoning up his coat and avoiding all eyes.

TWO

He was twenty-nine and a criminal attorney achieving success after success. The angels had bent low and touched him with the gift of jury persuasion.

He had won eleven difficult jury trials in a row and had won some regional fame in northern Arizona. For that, Sanchez could be grateful.

But Thaddeus Murfee came with his own baggage. While he now served on the State Bar Committee on Drugs and Alcohol, he had previously struggled with addiction.

Beginning back in Chicago, following his daughter's kidnapping and his own torture, problems had erupted. Sarai, his four-year-old, stopped talking. She ceased acknowledging anyone. At first, the parents blamed the kidnapping. Then the mother blamed the father, whose money invited the kidnapping. The father fought back. The parents had taken to attributing blame late into the night. Doors were slammed and nasty words spoken. Hearts broke and silence settled over the small family like a gathering of dark spirits.

Many nights they arrived home separately, sometimes very late. Sometimes one or both smelled of expensive fragrances not their own. Sometimes they were addled with alcohol. Thaddeus went down the black hole first, drinking heavier and staying out sometimes all night, when no good is ever done. Frustrated and frightened, Katy changed the locks early one evening and wouldn't allow him back inside even as he stood beneath their window and begged forgiveness. She had turned her back and returned to bed, pulling the pillow over her head and crying into its cool side. A conservatorship for his assets was established. A mutually agreed separation followed.

His life in disarray, Thaddeus fled Chicago.

Arriving in Flagstaff, he had wrangled admission to the bar and had made a go of it for six months. But then the roof caved in.

After his arrest for drunk driving and assault on a police officer, his case was assigned to Judge H. Ivan Trautman. The angry zealot had yanked his driver's license and consigned him to six month's probation. A public censure in the *State Bar Journal* was printed and distributed to 250,000 lawyers in Illinois and Arizona. Plus he had suffered a thirty-minute harangue by the judge in open court, while the young attorney's peers smirked and poked each other. Judge Trautman seemed not to notice.

Thaddeus had some days later cried with relief when the State Bar intervened and helped him get medical treatment for his drinking. Ever since treatment, he had remained clean and sober, the picture of a moth that had singed his wings at the flame. Now he spent noon hours in AA meetings, talking recovery. His law practice once again flourished.

THREE

When Judge Trautman asked if his own probation was up, it left Thaddeus' face burning. This time no one was laughing; all eyes were downcast. Even for his competitors it was too much to watch the judge slice and dice what little self-respect remained. He hurried for the double doors, fighting down the urge to break into a run.

He was determined to get Sanchez back to his family. After lunch, Thaddeus went to see the prosecutor. Her name was Roslin Russell—everyone called her Wrasslin for her propensity for throwdowns in the courtroom. Would the prosecutor sign an agreed order reducing the bail to a signature bond? Laughter erupted from Wrasslin and she hit her desk hard enough to cause her secretary to ask if everything was okay in there.

"We're fine," said the prosecutor. "Just lost it a second.

15

Thaddeus, get the fuck out of here. That guy had enough pot to fog up the city and kill mosquitoes. There's no way I'm agreeing to a signature bond. He'll flee to Mexico and never come back just as soon as he walks out."

Thaddeus shook his head. "I get that, but Hermano has a nine-year-old daughter who will probably be sexually assaulted if he doesn't get back pronto with a thousand bucks. Can't you give someone a break just this one time?"

"Why don't you just plead him instead?"

"What are you looking for?"

"Three years, no good-time, five years' probation."

"What the hell good does that do? He doesn't go home for three years!"

"Hey, you asked, I'm telling. No bail reduction, no probation without incarceration on the front end. Fifty pounds, Thaddeus."

"Your offer is rejected."

Thaddeus stood and began buttoning his coat. "I'll go give him the bad news."

"Doesn't he have anyone from Sinaloa who'll make his bail?"

It was snarky, Sinaloa being the drug capital.

"Cartel contacts? LMAO. This guy's as green as they come."

"Lucky he has you then. With your help he'll only wind up doing five years, 'cause you'll be bullheaded enough to take it to trial and lose and then Judge Trautman gets to blow the fuck out of his life and give him a maximum sentence. Poor schmuck. You were just leaving, please."

"Thanks for nothing."

"Anytime, friend. Go see your boy and give him the news. And why sweat it anyway? The state is paying you a hundred fifty an hour for your services. You'll make out."

"Right."

"Oh, and one more thing to remember."

16

"Yes?"

"It ain't the last drink gets you drunk, it's the first. Stay sober."

"Oh, so now you're an addiction expert? Any other super powers we should know about?"

Which is why Thaddeus paid the bail. Out of his own money. He knew it violated several ethical rules. He knew he was in deep trouble. But he did it anyway.

Just before five o'clock a bedraggled Hermano Sanchez appeared in the waiting room of Thaddeus' office in the Bank of America building. Thaddeus was down at the Sunshine Cafe with a client. He never saw Sanchez walk past on his way down to the Greyhound station. Nor would it have made any difference in the ultimate outcome: Hermano Sanchez was a homing pigeon on a straight-through to Nogales, where he would again enter the fight for the safekeeping of his little family. He was gone, Christine told Thaddeus back at the office. Long gone. Did he say anything? "*Gracias*. He said *gracias*."

Thaddeus' heart flip-flopped. He had actually broken the rules and given a jerk like Trautman access to his life.

There was not a shred of doubt in the young lawyer's mind that he would most likely never see Sanchez again and his bail would be revoked and the judge would look to Thaddeus to make up the other ninety percent. Much, much direr, however, was the certainty that the identity of the person who had bailed out Sanchez in the first place would come to the judge's attention. He would nail Thaddeus, a misfit judge's dream come true.

Which is exactly what happened seven days later when the case was called for arraignment and only Thaddeus showed up.

"Mr. Murfee," said the red-faced judge, his lower lip trembling, "I am not hearing good things. Where is your client Hermano Sanchez?"

That evening, back home, he told his estranged wife what had happened. It was time for their every-other-day catch-up call. He had been convincing his wife that he was done with drinking. The calls had been increasing.

"Repeat that again, please," Katy asked. "Go slow."

"I paid this guy's bail. Of course he left town and I haven't seen him since. I'm sure he's back in Mexico."

"That seems like a good thing to do, helping someone out like that. So what happened in court?"

"Judge Trautman found out I was the one who paid the bail with my own money. Now the court is after me for the other fourteen grand plus Trautman is having me appear in the morning on contempt charges."

"But I don't get it," his wife exclaimed, "you were only helping!"

"Katy, a lawyer is not allowed to make a client's bail. It's unethical. I wouldn't be at all surprised if he jerked my license to practice law."

"Can he do that?"

"In a heartbeat."

She went quiet.

"I was an idiot," he said. "I laid my license on the line for a guy I'll probably never see again."

"You trusted him to show up. He owed you that. Owes you that."

"Then I lied to this judge. In court, this morning."

"You lied? What for?"

He swallowed hard. "I did. He asked me where the money came from that I used for the bail."

"And you told him it was your own, of course."

"That's just it, I didn't."

"Go on."

"I told him a Mexican man I'd never seen before dropped it off at the office."

"Is that true?"

"Purely a figment of my imagination."

"You lied to the judge?"

"I was scared. And the courtroom was packed with other lawyers, Thaddeus haters. I couldn't stand to have him torture me again. So I lied and came up with this dog-and-pony story about a Mexican mystery man."

"You've got to go tell him you made a mistake."

"Judge Trautman doesn't do mistakes. He sends people to jail."

FOUR

The next morning he appeared before Judge Trautman at ten o'clock sharp. The courtroom was packed with the local bar and browsing reporters and sundry onlookers and gossips. To Thaddeus' dismay, the judge called his case first.

"Mr. Murfee, yesterday I asked you to bring me a copy of the receipt your office gave to the man who paid the bail in this case. Did you bring that to me this morning?"

"No, Your Honor, I didn't."

"May I ask where it is?"

"It doesn't exist."

"How could that be? This was a transaction required to be in writing."

"I made it up about the Mexican man with the money. I posted the bail myself."

20

"Out of your own money?"

"Out of my own money."

"Then you compounded that sin by coming in here and lying to the court about the source of the bail?"

You could have heard a pin drop. Every eye, every ear, was riveted.

"Since you put it that way, yes, that sin was compounded."

"Very well. I am going to make a referral to the district attorney's office and recommend to them that you be charged with perjury, which is a felony. And I'm also suspending you from practice. Effective immediately."

"Judge, I have other cases, I represent other—"

"Return the client fees. They can all find other lawyers. They'll have to."

"Can't you give me a lead time of thirty days to put my affairs in order?"

"Mr. Murfee, from the looks of things, your affairs are never going to be in order. And giving you another thirty days to wreak havoc on the public with your law license isn't going to help. You, sir, are formally suspended. Starting now. Madam Clerk, call the next case on the docket. Good day, Mr. Murfee."

He kicked himself back across street to his office. It was snowing again and slushy along Aspen Street. A four-wheeler blasted past, spraying a slurry of water and ice against his trousers. He stepped up on the curb and shook his fist. "Damnation!" he screamed. *Where was your head at!* Thaddeus cried inside. *Making bail for a client? Where was my thinking? I know better than that! Five years practicing law, that's a rookie mistake. No, not even a rookie would be that dumb. You allowed your heart to get involved in your law work and that's a no-no. You cannot afford to have feelings for your clients!*

The shame was overwhelming. He suddenly wanted to flee. But he couldn't leave. That would make him a fugitive. He was going to be charged with perjury. And he was guilty. Brother, he was very guilty. He could actually wind up in prison over this.

He checked his watch. 10:35. Too early for the noon AA meeting, too late for the ten o'clock. A deepening scowl settled across his face. He hurried inside the bank building and repeatedly punched the elevator button, wild with anxiety. He just needed to go inside his office and shut the door.

Fortunately for Thaddeus, the district attorney, John Steinmar, had a heart. He called Thaddeus over to his office, told him he had reviewed the file, and he had declined to prosecute for perjury. He was going to instead go with a misdemeanor obstruction of justice. Reason? Thaddeus was already on probation for the drunk driving charge. If he got convicted of a felony while on probation, he would lose his law license permanently and do some serious time in the penitentiary. District Attorney Steinmar wasn't comfortable with that happening; especially since he was up for reelection and he hinted that a sizable donation to his reelection campaign would help keep his thinking clear about it. Thaddeus got the message.

He returned to his office and told Christine she was to issue a check for ten thousand dollars to the District Attorney's Committee to Reelect. Then he went inside his office and shut the door. Following which, he shut his eyes and tried to understand what had happened to him in the past year.

An hour later he was no closer to an answer than he had been at the outset. He sent out for sandwiches and ate alone in his office, chewing a tuna sandwich and slurping coffee out of Styrofoam as he considered his next move. Law practice was definitely out. Then there was the problem of money. What he had was tied up in a conservatorship Katy had obtained from the court when he couldn't stay sober and was drunkenly burning dollars. Truth was, he was $1,500 away from being flat broke. He received $5,000 a month out of the conservatorship and that was all but gone. Income from clients went right back out for overhead. Thank heavens Christine had been paid Friday and today was only Tuesday. As of five o'clock he would owe her for two days. He would use the rest of what he had to give her severance pay and then it was all gone, all of it. He was actually going to have to get a job. But where? Doing what? A twenty-nine-year-old lawyer with no license? No law firm would touch him, not even for a paralegal position, not while he was disbarred.

Later that night, Katy would share with him by telephone, "From what my law friends tell me it's not much of an offense to bail someone out of jail. That's just an ethical violation."

"But then I lied to the judge."

"Hell, honey, every lawyer lies to the judge. That's why they call it court. You're appearing in front of a king in his royal court. You have to lie or face the consequences."

"What might those be?"

She made a slicing noise, as one drawing a finger across her own throat. "Off with his head!"

"But I got caught."

"That's because you told the truth. You had to. But I've warned you that honesty and lawyering are mutually exclusive. Yet you still insist on law practice even when you don't have to anymore. There's enough money for the rest of our lives and Sarai's life in the conservatorship."

"But I believe in helping people through law. It's what I do."

"It's what you did, you mean. You've been officially retired for one year."

He felt a stab of pain. He was going to hate not practicing. It defined who he was, for better or worse. He could think of no higher calling than helping people when the law threatened. He loved to interject himself into the middle of a dispute and say "No" to the process and turn it around in his client's favor. That was something worth doing with his life.

She drove home her point. "It's worth repeating. Law and ethics don't mix well, especially for someone like you who actually believes in a thing called justice. But you wouldn't listen. See? I'm not so dumb after all!"

"Nobody ever said you were dumb."

"Then why aren't you here with me instead of two thousand miles away? I miss you."

His face brightened. "Yeah?"

"Sarai and I need you to come home. You've lost your license for a year, you have nothing holding you there."

"I'd drive you nuts, being around all day not working. You'd be trying to go to med school, I'd be bitching and moaning about how bored I am. I don't think so."

"Take Sarai to the park. Take her to the zoo, the Shedd Aquarium. She'd even go with you to those damn Bulls games. She's great company."

"Except she won't speak."

"Having you around full time might change that. We won't know if we don't try."

"I hit a wall in Chicago. I couldn't stay sober there. I'm not sure I'm ready for that."

"Take your time coming home. Drive. Go down through the South. See the magnolias, it's like summer down there. Work on a shrimp boat for a couple of weeks."

"I think I need to just do something totally different for a while. Like driving a truck—good, honest work."

"Get real!"

"I am real. I'm thinking North Dakota. Oil Fields. Driving a truck up there."

"I hate fracking. Think of something else."

"I'll work on it. Call you tomorrow."

North Dakota? Where had that come from? He'd never been. But it represented a place where he had no history, a place where he could start over. But would it just be a geographic, the kind they warn about in meetings? Probably so, but so what? At least he'd be sober. That—sobriety—was one thing he wasn't sure Chicago could help him with. He flipped open the laptop and started clicking away.

It was a year and he knew nothing about North Dakota. It was time to start reading.

FIVE

During the twelve-month ban from law he spent a good portion of that time in North Dakota, driving a Ford F-250 with a monstrous diesel engine. He towed a fifth wheel flatbed and delivered drilling supplies to the oil fields. It didn't require a CDL and he didn't have to join a union.

He lived in a man dorm—a rented house with seven other men, two to a bedroom. Housing was extremely scarce and he considered it a huge piece of luck that he had found a place to crash while he put in his sixteen-hour days. He earned enough to support Katy and Sarai long-distance, plus they were keeping half of his conservatorship money each month. So the bills were paid and they were keeping up with Katy's med school tuition.

For a while, his outlook was improving and he began to have hope again. Sometime in the future he would complete his suspension and get his license back. That kept him going even on those cold, dark days in North Dakota when the wind howled like a banshee, his face and hands chapped from overexposure, and the snow blew in crazy circles around his truck as he made his way from delivery to pickup to delivery. He drank gallons of coffee, puffed away on e-cigs to help pass the time in the cab of his truck, and slept like a baby at night. Life was better than bearable; at times it was actually good.

At Katy's spring break, Thaddeus flew to Scottsdale from North Dakota while Katy and Sarai flew from Chicago to meet him. They spent a week relaxing poolside at the Phoenician. Sarai swam and spent hours slathered in sunblock at Surge, the interactive spray at the end of the Oasis pool complex. She squealed down the waterslide and enjoyed the falling buckets of water and misting turtles and water cannons.

In the afternoons when the sun would damage skin, they kept her inside their suite and encouraged her to play video games. She still refused to speak. The psychiatrist explained that the kidnapping had significantly altered her emotional health. PTSD was the official working diagnosis. The video games held her interest more than anything else. Thaddeus and Katy cheered her on to repeat the words and phrases the games delivered. It was a glorious day when the first word was uttered, and her parents held each other and wept. Sarai looked at them quizzically and went right back to the console.

At night the parents made love and talked for hours while relaxing at the in-room spa. They sipped coffee and devoured fresh pastries. Mornings saw Thaddeus working out while Katy babysat, then they would trade off and Katy would have her turn.

Then the mother and daughter returned to Chicago. Thaddeus returned to North Dakota and kicked it into high gear. The time flew by as long as he kept up the sixteen-hour days.

He received his license back six months later. His shiny new bar card was inspected and admired. He was free to practice again.

SIX

He took a week driving from North Dakota down to Flagstaff. He enjoyed the mountains and high plains and laid his plans. Just outside Flagstaff he found a house on five acres that backed up to national forest. Ponderosas dotted his land and flowed into the refuge provided by the two-million-acre forest.

He took to dining out with other Flagstaff attorneys, particularly those who weren't engaged in the practice of criminal law and might therefore need to make a referral here and there. There were plenty of steak and lobster dinners, Mexican restaurants, and a lunch date almost daily. Money wasn't a problem so he was free to spend; besides supporting Katy and Sarai, he had managed to squirrel away $75,000 in North Dakota and now was when he would need it. He hated to admit it, but he held a special gratitude for fracking, though he knew Katy would violently object.

DEFENDING TURQUOISE

Lunch with Shep Aberdeen was productive. Shep was a stout, muscular man from Durango who practiced criminal law and raised white-faced cattle. He was medium height with brown hair kept long in back, rimless spectacles, and a mouthful of teeth that produced a refrigerator-white smile. He twiddled his thumbs when his hands weren't busy animating his conversation. Perched on his middle finger, right hand was a turquoise ring almost as large as your palm. They had met and become friends through various CLE seminars. Thaddeus found Shep to be a likable guy and there had been an immediate affinity. More than once they had referred cases back and forth, and Shep was game to pick right back up where they had left off.

"Still think Trautman booted your ass on a bum rap," Shep said over mushroom burgers and tea down at Kathy's Kafe. "A public censure would have been more in line with the severity of the crime, which was bullshit to begin with."

"Agree," said Thaddeus between bites. "But Trautman has hated me since my DUI."

"Little bastard. He just can't stand the idea that someone might be having more fun carousing around in the bars than him staying home with his Bible. He suffers from short man syndrome and he's a ruthless dick besides a wild-eyed religious zealot."

"Thanks, but how do you really feel? Anyway, technically he was right to jerk my license. It sure as hell could have been a lot worse."

"Thank goodness the DA's office gave you a break."

"That's what I'm talking about. It could have been worse."

Shep took a swig of iced tea and leaned close conspiratorially. "Just watch your back. Little bird told me that Trautman's going to try to get you on something else and see you do time. Evidently he's not through with you, Thad."

"Thanks. I'll watch my step."

29

SEVEN

In the summer, Katy came out with Sarai. She had a summer internship with Indian Health Services. On the Navajo reservation, she began meeting new people with whom she had everything in common as she was Navajo and back home herself. And she began running into family members, people to whom she was related by blood but had never met. One of those was a grandniece named Turquoise Begay. She was fifteen and attending the small animal clinic in high school. Turquoise came to the medical clinic with an STD. Katy treated her and prescribed medicine. The girl began calling her and it appeared she had found a long-lost older sister.

They became confidants.

And Katy took up her cause. She promised the girl she would protect her. Turquoise was related by blood and she was a patient and

30

Katy would save her.

Gonorrhea was a family disease on the reservation; a family disease because it was passed around inside the family.

At least that was the story given to the caseworker by Turquoise.

EIGHT

Angelina Steinmar lived in a residential neighborhood northwest of downtown Flagstaff. Her husband was the district attorney and she worked for the Department of Children and Family Services (DCFS). People referred to the husband-wife team as double dippers: both on the public teat.

DCFS got wind that Turquoise had been treated by the Indian Health Services clinic for gonorrhea. She was a minor, so the DCFS through Angelina responded, facilitating an intervention.

She drove out to the girl's trailer and found her home alone, frying a hamburger patty on a griddle meant for waffles. The girl seemed to be oblivious to the juxtaposition of beef patty and waffle griddle. She poked and flipped the patty as she vaguely answered Angelina's first inquiries. In fact, if Angelina hadn't asked and been satisfied the answer was truthful, she would have thought the girl high on dope. But she wasn't; she was just immature and overly sheltered, not by doting parents but by the circumstance of living ten miles out on a remote highway, far from any neighbors, classmates, or other members of her tribe who might have provided support if they'd known of her *de facto* abandonment by her father. Angelina could see the girl just didn't know better than to be cooking a hamburger on a waffle griddle. It was a short assumption for her to make that the girl was equally naive about protection against STDs. Which traditionally, on the reservation, were the offspring of family rape.

"How did you acquire the STD?" was question twelve on the DCFS interview sheet > sexually transmitted diseases > sub-part C.

The girl crossed her arms defensively, a blackened spatula dangling from one hand. "Do I have to answer?"

"Please. It's my job to find out so I can help you."

"My uncle Randy. He's the only one who'll have me."

"What does that mean?"

The girl shrugged and one-handed a square of paper towel. She wiped spattered grease from the Formica counter. "He tells me he's the only one who'll ever want me. He tells me I've been ruined for anyone else."

"Heaven help us," muttered Angelina. "Where is this Uncle Randy right now?"

"Kayenta. He's selling a cow."

"Is he coming back here?"

"He's always here. When he's not at a party."

"Does he live here?"

"Pretty much."

"This is two bedrooms. Does he sleep on the couch?"

"He sleeps with me until sunrise, then sneaks out on the couch."

"So Uncle Randy has been sleeping with you. Having sex with you?"

"He fucks me."

"I want you to come with me tonight."

"Do I have to?"

"Yes."

"What if I don't want to go? What if I won't go?"

"Then I'll phone the police and have you removed. You don't want that, believe me."

"Can I eat first?"

"Certainly. Take your time. What time will Randy get back?"

"Probably late. Maybe in the morning. He goes to the party after he gets money."

"Sure he does."

Angelina removed the child that night. She drove her back to Flagstaff and made an overnight placement.

The next day she filed a petition for dependency. A hearing was held and a temporary placement in a foster home was made. Unhappy and missing her father, Turquoise hitchhiked out of Flagstaff, back to the reservation.

She arrived home on a Wednesday afternoon.

Randy Begay stormed inside the trailer that night, knocking over a lamp and burning a hole in the thin carpet with his cigarette.

He found Turquoise in the back bedroom and forced himself on her.

The next day she called Angelina and reported the assault. Then she called Katy Murfee and made an appointment at the clinic. She had pain in her pelvis and was afraid the STD had returned. Katy called Angelina and discussed the situation with her. Something had to be done.

Angelina was furious and swore to the girl she would protect her. But she also knew the uncle was going to be a huge problem because he would always find the girl and abuse her once again.

Something more was called for.

NINE

Then the summer was over and Katy found it difficult to return to Chicago. First semester was put on hold. It was more important to work through several family issues, beginning with Thaddeus.

Then there was Sarai. The little girl had come a long way and was talking now and even held out her hands to Thaddeus when he kissed her goodbye in the mornings. He would swoop her up and whisper in her ear and get her to smile. Then he would turn her over to her mom and head up to the office.

He needed another man to talk to. Someone who wouldn't ever turn around and repeat his words.

So, Thaddeus made the two-hour drive and spent a Saturday with his old friend Henry Landers. Henry was a Navajo shepherd who had survived over a century and was happy to tell how. He was still actively caring for a herd of 220 Navajo-Churro sheep, while his mind and physical health were as good as they had been at forty. Henry was also Katy's great-grandfather and he had saved Thaddeus' life, literally, at one time.

Henry listened over coffee and donuts and thought long and hard about what Thaddeus shared: He had described his troubles with Katy and his drinking and the problems with Hermano Sanchez when he paid the man's bail. H. Ivan Trautman was described in detail and his hatred for Thaddeus recounted several times.

"Your problems are bigger than the problems," Henry finally pronounced.

Thaddeus held a donut inches from his mouth. "What in hell does that mean?"

The old man smiled and blew on his coffee. "The problems are real. But your problems you are making up and telling yourself about the real problems—not good. There's what's holding you back."

"My problems are bigger than the actual problems. That's amazing."

"Yes. You're a good man, Thaddeus. You got in trouble because you are a good man."

"Thank you."

"The white man's law is never true, not to my heart. In our culture we do whatever we can to help one another. In the white man's culture—in your law—it is possible to do too much. That amazes the Indian. There are no limits on good in our world. There are in yours. But your laws are artificial and they exist for reasons that are always about money and greed. You can't pay a client's bail because that might make other clients come to you too. That's crazy. If you want to help, you should be totally free to help. You are to be held up as an example of what's good in a man, not made an example of by losing your license. How sad."

"I'm going to have to mull this over," Thaddeus said.

Henry smiled. "You be sure and do that."

On the drive back home, his thoughts took flight. *I'm a trial lawyer, dammit! I want to try cases, prove why many of these folks aren't really guilty of anything, and do what I do best! But for Hermano Sanchez and his beat-down family and the hell he was living in, I gave it all up. For one case I turned myself over to the hands of the prosecutors and a hateful judge. I've had enough deep periods of depression and paralyzing anxiety. Can I ever shine again?*

He vowed to himself that somehow, someway, he would scramble his way back on top. He would make the phones ring again with people who came to him for his reputation. It had happened before, it *would* happen again.

TEN

She attempted suicide two times, two weeks apart. On the second try, she was successful.

Her name was Hamilton "Hammy" Steinmar and she was seventeen and a freshman at the University of Arizona, where she had pledged Alpha Nu, made the freshman swim team in the 200 freestyle, and was turned down in tryouts for the cheerleading squad. It wasn't the cheerleading rejection that prompted the suicide, however.

It was her father.

Her father was John Steinmar, the duly elected district attorney of Coconino County, Arizona. He was married to Angelina Steinmar, the five-foot-eleven mother of Hamilton, member of the Northern Arizona Botanical Society, wine connoisseur, and caseworker for the Department of Children and Family Services.

38

DEFENDING TURQUOISE

DCFS was a full-time job and kept her away from home for long hours. As a result, daughter Hammy, while a preteen, had often found herself alone at night with her father while mother was away at work, intervening in the life and family situation of some poor abused or neglected child in a jurisdiction that stretched from Williams to Winslow, including a third of the Navajo Reservation. It was on those long nights that father forced himself on daughter.

It continued for four years. While at home from college on Thanksgiving break, Hammy made her first suicide attempt. She had never seriously considered killing herself before that Thanksgiving night, but this time was different. There had been a struggle in the bathroom as she was finishing with her bath, father against daughter. She had cried and begged him to leave the room. She told him she had been away to school and learned that other girls had never had sex with their fathers and, rather, their fathers kept them on pedestals and did everything possible to help them through life.

Her words had enraged him and he had choked her with a bath towel so as not to leave marks around her throat. She had passed out, only to regain consciousness with him inside her, panting heavily against her ear, their upper bodies semi-attached with sweat and bathwater. Wordlessly he had climbed to his feet and faced her while drying his penis with a washcloth. When he was done, he zipped up his pants and raised his right hand, index finger extended. "Not one word," he demanded. Then he had left her to her toilette.

She wiped herself clean and shrugged into her blue and white bathrobe. For several minutes she stood before the mirror, disoriented and staring wildly into her own eyes. "If only, if only, if only," her brain repeated on full loop. Then, as she struggled with forming a coherent thought, she pawed through the medicine cabinet. Spinning the bottles label-out, reading, reading, she had finally settled on one bearing her mother's name. Prescribed by Dr. Francis L. Prine, it was labeled Xanax. She dropped the bottle into the pocket of her bathrobe and disappeared into her bedroom.

Hammy had never tried cocaine but she had heard of doing lines. So she knelt down bedside and pushed and turned the medicine bottle. She arranged the Xanax into six lines of four tablets each, and began doing lines. A bottle of water washed everything down. She removed the bathrobe and stood nude before her open bedroom window. In one way she was wishing to startle and disgust; in another way, it was a cry for help; but in another, she only wanted to entice the next inappropriate suitor into her bedroom and her intimacy. She knew she was crazy. She no longer cared.

Two minutes later she was fully prepared to die, so she lay down on her bed, between her Elmo doll and her most-favored iPad, earbuds inserted, feet tapping toes in time to the music of Rosebud. She watched the empty medicine bottle as it rose and fell on her diaphragm, consistent with her breathing. Soon it shallowed and all but ceased.

She was found and rushed to the hospital. She survived this first attempt.

Two weeks later, alone in her dorm room, she hung herself from her closet door with a coat hanger.

This time there was no one to save her.

ELEVEN

In August the monsoons settled over Flagstaff and it rained every afternoon for three weeks. Late summer weeds and wildflowers burst forth in the Inner Basin, blue jays swooped into catch basins and took long, fluttery baths, deer and elk crept down off the mountain and drank deep, while black bears swiped fish from the ever-deepening Lake Mary. Thaddeus took to fly fishing in the early evenings before the sun settled behind the mountains and oftentimes would catch his limit, gut and clean them on the shoreline, and cook his supper before driving home and catching summer league NBA.

The house with five acres backed up to the Coconino National Forest, so it was quiet and serene, the highway traffic more than a mile away down a north-south gravel road.

He opened his eyes when the rain began hammering the skylight overhead. Katy was nude, rolled up against him, and charmingly

41

accessible. Instead of awaking her, he crept across the plank floor and slid open the glass door on the north wall. He stepped out onto the porch, unclothed and unseen, and let the rain drum down, matting his hair and running down in rivulets, draining away from his feet in a torrent.

At 5:45 he saw headlights approaching and ducked back inside. The rural newspaper carrier let fly with a wrapped *Coconino Examiner* that hit the lower deck with a *thump!* Thaddeus threw on Levi's and traipsed downstairs and retrieved the paper. He unsheathed it and was blasted with two-inch headlines, "DA Slain in Home!"

His name was John Steinmar, the paper said, and he was a local boy, born and bred, whose signature characteristic was the albino gene that had tagged him at birth, leaving him pink-skinned and white-haired.

His politics were impeccable. Just before he died he had been on the phone with several precinct committee members. They had just elected him chairman of the Coconino County Republican party. They recounted that he had been his usual, chatty self, that there was no stress in his voice and nothing to indicate any kind of torment in his life.

Thaddeus absorbed the stories about the death by gunshot wound, and examined the photographs. He absently shook his head. "Good grief, I wonder who gets the needle over this?" he said to Max, his pound mutt who shadowed him. Max responded to the query with a cocked head, which might have also meant he was hungry. Thaddeus wiped Max's bowl and shook in a cup of dry food. He went to the refrigerator and sprinkled Parmesan cheese over the pellets—the only way that Max would agree to eat the stuff.

He looked out the floor-to-ceiling windows on the north end of the house. Rain was still a downpour; his two horses were pressed together beneath their shelter, heads lowered into a rack of hay, stamping and blowing. Their names were Coconino and Charlie.

He rehashed the murder of the district attorney. The crime of the decade. Thaddeus immediately knew he would have no role in the drama—he was a pariah, an outcast since his disbarment. Another huge parade would roll off down the street without him.

He sighed and looked north at the San Francisco Peaks. It was time to go to the office. There would be more news about the murder of the district attorney. So the morning had some merit.

He slipped into court clothes. Ten minutes later he was strapped in the F-250 he had driven from North Dakota.

Just then he received a text from Shep Aberdeen. It was cryptic, saying only, *Call me. It's big.*

He studied the cell again and dropped it back inside his shirt pocket.

He wondered what Shep Aberdeen could want with him on a Monday morning. Maybe he was ill and needed cover at court. Or maybe his calendar was conflicted and he needed a warm body. Why he would be texting Thaddeus with the enigmatic "It's big," Thaddeus had no idea. But once he got to the office he wasted no time calling Shep's office.

"He's in court in front of Judge Gerhardt," said his receptionist. "He said if you call to, quote, get your skinny ass right over there, unquote."

"What's going on in Judge Gerhardt's court?"

"Initial appearance. Angelina Steinmar."

Thaddeus sucked in a deep breath. So, the DA's wife; the finger had been pointed at her. He blew out a long breath. Do you imagine— he stopped and didn't allow his mind to race away. "Okay, Maya. I'm on my way."

Thaddeus hurried up the courthouse stairs to the second floor. He raced for the courtroom at the far end. Honorable William A. Gerhardt, Criminal Calendar, said the notice posted outside the double doors. He let his eyes scan over the roster and saw that there was nothing listed referencing Angelina Steinmar. That's why they were holding court so early in the morning: they were having a fast session before the press could get wind.

He stepped inside and was greeted by twenty pairs of eyes turning to see who had come in. Five pairs belonged to armed deputies arranged directly behind the defense table. They effectively shielded that table's occupants from Thaddeus' view, but he already knew whom he would find there—Shep Aberdeen and Angelina Steinmar—defense counsel and defendant in the murder of John Steinmar, Coconino County district attorney.

"Morning, Mr. Murfee," said Judge Gerhardt from the bench. "Lock that door behind you, please."

Thaddeus did as he was told.

He turned back around. The courtroom was part of the original building of the Coconino County Superior Court. Its ceiling arched up two stories to a condemned gallery that ran around three walls on the second floor and remained locked. The lower walls were populated with portraits of judges reaching as far back as territorial days— bearded men, with their mutton chops and rimless spectacles, posed without any indication of character other than grim and serious—their posterity. Closest to Judge Gerhardt's bench was the current crop of six jurists comprising the Superior Court, robed and smiling, as if life had become more accommodating as the twentieth century gave way to the twenty-first.

Judge Gerhardt had drawn the Angelina Steinmar assignment over the five other judges for one reason only: among the six judges he was the only one who hadn't served as an Assistant DA under John Steinmar at some career point. Bill Gerhardt hadn't felt that call, the call to prosecute and put people behind bars. His pre-judicial law practice had been mostly commercial with just a smattering of minor criminal work—DUIs, disturbing the peace, retail shoplifting, and the two-bit stuff where not much was on the line. So his slate was clean to accept the assignment of the Angelina Steinmar murder case.

The case would be high pressure and high profile. Already it was clear the local district attorney's corps wouldn't be prosecuting. Thaddeus saw at the state's table a fortyish man, thin and bespectacled with a bald spot plating his crown. Thaddeus knew the man hailed from the office of the Attorney General in Phoenix. Big-time prosecutors. So, the cannons were in place, the press would be charging the door at any moment, and here he stood—but why?

Judge Gerhardt was hastily setting bail before the press could storm the courtroom. Bail hearings were the trickiest part of high-profile prosecutions because the availability of bail in a capital crime always came down to judicial discretion. Which meant the judge couldn't (nor would he) blame his ruling on something required by the law. Instead, the amount of bail would be his call. If he even allowed bail at all. He probably wouldn't, Thaddeus knew, where the "presumption was great and the evidence strong" of guilt. The morning was shaping up to be an all-out war, and Thaddeus had arrived just in time, though for what reason, he still was unsure. That part was up to Shep.

Thaddeus eased into the front row spectators' pew and got himself oriented.

The dull overhead fluorescents fluttered and blinked atop Judge Gerhardt's shiny blond hair, and reflected sharply from his bifocals as if he had X-ray vision to peer into the hearts of those who stood before him.

"Mr. Aberdeen," he said in a warm tone, "I've read your application for bail and I'm going to take judicial notice of the defendant Angelina Steinmar's contacts with the community. For the record, first out of the gate, I know this defendant, Mr. Aberdeen, and I want to be sure you understand that and that the record reflects my acquaintance with her. I have been to her house the past ten or twelve Christmas Eves. She and my wife once worked together at the

Department of Children and Family Services. She has appeared before me as a caseworker in hundreds of child dependency cases, most of them from the reservation where she is assigned. She and John have barbecued with me in my own backyard. In other words, I know things about her, sir. And while all that may be true, I would also like to state for the record that none of what I know about Mrs. Steinmar will affect my participation in this case to even the slightest degree. Flagstaff is a small town and I know many of the people brought before me, but so far no one's complained about how I have comported myself. Now, knowing these things, and having listened to me, do you, Mr. Aberdeen, or your client, Mrs. Steinmar, have any requests for a change of judge based on what I've just revealed to you?"

Shep was instantly on his feet. "Your Honor, I've discussed this very thing with my client, albeit briefly. We would both respectfully request that you remain on the case. We make this request even knowing that you might know such and such or mister or missus someone or other. And we waive any such possible bias with a greater eye toward your known ability to be fair and impartial to all who stand before you. Whether you know someone or not, you have always been fair to my clients. There will be no motion for a new judge, Your Honor."

The judge swung his gaze to the other table. "And what about you, Mr. Moroney? Does the Attorney General have any position?"

The AG didn't bother to stand. "No, we know of no reason why you shouldn't hear the case, Judge Gerhardt. Of course we would reserve our right to object if something later comes up, being as how we're brand new on the case and new in town."

"Fair enough," said the judge, nodding pleasantly at both lawyers. "We'll give it a whirl, then."

Several smaller conversations took place. It turned out that the AG was a man named Jimmy Moroney, and he was a first-line prosecutor from among the Attorney General's handpicked lawyers for the high-profile cases around the state. It came out that the AG's office had rented office space in the BOA building across the street from the courthouse. Wiring was now in place, networks were hooked up, and police officers from the City of Flagstaff PD and the Coconino County Sheriff's Department were assigned as full-time investigators. The local AG office would be fully staffed by Friday. In all, a major assault was underway. The state was pulling no punches.

Just then a clamoring and pounding arose at the courtroom door.

"Bailiff," said Judge Gerhardt, "this is an open proceeding. We might as well take a break while you let them in and get them settled with a good view. One TV camera welcome, no phones—you know the drill. Court stands in recess fifteen minutes."

Shep stood and put a hand on Angelina's shoulder, bent low, and whispered, then hurried back to Thaddeus and motioned him to join him outside in the hallway. They found a private spot midway between the stairwell and the courtroom, where Shep put his back up against the wall and shook Thaddeus' hand. "Thanks for coming," he said. "This is going to be wonderfully, magically insane."

"It is. I stopped counting at fifteen reporters when we walked out. You'd better press your best outfits and shine your boots."

The boots reference was to the fact that Shep wore cowboy boots with his courtroom attire. They were a deferential nod to his upbringing and family's history in the Wild West.

"Done. Got the call from Angelina around seven this morning. Cops were at her house. She called in the shooting herself."

"She pulled the trigger?"

Shep two-fingered a Winston from the hard pack in his pocket. He inserted it in his mouth but of course didn't light up—public building. He drew mightily on the unlit cigarette and exhaled through pursed lips as a smoker would. He shook his head and looked down at the courtroom entrance. "Yeah. Yeah, she did."

"Self-defense or something?"

"No, not self-defense."

"So she just shot him for no reason."

"Let me show you. These are shots on my cell phone. I had a real photographer take them at Dr. Sloane's office too, where I had the doc meet us before hours. Look here."

He flicked on the cell phone. He held it up for Thaddeus to view, all the while keeping his eyes focused on the courtroom doors. Thaddeus felt a sharp chill roll up his spine. He didn't know why—yet—but Shep was bringing him in on something. He was complicit. He reached and held the cell phone, viewing the picture this way and that.

"Is this what I think it is?"

"Pussy?"

"Uh-huh."

"It is."

"Is it whose I think it is?"

"Uh-huh. Mrs. Steinmar's."

"This is Angelina's puss—labia."

"Yep. Notice anything strange?"

"She's sitting back or lying back semi-reclined. She's wearing no underwear. She shaves her cootch like a landing strip. And there is a bright red scallop inside her uppermost thigh. Am I getting close?"

"Almost. Check out the next one."

Thaddeus flicked his finger across the screen.

"No way! This is her—her labia major. With deep impressions. Okay, Shep, what am I looking at here?"

"Bite marks."

"Bite marks. Serious?"

"Serious as a rattlesnake in your bedroll, serious. Son of a bitch chomped up her pussy."

"John Steinmar did this?"

"Yeppers. Mean son of a bitch, eh? Who would have thought?"

"So—what's this mean, legally? Where you at with this?"

Shep focused his gaze back on Thaddeus. He retrieved and pocketed the cell phone. He shrugged.

"That's what I want you to find out. Where am I with this?"

"You're asking me to help with the research?"

Shep grinned broadly. "Nah, I got paralegals can do that. I'm asking you to second chair. There's fifty grand in it for you."

Thaddeus exhaled in a whoosh. "I'd do it for nothing. Get to work with a star like you? Anybody'd do it for free, Shep."

"Don't go all soft on me, Thad, my boy. Fifty grand—you have to take it so there's an attorney-client relationship formed. Something of value for something of value. Your services for fifty thousand dollars."

"Which begs the question. Why me?"

"Angelina likes you. So do I."

Thaddeus was taken by total surprise. "*Likes* me? Likes *me*? I've never even spoken to her before."

"Oh, but you have."

"I have? Where?"

"You spoke to the Sunday Morning Mourners AA group two Sundays ago at the halfway house."

"Yes, I did."

"Angelina was there. She took a girl to Al-A-Teen. One of her client girls was there at the teen meeting. But she heard you speak when they dropped in on the AA meeting after."

"You are joking."

"Yeppers. She likes your program. She says she can't lose with you."

"AA sharing is no way to judge a lawyer. That's totally bogus," said Thaddeus.

"Lawyers get selected for a hell of a lot crazier things than that,

Thaddeus, my boy. How we doing on time?"

"About up. You should get back in there."

"*We* should get back in there. You on board or not?"

There was no hesitation. "Hell yes. I was on board when I got the paper this morning."

"That's the stuff. Now let's go kick some ass. This is going to be good."

At counsel table, Shep told Thaddeus to introduce himself to Jimmy Moroney, the Assistant Attorney General. Thaddeus stuck out his hand. "Looks like I'll be joining the defense team, Mr. Moroney. I'm Thaddeus Murfee."

Without looking up from his tablet, Moroney waved him off. "I'm Jimmy, thanks."

Thaddeus looked over at Shep, who shrugged.

"We've got your boy," Shep announced to Angelina Steinmar. "Officially meet Thaddeus Murfee."

She stood and he realized she must have been five-eleven, and that an exquisite female body was barely concealed under the tight gray silk slacks and white silk blouse beneath which her breasts swayed as she swiveled to come face-to-face with her newest lawyer. Her hair was brown and cut quite short in a pageboy. She looked Thaddeus directly in the eye. Four silver bracelets slid up her wrist as she lifted her hand to shake. The flesh felt cool and her pale blue eyes met his gaze head-on. "At last," she said with an affectionate smile. "I've heard nothing but good about you, Mr. Murfee."

Thaddeus was immediately struck by how calm and self-assured she came across for someone who had just shot her husband to death. Was he missing something here? And what was with the get-up? She looked like a *Vogue* model coiffed and donning the latest in casual office wear. Had she actually had time to get cleaned up and styled after the shooting before the cops arrived? Or had she been dressed this way when she fired the gun? A thousand questions raced through his mind, for which he had no plausible guesses. The case just turned the dial one more click toward ODD.

"I hope to bring a lot of help to the team," was all he could think to say. But he returned the smile and turned away as Judge Gerhardt returned to the bench. Everyone took a seat as the judge tugged his shirtsleeves under his robe and then looked out over the crowded courtroom, ready to proceed to bail.

"Mr. Aberdeen, earlier today you filed a motion that bail be allowed in this case."

Shep took to his feet. "Correct, Your Honor. Defendant is requesting bail in a fair amount. She owns no property except her half interest in the house on Mountain Drive. Two web searches peg the equity at around eighty thousand. So she could post a property bond in that amount."

Judge Gerhardt looked troubled. "Assuming bail were ordered— and no one's done that yet, I'm just saying 'assuming.' Assuming bail is ordered, are there other assets that could be placed in the pot?"

"You know, Your Honor," said Shep in his resonant baritone, "the only other asset is the decedent's retirement through the state employees' retirement fund. And that's not available until the age of fifty-five. Fact is, now that John's passed on, I'm not sure there's anything there she can tap at all."

"Object," said Jimmy Moroney, leaning back in his chair and still refusing to stand even though addressing the court. "Object to the use of the term 'passed on.' John Steinmar was shot down in cold blood; he didn't just pass on. And for this woman to even whisper the word 'bail' is an insult to this court. She murdered him in cold blood. She's even admitted to it, in case anyone in here is guessing."

A clamor arose among the press corps as laptops were flipped open and iPads tapped. Notes were made; blood had just been let: she had admitted committing the crime! Three reporters charged up the aisle toward the double doors.

"Ladies and gentlemen in the gallery," said Judge Gerhardt evenly and politely, "please try to remain in your seats until this session is completed. I realize this is a small town and I realize this might be considered a case of no small notoriety, but this is still an official court session and I would appreciate an effort at decorum in my courtroom. Thank you. Now, Mr. Aberdeen, you were about to tell the court why you believe this is a bailable offense."

Shep was bent down, whispering to Angelina. He rose back up. "One other asset I didn't know about. There's also a Harley Davidson Sportster that's titled in my client's name. A birthday gift from her father on her fortieth birthday. The bike is just a few years old and has forty-seven hundred miles on the odometer. She guesses its value at around seven, maybe eight thousand, tops."

"Well, we don't want to touch her birthday present," said the judge, "but thanks for the additional information. Now please address my question. Why is this a bailable offense, Mr. Aberdeen?"

Shep, who hadn't sat following his first comments, nodded and spread his hands. "As the court knows, the Arizona legislature in Section 13-3961 has made it a rule that a person in custody shall not be admitted to bail if the proof is evident or the presumption great that the person is guilty of the offense charged in a capital murder case. Of course we don't know yet whether this is a capital offense or not, as the state hasn't made that election."

Moroney climbed to his feet and assumed the posture of a bouncer, arms crossed, chest thrust forward, scowling face. "That election can be considered made. The state will be seeking the death penalty in this case." The veins bulged in his neck as he spoke, a well of anger barely suppressed. Thaddeus could only guess the man had known John Steinmar and was maybe even close to him, which would explain the personal anger. Or else he was an accomplished actor. Probably both.

Again, much muttering and sighing arose from the gallery at the mention of *death penalty*. One reporter stood but thought better of it, heeding the judge's earlier admonition, and quickly sat.

But Shep had smoked them out. Now he knew for sure what his client was facing and he could begin whittling away at the charges. He didn't hesitate.

"Judge, the proof is anything but evident in this case and there can certainly be said to be no presumption, given the facts I have outlined in my motion. With the color photographs."

"And those would be which facts?" the judge asked, as he paged through the motion bound within the manila file folder.

"The fact that at the moment she fired the gun she was being attacked by the decedent. I'm talking specifically about him biting her genitals."

The judge had to bang his gavel for order this time, and a threesome of reporters did head for the doors despite the judge's admonition. Judge Gerhardt finally quieted things down with his pounding gavel. He turned to the bailiff. "Deputy Baker, please walk up and lock that door. No more disturbances will be abided without someone going to jail for contempt." The bailiff did as he was told.

Moroney was yet on his feet and shook his head violently at the "genitals" comment. "Your Honor, that allegation by counsel is outrageous! For all we know the photographs could have come from many different sources!"

"I'll submit my client to a forensic examination so that the bite marks on her genitals can be matched to the decedent's bite, Your Honor. Happy to oblige."

"Judge, can we agree not to refer to Mr. Steinmar as the decedent. He had a name and that name was John Steinmar, not 'the decedent,' much as Mr. Aberdeen would like to depersonalize our murdered district attorney."

"Point is well taken but unnecessary, Mr. Moroney," said the judge. "We all have fond memories of Mr. Steinmar and he won't ever be depersonalized. However, for want of a better term, 'decedent' is accurate and cognizable by the court. If you were objecting, your objection would be both noted and overruled."

"The state would further move that the defendant's photographs be sealed by the clerk of the court."

A groan arose from the spectators.

"So ordered," said Judge Gerhardt. "The clerk will seal the photographs attached to Defendant's Motion for Bail."

"Your Honor," Shep said, "the purpose of bail is to ensure the appearance of the defendant to answer the charges against her. In our case, Mrs. Steinmar was the one who called the police and waited for them to arrive. There was no attempt to clean up the scene or hide the body, there was no attempt to run, no attempt to blame intruders. She voluntarily called the police herself and has voluntarily given them a full statement and cooperated much more than I would have liked, but it was done before I was called."

"But there's no guarantee she won't leave," said Moroney, "especially now that she knows the state is seeking her death."

"Consider her connections with the community," said Shep. "She was born and raised here, educated at NAU where she earned her Master's in Educational Psychology, twenty-year veteran of the Department of Children and Family Services—but even more than all that, Judge, she has no money to run on. There's no hidden money to make a getaway."

"Which means she has nothing keeping her here," said Moroney, "she has nothing to lose by leaving."

Shep ignored him. "Most of all, I need her free so she can take up a collection among relatives to pay my fee."

"I was going to ask about that," Judge Gerhardt said with a smile. "I'm sure you don't come cheap, Mr. Aberdeen. And now I see another attorney with you at counsel table, Mr. Murfee. I'm sure he isn't free, either. Will you be entering your appearance, Mr. Murfee?"

Thaddeus decided to lighten the moment. "I *was*, but now that there's no money to go around, I'm having second thoughts," Thaddeus said in all seriousness.

Judge Gerhardt couldn't help but laugh—before catching himself. But the moment had been won: what had been a very grave proceeding had been lightened, which was the first rule in criminal cases, to get the judge and jury smiling. So far the judge had smiled, at least to some small extent. The jury would come later.

"Mr. Murfee's point is well taken." The judge inclined his head toward the defendant. "Mrs. Steinmar, I've known you for a long time. While my personal proclivity is to allow you to remain free on your signature, I have official duties placed on me by my office as a judge. I'm sure you understand." She nodded and returned his gaze. "But I'd like to ask you, will you come to court as required if I allow bail?"

She nodded solemnly. "I will do that, Judge Gerhardt. Whenever you say I must be here, I will be. I've spent hours in these courtrooms and I take my obligation very seriously, Your Honor."

He smiled, and in just that moment, the thought occurred to Thaddeus that the judge and defendant might know each other a lot better than either was letting on. He decided to file that in his mind for future reference. He would ask Shep about the moment he had just witnessed.

Addressing both attorneys, the judge said, "Gentlemen, my inclination is to set bail at one hundred thousand dollars."

"Ten percent?" asked Shep.

"Of course. She may pay ten percent and post her house as surety. It's so ordered. Now we still have the matter of the autopsy. Are you gentlemen prepared to address that motion?"

Shep didn't miss a beat. "Ready, Your Honor, and if I may say so, we'd like to amend that motion to add the Coconino County Medical Examiner. He's the one who will be performing the autopsy."

The judge raised a hand. "As I understand it, Shep—Mr. Aberdeen—your client is claiming the decedent was biting her before or at the time the gun was fired. Is that correct?"

Shep nodded vigorously. "Oh, yes, John Steinmar had his teeth buried in my client's crotch when she blew off the top of his head. He wouldn't let go and the pain was excruciating. He was warned, as well."

Angelina lowered her head and began sobbing as if on cue. She shifted uncomfortably in her chair. Pain between the legs? Thaddeus wondered. Was she cuing the viewers to some degree of painful distress to make her point? If it was intentional, she was a great actress. If unintentional, then the gods were smiling on her case because it was playing beautifully over the airways right now and would on tonight's *News at Six*, as well. His respect for her sense of theater rose ten points. She was good.

"Objection!" cried Moroney. "These are allegations, pure allegations. There's absolutely no record of what she's now claiming. In fact, she never mentioned to the police that he was attacking her when she pulled the trigger. The state claims surprise and objects!"

"We will be supplementing the defendant's motion for dental impressions of Mr. Steinmar's mouth this afternoon, Your Honor. We have forensic photographs we'll be attaching and amending our motion. For now, if the court would issue an order to the Attorney General and the Medical Examiner requiring that dental impressions be taken of the decedent's bite and preserved—that's all we're asking. Next thing you know they'll be trying to hurry him into the grave so that exhumation is required, if we don't do this now. Worse, he could be cremated and we lose the evidence of his bite altogether."

"The court is inclined to agree, gentlemen. It costs the state nothing to preserve evidence of the decedent's bite. It is ordered that both the Attorney General and the Medical Examiner take and make available to defense complete dental impressions of John Steinmar's bite. It's a simple autopsy procedure and the court has seen it done many times and the results are always accurate and convincing. The impressions shall be made by means common to such procedures and X-rays of the decedent's teeth taken as well."

"Judge, *X-rays*?" said Moroney, pounding his fist into his hand. "For what possible reason would the defendant want X-rays?"

The judge looked coolly at AG Moroney. "The X-rays are for me, Mr. Moroney. The court wants X-rays for its own purposes. Now go forth and do what you're told."

"Yes, Your Honor."

"Thank you, Judge," Shep said quickly.

"Have I missed anything?" Judge Gerhardt asked.

Both attorneys said he hadn't missed anything.

The judge smiled and looked straight at the red light on the TV camera. "Will that be all?"

Both attorneys said that would be all.

"Very well. Mr. Murfee, I'll expect to see your entry of appearance as co-counsel filed by close of business. Fair enough?"

"Yes," said Thaddeus, fighting to restrain his enthusiasm for being invited on board. "I'll have it back before noon, Your Honor."

"Ladies and gentlemen, please remain seated while Deputy Baker unlocks the door. Court stands in recess. Defendant is remanded to custody of the sheriff pending bail."

Chairs scraped back and briefcases were packed. A seventy-year-old deputy everyone called "Hoss" laid a gentle hand on Angelina Steinmar's shoulder. "Please come with me, Mrs. Steinmar." She held out both arms for the handcuffs—mandatory—and looked at the floor while the iron was placed around her wrists.

"I'll speak to your father as we discussed, Angelina," said Shep. "We'll have you walking in the sunshine by noon."

She nodded and allowed herself to be led away.

JOHN ELLSWORTH

TWELVE

Katy was playing Barbie's with Sarai when her cell phone chimed. She touched her daughter's hair and stood to retrieve the phone from the kitchen island.

"This is Katy," she said.

The voice sounded distant and very small.

"Dr. Murfee? This is Turquoise Begay."

"Turquoise. We haven't spoken since the clinic. How are you?"

"I'm not so good."

"Why not?"

"My uncle, he's—he's—"

She could hear the young voice break and begin weeping.

"He's what, Turquoise? Is he hurting you?"

"Y-y-yes. He's fucking me."

"When?"

"Every night."

"Is that where you got the STD, from your uncle?"

"Yes."

Katy felt the old rage work its way up inside her. Old feelings, old body memories, came rushing back. She wanted to fly to the girl, take her in her arms, and rip her out of that place. Sometimes she hated the reservation. Sometimes she hated the people there and how they preyed on each other and how sexual abuse was twelve times what it was in the rest of America. Two out of three women by the age of twenty-three had been sexually assaulted, fifty percent of the time by a family member. She knew the statistics, she was just about a doctor and she knew how important health statistics were to a statistical population. But she was more than that. She was also a survivor herself, a survivor of sexual abuse on the reservation, and her personal rage instantly overlaid on the rage she was feeling toward Turquoise's abuser. She wanted to see that person behind bars. Or worse.

But more than anything, the abuse had to be stopped.

Small chance of that. It was the reservation. Women's—and girls'—bodies were there for the pleasure of men. While it was a matriarchy—the Navajo Nation—when it came to crimes against women, the place was a good old boys' club.

She had to do something.

"I'm coming to get you. Are you still living in the trailer where I dropped you after clinic?"

"Yes."

"Is there anyone there with you?"

"Uncle Randy. He's passed out in my bedroom."

"Asleep on your bed?"

"Yes."

"Anyone else there?"

"My dad hasn't been home in three days."

"Okay, I'm going to see what I can do. Go someplace safe. I'm going to first go by the clinic for help. Then I'll come over and get you. Go outside and hide. When you see my car, come running. It's a maroon Toyota Highlander."

"Maroon SUV?"

"Yes."

"Okay. I called my caseworker, too. Someone will come for me."

"That won't hurt. Whoever gets there first, you go with them."

"Thank you."

"You're welcome."

She was seeing red—in fact, she wasn't seeing anything. She was in a rage and she meant to stop the perpetrator before he could act again. That was her sole aim in life at that moment. Stop him. She changed from shorts into Wrangler's blue jeans and the red roper boots with the walking heels, and shrugged into a T-shirt that said "Chicago Medicine."

She made arrangements for Sarai and waited while Mrs. Johnston from across the street waved her over. She carried Sarai over and deposited her with the friendly woman.

"One hour, maybe two. You know Thad's number if you need him."

"She'll be fine here with me. Looks like we'll play Barbie's."

"Thanks, Mrs. Johnston."

"Of course, honey. Go do what you need and we'll be here when you get back."

"So long."

So long, she thought. Maybe it was a Freudian commentary. She hated herself for even thinking that and hated the world that had taken away her innocence that would even let her think something like that. She furiously marched back across the street and left for the reservation.

He had to be stopped.

THIRTEEN

Angelina was home from court by 2:30. First thing was to strip down and take a long, hot shower. She washed her short hair and shaved her legs and armpits. The loofah felt great across the back and butt. Then came the facial scrub and conditioner for the short hair. Then a five-minute soak and rinse, almost unbearably hot.

She stepped out and toweled dry. Angelina would let her short hair air dry, of course, and she wiped away the steam from the mirror over the double his-and-her sinks.

An enlarging mirror was held to reflect her vagina. She twisted it this way and that, pursuing the elusive wound. She peered into the mirror and watched her fingers carefully lift the left labia away from the vagina. A definite two chords of bite marks were revealed. She uncapped the antibiotic ointment and applied a small dab inside and outside the labia. It burned but quickly relented in intensity. A very

62

sensitive place to have someone bite you, she thought. She replaced the enlarging mirror on the cabinet top. She washed her hands and slowly dried them on the hand towel on her side of the counter.

Across from her own sink, her dead husband's electric toothbrush was still in its charger, green light aglow. He won't need that, she thought. She resumed the preparations she had missed just before dawn, thanks to the incident with John.

Teeth brushed, deodorant applied, small spray of Canoe across the shoulders—very light, just a mist. Satisfied with her preparations, she went into the bedroom and stood at the double windows looking down on the front yard and street. She was nude and would have been seen, but no one looked up at the figure in the window. She finally smiled and turned away. It was such a relief not to have to face them and force more tears. She had done all the crying anyone could hope for with the detectives just before dawn.

KTVK Channel 3's van was still parked in front, its satellite pointed aimlessly at the sky. Three other news agency SUVs were parked along the front yard, and reporters milled about, talking and comparing notes. When she arrived home they had gawked as she clicked and the garage door opener raised the door. Inside, she closed the door behind her and passed directly from garage to kitchen, avoiding the throng out front.

The police cars and CSI van were gone, thankfully. They had cut out a huge section of carpet in the family room where John had marinated in his own blood and brain matter after she blew away the top of his head. Prints had been dusted and lifted, photographs taken from every conceivable angle and distance, drawings made, and evidence collected.

Two detectives had questioned her. She had sobbed and appeared distraught. Through a wash of tears she had called Shep and he had shut them down. They had allowed her to retreat to the couch in the family room, where she lay on her back and moaned as if pierced by the horror of what had happened. She was dying for a cigarette the whole time, but didn't dare light up.

The gun was gone, of course, and she was sure they'd also found the bullets in the desk drawer. It was John's gun; he kept it for self-defense and as the chief law enforcement officer of the county it had always made perfect sense that he have it around. While Flagstaff was a small town, it still saw enough transient blow-by that one could never tell what might be coming up or down the interstate next.

John had been in the Army and knew all about guns. She knew almost as much, as he'd wanted her to take the self-defense course and become licensed to carry concealed, so she had acquiesced and done the course. The police hadn't found her own gun, of course, and wouldn't. She kept it stashed in the black and gray Coach purse on the closet shelf. It would go with her on her mad shopping sprees in Scottsdale. She loved having the Coach on her arm at those times; she believed it made a statement she liked. John insisted she carry the sidearm when she went to the Valley anyway. It made him happy.

She was dry and she disappeared back inside the bathroom. She applied powder, moisturizer and a light blush. No eye makeup, no lipstick. No need for much; she wouldn't be giving any interviews and she had no plans to go out, orders of Shep, who'd told her to stay home no matter what.

She was slipping into her Ralph Lauren pants when her county-issue cell chimed. Calls from the Department of Children and Family Services reached her on that number. She went to the dresser and looked. Navajo Reservation number trying to reach her. It might be one of her kids from her caseworker duties, so she answered.

"This is Angelina Steinmar, how can I help?"

"It's Turquoise, Mrs. Steinmar. You said I should call if he did it again."

"I did, Turquoise. Where are you right now?"

"Home."

"Is he there?"

"He's in the back bedroom. I think he passed out after he did it to me."

"Are you bleeding?"

"No."

"Did he hit you?"

"No. He only threatened."

"With the gun?"

"He showed me a knife. A switchblade. He asked me to choose."

"Choose what?"

"He said I could choose what went between my legs. Him or the knife."

Son of a bitch! She swore in her mind. "Can you leave the trailer?"

"His truck's out front. Dad hasn't been home for three days."

"You were going to call me," Angelina said. She used a tone that wasn't blaming. It was only a reference to their agreement.

"I know. I forgot."

"Then your uncle came over. He must have known your dad was missing."

"Yes."

"Can you find the keys to the truck?"

"He always keeps them in his pocket."

"Okay, here's what I want you to do. You slip outside and start walking west along the highway. I'm going to come get you."

"You will?"

"I told you I would, Turquoise. I said you only had to call me."

"I'll go outside right now. Please don't forget me."

"Turquoise, I'm on my way. Don't accept any rides from anyone else. I'm one hour away. Take a bottle of water with you."

"Pepsi. I only have Pepsi in the fridge."

"Take that. One hour, Turquoise. I'm on my way. Remember,

65

you're to walk west, toward the mall."

"Thank you, Mrs. Steinmar."

She hung up the phone and resisted the urge to fling it against the wall. She hated that son of a bitch, Randy Begay. Hated his guts. He was damn lucky someone hadn't blown him away. Someone should, she thought, then her mind kicked in and she was thinking.

Sitting on the bed, she kicked out of the RL pants and opened the bottom drawer of her dresser. Black Levi's, hiking boots, and a Harley T-shirt quickly were assembled and tossed on her thin frame. She shook out a Harley bandana atop her head and pulled it together in the back. She tied a knot and looked at herself in the mirror. The bandana looked good, all Harley. She turned.

As tall as she was, it was an easy reach to the closet shelf and her Coach purse. She retrieved the .38 Detective Special, snapped open the cylinder and spun it once, slapped it shut, and dropped the sidearm into the right pocket of her denim Harley jacket. She slipped it on and spun before the mirror. The American eagle embroidered on the jacket flashed by as she turned. "Born in the USA," the eagle cried. She dropped her cell phone in the left pocket and hurried downstairs.

Downstairs she crept out the back door into their fenced yard. The Harley was kept on a cement slab behind the garage, beneath an awning. She removed the tarpaulin from the bike and pushed it to the back gate, out the gate and down the alley to the far end where it intersected Hoover Road. She inserted the key, hit START, and the engine caught on the first try. She reached behind and removed the helmet from the bungee and placed it on her head, shield fully down and covering her face. She looked both ways. So far, so good. No one was aware she was gone, no press, no police, nada. She toed it into first and slowly pulled out of the alley onto Hoover eastbound.

Turquoise would be walking west on the highway; Angelina would come in from the east.

DEFENDING TURQUOISE

◇◇◇

Ninety minutes later the woman spotted the singlewide where Turquoise lived with her father and brother. The father's gray primer Ford was missing from the front yard, but Randy Begay's red Chevrolet Silverado was pulled up almost to the front stoop. It was missing the rear license plate.

She shook her head and shut off the engine. A perfect stillness settled over the scene. It was almost five, but the sun was still high in the western sky. Overhead a chicken hawk curled lazily on a high desert thermal and a gentle breeze pushed in from the west. No other traffic for probably ten minutes, as it was a fairly deserted reservation road. It was blacktop, one lane either way, and she could see a good five miles in both directions.

She squinted her eyes and looked west but couldn't see anyone walking. Never mind; she would catch up to Turquoise. She patted the side pocket of her denim HD jacket, making sure that the gun had come on the long ride. Satisfied, she entered the trailer without knocking.

FOURTEEN

The sun was high in the sky and Turquoise was hot. Then she chilled in the breeze and was cold. The area was at 5,000 feet and wind currents blew hot and cold almost by the minute.

She paused and took a long drink of the half-cold Pepsi she had carried along. It felt good on her parched throat, and familiar.

She wiped her mouth with the back of her hand and looked back behind. She was almost two hours into her walk and had covered maybe ten miles.

The landscape looked vaguely familiar, but less so than it did at seventy miles an hour, her customary speed in her father's truck as they drove west to Flagstaff.

A rock in her right shoe was painful, so she balanced on her left foot, removed the troubling shoe, and dislodged the small pebble and a spoonful of sand. The grains gathered and blew away in a single puff as the wind rustled past.

She replaced the shoe and bent to tie the lace. Blood rushed to her head. She blinked hard. For just a moment she was afraid she was going to faint, but kept her head down long enough that the spinning ceased and she regained her balance. Then she was fully upright and telling herself she could do this. Put one foot in front of the other, she commanded, and she stepped west. A second step followed and she was moving again.

After ten steps she realized she needed to urinate. *Even out here in this sunshine*, she thought. She stepped off the road and slid down into a dry arroyo, where she relieved herself. She could hear a vehicle thunder past on the highway and hoped she hadn't just missed her ride. "Damn," she swore at the sand, the dirt banks of the arroyo, the sun and the sky. "Damn, damn, damn!"

FIFTEEN

The girl was nowhere to be seen. She had thought she might catch sight of her outside, maybe along the road, as she drove in from the west, but there had been no sighting.

Inside the trailer, the woman paused and listened. There—she tilted her head. Again—clearly the soft rasp of Randy Begay snoring. She crept down the hallway and peered inside the back bedroom. It was a mess; newspapers stacked three feet high, *Truck Traders* everywhere, a Winchester .30-.30 leaning in the corner, and two neon Budweiser signs adorning the south wall. Clothes were piled in great lumps; a pair of Nikes on their side and almost beneath the bed; and there, stretched out full length, fully dressed, lay Randy Begay. He was on his back, mouth wide open, his right arm draped across his forehead. His rimless eyeglasses lay folded on his chest, focused on the white plastic ceiling of the trailer. For some odd reason his left

70

hand was shoved down inside the waistband of his Wrangler's, all the way to the crotch.

Must have been playing with himself, the woman thought.

She watched and listened for several minutes. She worked to fight down the hatred she felt for the child rapist, but could not. It even came up in her throat as hot, sour foam and she swallowed hard to make it go away, but it would not.

A thought came to mind and she was immediately grateful. The Winchester .30-.30. Was it loaded? There was one way to find out. She retrieved the rifle and retreated back down the hallway. In the living room she worked the lever action. A long, fat .30 caliber bullet was visible in the chamber. She worked the lever up and closed the action. Was there a safety on the thing? Then she remembered. She found the stop/safety and saw the "S" indicating the safety was on. She pushed the safety forward until the red dot appeared. Now it was off. Now the gun would fire. The gun was an exact replica of the .30-.30 she had carried when guarding the animals. It felt very familiar in her hands.

She crept back down the hallway. At the door to the back bedroom she paused and raised the rifle to eye level, placing and holding it against the doorframe to steady her shaking hands. She pointed the muzzle at Randy Begay's head and squinted down the barrel. The rear sight lined up with the front sight and she drew a shallow breath and held it.

She suddenly wanted to turn her head and look away and run from the trailer, but she caught herself and planted her feet again.

Sighting down the rifle, taking and holding one last breath, she slowly squeezed the trigger. "Blam!" The gun exploded inside the closed space and her ears were instantly ringing. Randy Begay never moved but now had a hole the size of a quarter leaking dark blood out the side of his head, just forward of the left ear, exactly where she had been aiming.

She reentered the bedroom and took a black T-shirt from the nearest pile. She replaced the gun where it had been leaning in the corner and, without touching it with any part of her skin, began wiping it down. It wasn't easy, the gun flopping one way and then the other as she worked the T-shirt up and down on its metal and wood parts. But in the end she was satisfied. She had left no prints and no DNA. She stuffed the T-shirt inside her Wrangler's and headed for the hallway.

She made it halfway when the vomit came up in her throat. She was shaking and diving for the toilet, just off the hallway. She threw up from her mouth and from her nose and then had a sudden urge to move her bowels. She sat on the toilet and felt the defecation leave her body and flow out of her in a long stream. Then she was shaking and holding her head between her hands at what she had done. She had killed living things before, but never a human being. She went to wipe herself. Nothing. No toilet paper.

"Son of a bit—" she muttered, and then stood upright without wiping and began looking under the sink for tissue paper. Nothing there, so she began opening drawers. Third drawer down on the side of the vanity nearest the toilet stool, she found napkins. Small white dinner napkins such as a fast food restaurant might dispense.

She grabbed several and resumed her seat on the toilet. She wiped. Then she flushed, wiped the toilet ring with napkins wet from the sink faucet to rinse away all traces of DNA, and flushed again, this time with the aid of the black T-shirt. "Damn Indians," she muttered.

She hurried into the living room where she let herself out through the metal door and paused on the porch. Again with the T-shirt, this time wiping the door handle. She was positive the handle was all she had touched with her skin.

"You have the right to remain silent, Mr. Begay," she said to the trailer and the window where she knew the less threatening, newly

72

improved Randy Begay lay dozing in his own blood. Oh, that's right, he wasn't dozing. He was dead, exercising his right to remain silent.

And damn good riddance.

SIXTEEN

She thought she heard the report of a gun bouncing around the mountains, but she wasn't sure. The young girl shielded her eyes with her hands, even though the sun was behind her, and squinted back toward her home. She couldn't see the trailer, thanks to the groundswell as she made her way west, but she was almost certain she had heard a gun. It sounded like the gun she sometimes fired to scare critters away from her sheep.

Then she ducked her head and moved toward the sun again, one foot in front of the other. Someone would pick her up soon. She was sure of it.

◇◇◇

The leather gloves protected her hands against the rush of the wind and would save acres of skin if the bike went down with her on it, as would the denim coat.

The guy was clearly dead, half his head blown away.

Angelina Steinmar closed the front door and stepped from the stoop and strode quickly out to the motorcycle. She twisted the key and hit the starter. It immediately roared to life and she left it running as she bent and studied the ground around her feet.

She located her tread marks in the sand where she had turned off the road coming in, and began walking backwards on her path, returning the sand to a smooth state with the Harley bandana she had been wearing on her head, wiping it left and right across the tread and her footprints. She reclaimed the bike and kicked it through the gears up to eighty-five and eastbound. She absolutely couldn't be seen in the area.

She meant to retrace her earlier path coming in to the trailer. No one had seen her; no one saw her now—not that she could see. Wait; there might be a truck far, far behind. She watched it disappear in her rearview as she crested a hill and dropped away onto a long flat plain. Once again she was alone.

Miles east of the trailer she stopped to use the pay phone at the New-Nav Trading Post. She kept her back to the windows of the store and kept the call short. Navajo Family Services answered and she told them where they would find Turquoise. She told them the girl had been raped and a medical exam was necessary. They agreed to go out and pick her up and find a foster home until her dependency could be taken up in court.

She then jumped back on the bike and drove home without stopping. She shut down the engine a block away from her back fence. The sun was going down and no one was about. She pushed the bike up the alley. Back inside the yard she bolted the gate and returned the bike to storage beneath the awning and tarpaulin. The cooling engine popped and hissed metallically as it began contracting in the cool air.

She changed clothes and went back downstairs. She asked the press, "Would anyone like to use the bathroom?" She had three takers. "I saw it was almost eight o'clock," she told them, "and I thought, now someone out there might need to go potty."

They thanked her, she declined to give a statement, and they returned outside, though for what purpose she wasn't sure. Evidently neither were they, because one by one, over the next three hours, they all pulled away and left until she was again alone on her street.

She fired up the 1971 *Bonnie Raitt* debut album and danced around the kitchen. Her ethereal dance partner was a cross between Shep Aberdeen and Thaddeus Murfee. Then she danced with each of them separately. Randy Begay asked if he might cut in, but she turned away and ignored him. She poured wine and toasted the air. It was a stirring dance and there were many partners, none of them John Steinmar.

At long last, the man she had come with to the dance was gone.

SEVENTEEN

Katy hadn't found Turquoise. So she had stopped at the clinic and called the Navajo PD. The girl had been found walking along the highway after someone called it in.

As she was driving back from the reservation, she called Thaddeus.

He was dozing on the couch. His eyes came open and he lay there, disoriented and wondering—there, he heard it again. Cell phone.

"Hey," she said, "is Sarai okay?"

"Fast asleep. Curled up with Jack the T-bear."

"You got her from the sitter's after work?"

"Done."

"I had to run back out to the reservation and I've been doing some thinking."

"And?"

"I'm staying here."

"You're *what*?"

"I'm staying in Flagstaff."

"Sure. Why?"

"I want to help a kid out here. I'm going to withdraw from school tomorrow. I'll still graduate in June because all I'm taking right now are electives."

"Fantastic. What do you want to do?"

"Counsel her. Take her wherever she needs to go. She needs a surrogate right now. It could make all the difference in her life. She's me, Thaddeus, ten years ago."

They talked some more, envisioned the girl as a foster child and wondered whether they could make that happen.

Katy determined she would try.

EIGHTEEN

News of the Turquoise STD had made the rounds.

Indian Health Services had notified the father, Garcia Begay, of course, and Mr. Begay called his great-grandfather and family patriarch Henry Landers.

Henry was in Window Rock when he received the call. He listened and asked several questions about his great-great-granddaughter's plight. He was terribly concerned and, as usual, on the front lines where his family was concerned. He heard the whole story. He told Mr. Begay that he would look into it. Mr. Begay pursued the issue. He asked Henry what should be done about his brother, Randy Begay, the rapist. Again, Henry replied vaguely that he would look into it. He did ask the father not to take any action—yet. He asked the father to act as if nothing had changed. He wanted to come and talk to Randy Begay himself and he would prefer to find him at home, unaware that his crimes had been uncovered. Henry said he wanted to catch him off-guard. Henry was like that, the father understood. He preferred to catch people off-guard.

The day Randy was shot, Henry had driven in from the east. When he neared the trailer, a motorcycle was just pulling out of the drive.

From two miles east, he thought he saw the rider first park the bike on the highway and then stoop down. It looked as if the gravel drive were being swept, back and forth, back and forth, the rider apparently retracing his bike tracks. Henry thought that odd, so he swung around in the trailer driveway and followed, lagging a half-mile behind the biker.

At the New-Nav Trading Post the rider pulled up to a pay phone. He removed his helmet and Henry, who had pulled in at the gas pumps, saw that the rider wasn't a "he" at all. It was a she, a woman in her forties, Henry guessed. She spoke briefly, hung up, and remounted the Harley. Henry allowed the bike to distance itself and then he unnoticeably fell in behind once again.

Ninety minutes later, winding through the east side of Flagstaff, he spied the rider dismounting the bike at an alley. The engine shut down and she began pushing. Fifty yards up, she opened a redwood gate and shoved the bike through. The gate was closed and Henry followed into the alley. With his cell phone he took a picture of the gate where the bike had entered. He peeked over and took a shot of the bike under its tarp, cooling and popping. He drove out the other end of the alley.

He circled around front. A news van and other media vehicles were parked out front and the house's curtains were drawn. Henry wondered what the press was about? And why was the woman hiding from them? She—or someone inside—was being extra careful in her comings and goings so as to keep the press unaware. Henry snapped a picture of the media vehicles as he passed by. Then he returned to the reservation.

Arriving back at the trailer, he found it surrounded by Navajo PD vehicles. He wasn't allowed to enter the driveway and was told to move along.

He did as instructed, heading into Kayenta, where he drank coffee for an hour.

Returning to the trailer, he again asked to check up on his great great granddaughter. Again the police blocked his entry and told him stay away. He followed their orders and returned to his hogan in the high desert.

He followed up with Garcia Begay the next morning by phone and learned the police had taken his great-grandson's daughter away. Uncle Randy had been shot to death.

That's all anyone knew so far.

NINETEEN

Monday morning dawned humid and overcast. Across the meadow and up 12,000 feet, the summit of the San Francisco Peaks was hidden away by low, sliding cumulus clouds gray on the undersides. Angelina Steinmar had shot District Attorney John Steinmar to death the week before. She was still out on bail and, as Shep relayed to Thaddeus, didn't seem to be suffering all that much.

Judge H. Ivan Trautman had summoned Thaddeus. It was just beginning to sprinkle when he dodged across Aspen Street to the Coconino County Courthouse. He cooled his heels in the waiting room of the judge's chambers, feeling uncomfortably damp under his arms. He knew he was sweating profusely, and he knew there was more to his distress than simple humidity. Fact was, he had managed to avoid Judge Trautman's court since pleading guilty and taking a

82

year off. Now he felt as if he were returning to the scene of the crime. Why would that judge be sending for him now? As far as he knew, he had been totally circumspect and had in no way violated any rule or law, whether criminal or ethical. He had learned that lesson and it would not be repeated. Alcohol gave the cops access to your life, so it was verboten. Ethical violations gave moral midgets like Judge Trautman access to your law license, so they were verboten, too. He would fight like hell for his clients in court, but he would never again give a court access to his license to practice law. Those days were over.

Thaddeus wore his newest three-piece navy pinstripe suit, and he had touched up his shoes after checking his messages and finding the judge wanted to see him at ten.

He watched Nancy Jo Evans, the judge's court coordinator in charge of his chief judge duties. She toiled at the flat-screen computer, presumably scheduling new cases for the six judges of the Superior Court. Nancy Jo decided which cases went to which judge; to the attorneys she was a god, as her preference of judge for a case could mean the difference between doing probation and doing time.

Her fingers flew across the keyboard as Thaddeus absently observed. While he was sitting perfectly erect and seeming to appear inflated with confidence, he knew, deep down, that he was really terrified of this mean, spiteful son of a bitch who had demanded to see him. Truth be told, Thaddeus had once been full of confidence and the swagger of youth. Then alcohol had taken him way down and the confidence had evaporated. Now he was scared and frightened, trying to remember how to again feel strong and nervy, but failing. In fact, he felt like a criminal again as he sat and waited, the sweat rolling down his back and soaking through his shirt to the suit fabric.

Finally the court coordinator seemed to acknowledge he was alive. She looked up from her screen and gave him her best phony smile. He smiled back at her. "Nancy Jo," he muttered in acknowledgment.

"Judge thinks you can help us today, Mr. Murfee," she said in a voice laced with a definitely southern drawl. She placed a finger on her screen. "He's looking to appoint you to a case. Defendant's name is Turquoise Begay. A Navajo. Capital murder, case number—write this down—2014 CF-11453. Would you be able to help with that?"

Thaddeus was shocked. Judge Trautman? A court appointment for Thaddeus Murfee? He felt like he had stepped into a parallel universe where he operated without a criminal history. *Some*thing had changed for the court to appoint him to *any*thing. He jotted the case number on his tablet.

Capital murder paid more than any other appointment. Better yet, a capital murder case always meant your name in the newspaper and at least two stories on the local TV news. But why him? A hundred doubts plagued him as he felt for an answer to her question. Could he help them with the case?

Thaddeus asked, "Who is the victim?"

Nancy Jo re-found her place on the screen. "Another Indian. Randy Begay. Same last name—but 'Begay' is like 'Smith.' Millions of them."

"Maybe related, though," Thaddeus mused. "Maybe she's accused of killing a family member?"

Nancy Jo shrugged. "Could be, I honestly don't know. All I know is the case came over from the DA and Judge Trautman said to call you for the appointment. It's been a long time since he appointed you. Maybe he figures you've done your penance. He wants you here at 11 a.m."

"It's 10:15. I'll definitely be back."

"Good. I'll let him know you accept the case."

TWENTY

After the Trautman drop-in he disappeared downstairs to the coffee shop and sat alone for a half hour, reading emails and checking case law on the issue of capital murder bail. The bail issue would reincarnate itself on the Turquoise Begay case, so he was getting ready to speak to it.

At 10:55 he returned to the chambers of H. Ivan Trautman. He told Nancy Jo hello again and took a seat. She asked him whether he had ever heard of the fifteen-year-old Navajo girl, Turquoise Begay. He said he had not. She had only smiled. "Good," she whispered to herself as she went back to her screen.

Just then, Wrasslin Russell, the guilty-verdict-queen and district attorney, showed up. He looked her over from the corner of his eye. She was short, maybe five-two, and stocky for her size, scaling out at 140, but she had a mean streak wide as Interstate 40 and a desire to

85

see all evildoers behind bars. It didn't even matter if they were guilty, the defendants. "I'll convict each and every last one of the sons-of-bitches, guilty or not," she told her supervisor when questioned about the negligible amount of cocaine seized from a college student whom she was bent on sending to prison. "I'll put each and every one of the fuckers behind bars that I can, let God sort them out!" All Thaddeus knew was that she seemed to be short in stature but long on attitude. He absently shifted in the seat so as to move away from her.

"Crowding you?" she asked without looking over.

"I'm fine, thanks."

"You're not here on the Turquoise Begay case, are you?"

"I don't know. Nancy Jo asked me if I knew her or not."

"Do you?"

"No. Do you?"

"Naw. Just another shooter."

"Who did she allegedly shoot?"

"Uncle. Blew the side of his head off."

"Poor kid. Wonder what he did to deserve that?"

The DA rolled her eyes. "Oh fuck, here we go," she muttered as she flipped the pages of a faded *People* magazine.

He looked over at her with mock chagrin. "So she's guilty—in your eyes? Already, without a trial?"

"Aren't they all? You're starting to sound like a defense lawyer. For a minute there I mistook you for a human being."

"Now don't go getting all up in my face," he said sweetly.

She tossed her Afro to the side. "As if you know 'up in my face,' cracker."

"Pardon?"

"We're done here."

"What did you just call me?" he asked, his voice climbing in pitch. "Cracker? Are you fucking kidding me here?"

At which point Nancy Jo looked up from her screen. She raised a hand. "Boys, girls, let's all play nice. Judge has had a long morning and this nasty talk won't make him happy. Suggest you both leave the 'tude out here with me. I'll watch it while you're in with him and when you come back you can have it. Save it for the playground, not in here."

"Sorry," said Thad. He settled his gaze on the far wall and withdrew. This was going to be one hell of a hearing. He could just feel it coming on. Wrasslin and Trautman in the same room? He wondered if he would wind up worse off than Turquoise Whoever when all was said and done. He half-expected it.

Suddenly he was tired and his $100 million—remaining from the casino he had once owned—looked like a good way out. He was beginning to feel very sorry he'd ever left Chicago, no matter the good reasons he'd thought he had when he fled. He realized what they said in AA was true, that even when you take a geographic you take yourself along. It applied to him and he wished he knew more about "living right" than he did. Maybe he should just get up, leave, and never look back on any of this.

He sighed and drew a deep breath. Wrasslin leaned away. Cooties, he thought, and suddenly grinned. He was back. These sons of bitches needed a good fight, he decided, idiot judge included. Now who was Turquoise Begay again?

Those were his feelings when Nancy Jo's phone buzzed and the judge asked for them.

Thaddeus went first. He knocked once on the judge's door and heard a shouted, "Enter!" from within.

He twisted the brass doorknob and pushed on through, Wrasslin close behind and then flanking him to take the far right-hand chair.

Thaddeus nodded to the judge and took the one remaining counsel chair.

The Chief Judge's office was spacious and took up the southeast corner of the courts building, looking down from the second floor onto Aspen Avenue below. The drapes were open and the window was cracked so a soft breeze lazily swayed the sheers. Thaddeus looked around, as the judge was still studying an orange-colored file open before him on the desk. H. Ivan bit his lip and nodded, alone with his thoughts.

Directly behind the judge was a doublewide bookcase that, from eye level up, was decorated with churchy knickknacks—in case there was any question about the judge's religion, here was the smoking gun. The judge also kept two sets of crossed American flags at either end of the iconography, plus a photograph (in 49ers uniform) of Steve Young, ex-BYU/SF 49ers quarterback.

Thaddeus grimaced and looked away, whereupon the judge fixed him with his eyes and said, "Are you uncomfortable here, Mr. Murfee?"

"Yes, Judge, just too much horseback time yesterday. Feeling a little sore."

"Good enough. We don't want you in anything but top form today. We need your best game for what I have in mind."

Thaddeus smiled. "And what might that be?"

"I'm appointing you to represent a young woman by the name of Turquoise Begay. Notice that is an Indian name."

"I noticed."

The judge pressed the fingers of both hands together. "Problem with the case is, we're pressed for time. I can give it three trial days, period."

Thaddeus inched forward in his chair. "Hold on. How old is Turquoise?"

"Fifteen-sixteen, thereabouts."

"And she's what, being prosecuted as an adult? Or is this a juvie case? I'm not at all familiar with juvie procedure and constitutional law and I might have to pass on this."

"She's being prosecuted as an adult," Wrasslin declared. "While she's young, she's very mature and understands the charges against her. You'll be asked to waive any competency hearing as she makes straight A's in school."

"What do straight A's have to do with competency? And you still haven't answered my question. Is this an adult or juvie case? How's she charged?"

"As an *adult*," the judge declared with a frown. "I wouldn't get you over here and interrupt your terribly busy day with a juvenile dependency petition, Counselor. Give me some credit, please."

"I do, sir," said Thaddeus. "I hold Your Honor in the highest regard. I'm just trying to understand what I'm being handed here."

"According to the police reports, she had sex with her uncle. This is based partly on a rape exam and partly on pure assumption it was the uncle. The assumption was made about the uncle because an hour later, while he was passed out, she took her dad's rifle and shot the poor man."

"Poor man? Statutory rape equals 'poor man'? Am I missing something here?"

"Rape is a penitentiary offense, you're right. But he didn't deserve to be executed for it. Not by a fifteen-year-old."

"Fifteen-year-old victim," said Thaddeus. "You calling him the victim ignores that she was a victim too, I believe."

"Counselor, are we going to have a hard time with this?" said the diminutive judge, pushing himself away from his desk. He adjusted his black eyeglasses and fixed a hard stare on Thaddeus. He crossed one leg over a knee and Thaddeus saw he was wearing cowboy boots, all nice and shiny. "I'm trying to give you some work that pays seven hundred and fifty bucks a day for court time. I know you need the work and I'm extending an olive branch here, willing to let bygones be bygones. But this isn't a case to make a huge commotion about. Ask the DA."

Thaddeus looked at his counterpart. "Roslin—you're the DA?"

For the first time, she smiled. "Sworn in less than one hour ago. New DA. First case, here we go!"

"Besides," the judge said, "this is an Indian case. You know what problems that presents for the court."

"What does being an Indian have to do with anything?"

"My great-grandfather settled Arizona up around Lee's Ferry. Back in the day, Indians were called Lamanites. Look it up. My family fought them off. Now they're drunk on firewater most of the time, swimming in their sins too many to count, and killing each other. There's so much of it pouring into my court from the reservation that time constraints kick in. We just don't have the time to drag them out like regular cases."

"Well, Your Honor, in this case I would at least like to meet with my client. As you know, I've already got one black mark against me with the bar association and don't need another one for neglecting a client."

"Two," said Trautman, "you have two black marks."

Thaddeus stared at him and sighed. "Two, then. Which makes it all the more imperative I talk with my client before we go ahead."

"You do that," spat the judge. "And let me tell you what else is going to happen in this case. I know you, Mr. Murfee. You are also known for not being entirely forthcoming in all you say. In fact, you've lied to me in open court before. You were suspended for a year for that. Beware, sir, that if you come into my court and plead this girl not guilty and then take her to trial and lose, I'm going to view that as one more lie you've told me and I'm going to personally jerk your law license permanently."

"Judge, pleading not guilty and going to trial is not—"

"Hold it, mister! Before you say something you might regret, let me remind you this meeting will be reflected in the record. DA Roslin Russell, sitting just to your right, is a witness to all that's being said in here. Are you not, madam?"

Wrasslin looked away from the window. "Haven't missed a word, Your Honor. You're trying to impress on Mr. Murfee the necessity to be forthcoming with the court."

"And if he pleads not guilty and goes to trial and loses, I'll be after his blessed license."

"Well—" Wrasslin began to say, but the judge cut her off.

"And I want you to make notes about what's being said here."

The judge cleared his throat.

"Here's some more. The state will turn over all discovery within seven days. Defense counsel and DA will then meet and negotiate. If there is no bargain, then trial will begin thirty days hence. Three days maximum for trial. Court will conduct all *voir dire*. Counsel will not be allowed *voir dire* with jury."

"So the defense will get one-half or one-point-five of the three days to present the defense case?" Thaddeus said to confirm. He was entitled to at least half the time. What the judge was ordering was also in error, which would give major grounds for an appeal. Of course the girl would be languishing behind bars for two years while the appeal went through the courts.

"State has the burden of proof, so state gets two days, defendant gets one. That's my usual stacking on these fast-track cases, Mr. Murfee."

"Judge, please. Can we get a court reporter and make a record on this? I would like to voice my objections on the record."

"You will be given a written order confirming all this. Make your objections then. Your objections are also overruled, incidentally."

"Judge, you don't even know what my objections are!" cried Thaddeus. "How on earth can you overrule before I even make them?"

"That's how it goes in my court, Mr. Murfee."

"With all due respect, I must decline the appointment. You'll need to appoint someone else to defend the girl. Someone in better standing with the court than me."

The judge's eyes narrowed. "Are you suggesting the court is prejudiced against you?"

"Do you treat all defense lawyers like this? Even the hotshots from Phoenix?"

"I told you, these Indian cases get the amount of time we can afford. No more, no less. I have standing orders with all judges to limit these Native American cases to three days, max. You're not being treated any differently than anyone else."

"Please, Judge, give this case to someone else. I think I'm leaving town, anyway."

"Not so fast. You'll leave town when I say you'll leave town. Your appointment to defend Turquoise Begay stands. The order will issue this afternoon. You can pick it up from your courthouse box. Is there anything else?"

He stared at Thaddeus straight on, just daring him.

Thaddeus swallowed hard. "No, sir. I'll go speak to her this afternoon."

"Seven days. A plea in seven days or trial in thirty. The case has been charged as a capital case, a mandatory crime. Her age is no defense against prosecution as an adult. Your client is looking at spending her natural life in prison plus one hundred years."

"Judge, she's a teenager, for crying out loud!"

"And?"

"Forget it," Thaddeus muttered, but not so loud as to be heard. He fled the chambers, Wrasslin close behind.

"Welcome to the Turquoise Begay sham," he growled.

"Don't say you weren't warned, hot shot."

TWENTY-ONE

Thaddeus downed a quick sandwich at Kathy's Kafe and thirty minutes later he hoofed it back east to the Coconino County Jail Complex, a liver-colored two-story edifice containing not only the jail but also the sheriff's office and public windows where visits could be arranged and bail could be posted.

The duty deputy buzzed him through the visitors' door and he was told to go hole up in conference room three, that Miss Begay would soon be brought to him.

He was buzzed into the room. He looked around and groaned at the sterility and lack of humanity in such places. Miserable vomit-green walls, fixtures and pipes overhead, glass brick windows, barred, that let in light but couldn't be seen through, and threadbare linoleum that must have been World War Two vintage as all pattern had been worn away and only a faint gray remained. Furniture and decor consisted of a stainless steel table, maybe four by six, bolted to the floor, a stainless steel bench along either long side, also bolted to the floor, and a Plexiglas encased Jail Rules bolted to the wall for those who might forget where they were and need a refresher in jailhouse etiquette.

He was just beginning to get angry at the long wait when the door suddenly buzzed, startling him from some kind of reverie and jolting him upright at the table. First through the door was the female deputy and a hurried comment, "Fifteen minutes and I'm back here and jerking her out." She disappeared as quickly as she had entered.

A young woman entered.

She was neither manacled nor fitted with leg irons, but entered with a shuffle step nonetheless, thanks to the jailhouse-issue flip-flops required on all prisoners.

Turquoise Begay wasn't beautiful, Thaddeus saw, but her face contained a kind of ageless wisdom in the eyes and affect. She was beautiful in the respect that he had found all Indians to be both beautiful and tragic at the same time: a result of their quiet acceptance of their always-near-tragic circumstances out on the reservation where the government had sentenced them to be born and wither a hundred years before.

Physically, she stood 5'2", thin-framed, high cheekbones, thin lips, aquiline nose that starlets would kill for, and, when she grimaced as she sat, she revealed a perfect row of bright white teeth not unlike the kernels of a perfect ear of corn all in a row and gleaming. Her hair was Navajo black and shone as if ramped up by an interior light. Like all Indians she was withdrawn and acknowledged him with neither a facial response nor a word as she silently sat and waited.

"I'm Thaddeus Murfee," he said, and gave her his professionally distant smile.

She returned his smile with a stare. Evidently she could think of nothing to say in return.

"I've been appointed by Judge Trautman to be your lawyer."

She brushed a wisp of hair from her eyes and chewed her lower lip. "I'm in trouble, aren't I," she said, not as a question but as confirmation she understood her plight. "They think I shot Uncle Randy."

Thaddeus turned the yellow legal pad over. He wrote the date at the top, and her name.

"Tell me about that," Thaddeus said. "You can speak freely in here. No one's listening and what you tell me is confidential."

She arched an eyebrow. Her looks were natural, no makeup required, and her complexion was unblemished and of light mahogany cast and she reminded him, for some reason, of a wonderful wild raven shining with youthful health and the beauty of childish innocence. She hadn't outgrown that aspect of childhood, the innocence, Thaddeus saw, and because of its presence in her soul he immediately felt protective of her. Clearly she was guilty of nothing, much less shooting anyone, and he only asked about it because he had to.

"Did you shoot him?"

"I don't even squash spiders. I don't know who shot my uncle. But I'm glad."

"You're glad he got shot?"

"I am glad. And I'm glad it killed him."

"Did he hurt you?"

"Yes."

"Did he rape you?"

"Yes."

"How many times?"

"Every day."

Thaddeus swallowed hard. He couldn't imagine but had to find out.

"How long had this daily abuse been going on?"

95

"Every day."

"I know, but how long? Months? A year?"

"Since I was ten."

"Ten?"

"He raped me first time on my tenth birthday. I had just got my first bike and he followed me down Weller Wash Road. As soon as I went over the hill he started running, threw me in the sand wash, and tore my clothes off."

"Where were your parents?"

"My mother left when I was so little I don't remember. Forever, I guess. My dad was passed out. He always gets drunk on my birthday."

"Were any other adults there?"

"No. We just have my uncle and my dad has a sister but she lives in Green Valley with an Apache."

"Any siblings?"

"No. Just me."

"Did you ever tell anyone?"

"I told Mrs. Steinmar. My caseworker."

"When did you tell her?"

"Two weeks ago."

"Anyone else?"

"I called my doctor and told her, the last time he did it to me."

"You're fifteen-sixteen now?"

"Close enough."

Thaddeus thumped his pen against the yellow pad, thinking.

"Why did you wait six years before you told someone?"

"I got an STD from him. He gave me the clap."

"So you told your caseworker."

"Indian Health Services told her. I had to go to IHS for medicine. The doctor put it in my file, my file went to Children and Family Services, and my caseworker found out. Mrs. Steinmar."

"Angelina Steinmar?"

"Yes. She's very nice to me. She wants me to get moved out of my trailer. But my dad needs me, so I told her no."

"When was the last time Randy Begay raped you?"

"He did it the day he got shot."

"Did you tell anyone?"

"Mrs. Steinmar found out. I didn't want to tell anyone, but I was bleeding and scared. So I told Mrs. Steinmar. I was afraid I had the clap again. I didn't know what was wrong."

"What did she do when you told her?"

"She said she would come get me. She was going to take me away."

"Did she?"

"The police found me walking on the road first. Before she could get there."

"What did the police do?"

"They took me back to the trailer. I was going to get clothes. Then they were taking me to wait for her at the IHS. Instead we got there and they found Randy dead."

"What did they do when they found Randy?"

"They asked me who did it."

"What did you tell them?"

"That I didn't know."

"But you didn't do it."

"I've never shot anything but coyotes when they're hunting our sheep. Only then. And I don't shoot them to kill them. I shoot at them to scare them away. But I make sure I miss."

"So you've never killed a coyote?"

"No."

"A wild dog? They come after sheep too."

"No. I told you, I don't kill things."

"Fair enough."

Thaddeus leaned back from the table. At which point the door buzzed and the same deputy reinserted her head. "Time's up. C'mon, sugar."

"Five more minutes?" Thaddeus asked. "Just about done."

"Five. You got it."

"Turquoise," Thaddeus said, "has your dad been to see you in jail?"

"No."

"If he comes, don't talk about the rape or anything with him, okay?"

"I won't."

"And of course don't talk about it with the police."

"I already talked to the police."

"Who else?"

"The doctor."

"Who else?"

"District attorney. A lady district attorney came to see me. She took my statement."

He frowned. Great, he thought, the die is cast; the facts are set in stone.

"Well, don't talk to them a second time. It would only hurt."

"If you say so."

"I say so."

"Are they going to keep me in jail?"

"For now, yes."

"Can you get me out?"

"I'm going to try."

"Someone told me they have bail. Can I get that?"

"I'm certainly going to try."

"Mr. Murfee. I didn't shoot my uncle. Honest." She began to cry. "It's awful in here and I miss my friends."

"I'm sure. I'll take you right back into court and ask for bail."

"When?"

"This week."

More tears rolled down her cheeks. He slipped the white handkerchief from his coat and passed it to her. She wiped at her eyes but the tears kept flowing as she cried without sound. He guessed she had cried without sound many times when her uncle was taking advantage and the father was home and passed out. He realized that she had been taught to cry without noise so no one would know, and she did that now. It touched his heart and he wanted to reach and squeeze her shoulder, but did not. She would take that wrong, probably, and he needed to get close to her, not risk pushing her farther away. His own eyes moistened as he felt her grief. Then he caught himself. You're not going to allow your own feelings to get in the way here, he ordered himself. For once, you're going to keep your distance between your heart and your client's difficulty. Stay professional and stay focused on that!

The door buzzed and this time was flung wide open. The deputy came in and motioned Turquoise to stand and go with her.

"I'll be back tomorrow," he said to Turquoise as her back disappeared out the door.

She left without another word, resigned to the world she now found herself inhabiting. Always resigned to her fate, like Indians were always resigned. They had given up so many years ago it had become an epidemic among them, he believed. That accounted for the hopelessness of their alcoholism and drug abuse and for their preying on each other and for the sexual abuse in families. There was just no hope and so no one cared. It was heartbreaking and Thaddeus had to once again remind himself to stay focused and stay aloof. At all costs, he reminded himself. This is an H. Ivan Trautman case and you simply cannot get emotionally involved. Period.

He sat at the steel table another ten minutes, writing down his thoughts and impressions. One thing had become abundantly clear and that was that H. Ivan wasn't going to be happy with him. Because there was no way in hell he would ever plead this girl to anything. H. Ivan could go screw himself, as far as Thaddeus was concerned. You want a trial in thirty days? Fine, we'll give you a trial. But I'm going to need some help—that was his next thought. There was a world to do before he would be ready to try to give her her life back by jury verdict.

TWENTY-TWO

They've got her cold," he told Katy that night. "They've got gunshot residue on her shirt and they've got overwhelming motive, with the six-year history of rape."

Katy flew into a rage, which alarmed him, as he'd never seen her touched off like that. She became furious and cried; she wanted to hear no more. She clambered upstairs and slammed their bedroom door. While she did whatever she had to do, Thaddeus geared up and headed out behind the house, where the property abutted the Coconino National Forest. For miles around that night he could be heard out back, shooting the kitchen rifle at Coke bottles. He more or less kept count of the shots in the back of his mind. He was sure he had run through at least three boxes of ammunition when he returned inside.

After supper, when Sarai was tucked in bed and stories were

read, Katy came back down. "Sit," she ordered, and he went into the family room and wedged his back against the armrest of the white leather couch, and removed his hiking boots. He dumped the boots on the floor and then pulled his legs up and stretched out, facing the side windows. Outside the pines loomed large and black against the moonlit sky. He balanced a mug of coffee in one hand and rubbed his temples with the other. He was headachy and not in a very good mood. But he always felt that way after a round with H. Ivan Trautman.

"This girl—Turquoise is her name?" asked Katy.

"Turquoise."

"Last name Begay?"

"Yes."

"I'm related to her. I know her. I know about her uncle. She's the main reason I dropped out of school this fall. She's the one I stayed to help, really try to help."

"You never mentioned her to me."

"She's a patient. Confidential."

"Got it."

"And Trautman has appointed you to defend her?"

"Yes."

"And there's no way you can get out of that?"

"No."

"My father's cousin."

"Pardon?" he absently asked. What was this about her father's cousin?

"He was *my* uncle Randy."

"His name was Randy too? I'm afraid I don't get it, Kate."

"I didn't say that. He was the Uncle Randy of my life. My rapist."

"What? This is new information."

A dark pain crept into her voice. "That's because I've never told anyone before. You're the first."

"When was this?"

"In high school. And eighth grade. That's when it started."

"Is this son of a bitch still around?" Thaddeus was the one enraged now. If only he could lay hands on the guy. Like Turquoise, Katy too had grown up on the reservation. In a different part of the state, yes, but it was the same Navajo reservation. Same squalor, he had learned over the years, same hard times.

"He is still around," she said. "He lives in Window Rock."

"What are you going to do about it?"

"Nothing. He's an alcoholic failure at everything. He's worthless."

"But what if he does it to someone else? Then how would you feel?"

She sighed long and hard. "I've thought about that. I don't have any younger siblings for him to violate in my immediate family. Beyond that, there's really nothing I can do."

"So...have you gotten any help for it ever? Seen a professional to talk about it?"

"Not yet. Maybe I will someday. I've adjusted and learned to live with it. It's just sort of become a part of my life and I'm smart enough to keep it compartmentalized."

"This is awful. I'm so sorry."

"Well, back to Turquoise Begay. I'd like to help her."

"Sure. What do you have in mind?"

"I don't know. I'll have to think about it. I'll get back to you on that."

"Sure."

They talked another five minutes about nothing and finally said good night.

TWENTY-THREE

The next day he visited Turquoise for the second time. He had decided he needed to know more about her before he began his investigation out on the reservation. She came into the conference room, led there by a female deputy dressed in the liver and brown uniform of the sheriff's office, an unsmiling woman who wordlessly steered the young girl into a seat at the table, where she cuffed her through a hasp that kept her bound to the table. "Why the upgrade in security?" Thaddeus asked, indicating the cuff and restraining hasp.

"She's been talking about killing herself. She's on suicide watch. I'll be right outside the door but I'll be watching through the window. You've got five minutes, mister."

"I'll take as long as I need, thank you."

"Five minutes. Then she's got to be somewhere else."

"BS. I'll knock when I'm done."

The door closed just as quickly as it had opened and Thaddeus was alone with Turquoise. The girl's eyes were red and swollen. Crying and who knew what else, he thought, and he immediately wondered what he might have to say to a teenage girl bent on killing herself.

"Suicide watch?" he began slowly, and then stopped. He looked at her, waiting to see if she would swim to the surface.

"I hate myself," she said in a whisper. "They all think I killed Uncle Randy."

"But you know you didn't. I know you didn't. I think I might have a suspect in mind, but I can't tell you that yet."

"When I left the trailer that day, he was alive. I could hear him snoring in the back bedroom. I hated how he snored. Sometimes he would pull me close after he raped me. And make me sleep with his arms around me, touching me all over. I hated him. I wanted him dead. But I didn't kill him. I don't even kill spiders."

"I believe you, Turquoise. So we need to talk about who else might have been mad enough at Uncle Randy to shoot him."

She looked up from the table. "I know he did drugs. Maybe one of those people he knew."

"How do you know he did drugs?"

"He used to make me take things."

"What kind of things?"

"He made me snort cocaine five times. He said the sex would be better."

"What else?"

"I took ecstasy lots. He said it made me sexier to him. I didn't feel sexier, so I don't know."

Thaddeus was making his notes. "Anything else?"

"I just know he was always outside taking pills. Especially when my dad was home. He never took drugs around my dad. He always went outside in the driveway for that. I watched him out my bedroom window."

"You could see him outside?"

"Uh-huh. My bedroom is in front."

Thaddeus stopped writing. "I want to make a deal with you, okay?"

"I guess. What kind of deal?"

"If you promise me you won't kill yourself, I promise you that I will get you out of this."

She looked suspicious. Her eyes narrowed and she reluctantly looked more alert. "How are you going to do that? Everyone thinks I shot him."

"Even if you shot him, I will get you out of this."

"But I didn't!" she cried. "I didn't shoot him, Mr. Murfee."

"I believe you. I'm only saying that I will get you out of this no matter what—if you will promise me you won't kill yourself. Can we have a deal?"

She pressed her fingertips together. Her eyes fell back to the table and she slowly nodded. "If you promise. But one of the matrons told me I was going to spend my life in prison and I should start reading the Bible. I don't want to read the Bible. I want to go home and go back to my school and see my friends. I hate the Bible."

"Do us both a favor and don't talk to anyone else while you're here. If someone like that matron starts in on you again just politely tell her your attorney has asked you to discuss nothing—including reading materials. Because that's what I'm asking you to do now. Whether you read something or not is nobody's business but yours and mine. Are we cool on that?" He thumped his pen against his yellow legal pad, waiting.

"We're cool. If I was going to read anything, it wouldn't be that."

"So, do you want me to bring you something to read?"

"Yes. I like stuff about girls my age, please."

106

"Listen, let's do this. My wife wants to meet with you. Her name is Katy. She wants to work with you and work on your case. She's Navajo, like you. Not but about ten-twelve years older than you, either. She can bring books."

Again, the narrowed eyes and head tilted to the side. "Why does she want to meet with me?"

"You'll know her when you see her. She'll tell you what she has in mind. My question is, would you like to meet with her? Check her ideas out?"

"I'll check her out. If it makes you feel better."

He sat back and spread his hands. "Hey, Turquoise, this isn't about me. This is about you. Everything we're going to do is about you."

"That's cool. I'm okay with her coming and talking."

"I'll pass it along. She'll be here in the next couple of days."

"Am I going to be here two more days? Really?"

"Just until we can have a bail hearing. I'll be filing that motion today and then I'll get word back to you about a hearing date. After that we just might get you out. We'll see."

The matron rapped on the glass with her keys. "One minute!" she cried through the glass. Thaddeus nodded.

"Remember," he said gravely, "knock off the suicide stuff. We want you around for a long time. Besides, we've got a deal. Do you remember our deal?"

She sighed. "You'll get me out if I don't kill myself. Even if I shot him. Which I didn't."

"Good. You're a smart young lady. And you're tough if you lived through the hell of Uncle Randy since you were ten. Tell the truth, you had every right in the world to shoot the son of a bitch and I wouldn't blame you if you had."

For the first time in two days, she smiled. "That's what I'm thinking deep down. Son of a bitch had it coming."

"My sentiments exactly. One other thing: Do you have a boyfriend?"

"Tommy Begay. He lives in Wells. He's a senior and loves working on his car."

"Did he know about what Uncle Randy was doing to you?"

"Why?"

"I'm looking at everyone who had a reason to shoot Uncle Randy."

"Tommy didn't know. I never told him or anyone. Except the clinic. But I told you about that, the clap and all. So Mrs. Steinmar knew too. But she wouldn't tell Tommy. I don't think I ever told her about Tommy."

"Okay. Well, they want to shut us down, so let's say goodbye and we'll be in touch about the bail hearing."

Before the girl could answer, the door swung open and the same deputy barged inside. "C'mon, little sis," she said. "It's almost lunchtime for B wing. Sloppy Joe's and fries today."

"Later," Thaddeus said as she was being freed from the restraint.

"Later," she said.

TWENTY-FOUR

Henry Landers once told Thaddeus he took sheep temperatures anally. This was when they were ailing. "It's just like with a man," Henry said. "No matter how big a lie the mouth is telling, the asshole never lies. Stick your thermometer up his ass if you need the truth."

Which was exactly what Thaddeus was intent on doing Monday morning when he walked across to the district attorney's office. He had a meeting with DA Wrasslin to learn what evidence they had collected against Turquoise. It was a process known as Discovery, and it was based on the 1963 Supreme Court case of *Brady v. Maryland*, where the Supremes ruled that if the prosecution withholds from the defense exculpatory evidence, it violates the Due Process clause of the Constitution. Which means the defendant goes free.

"Brady Day" in Arizona courts was the day defense attorneys met with prosecutors and, as *Brady* had seeped throughout the system, basically opened their files to the defense attorney. In theory, any and everything got revealed because the prosecutor didn't later want to be accused of withholding evidence that might have helped the defendant. To do so could cost a deceitful prosecutor his or her license to practice law. In practice, prosecutors still played hide-the-ball and required the highest degree of investigation and intuition or guesswork the defense attorney could bring to bear. For it was always up to the defendant's lawyer to ferret out the truth and the whole truth from the DAs.

Thaddeus rubbed his hands together gleefully as he swung inside the courthouse. Today he was going to take their temperature. And he was going to stick it up their ass if they lied. He figured he already knew Turquoise wasn't guilty and knew they would be hard-pressed to turn up evidence that she was. Why? Because she had told him she didn't shoot her uncle. And he believed her. Hell, she didn't even squash spiders—what more did you need?

In the DA's waiting room, from a stiff plastic chair, he could see straight into the newly minted district attorney's office. She was huddled at her sumptuous desk, green phone jammed against her ear, examining her nails, touching up here and there with a nail file as she spoke. She didn't see him come in and wasn't aware he was observing her. She held one hand up to the light and focused on the nails. Then she again undertook the task of getting them under control with the metal file. File-examine-file was how it went several times as he watched.

Actually he was trying not to stare, but another part of him—the lawyer part—was sizing up his adversary. Was she worthy and fit? He honestly didn't know, but she had the reputation of a brawler. The few times he had gone up against her on felony DUIs and miscellaneous misdemeanors she had come across as nervous and harried. Her right eye was a tell, twitching and jerking spasmodically as courtroom pressure mounted, on those occasions when Thaddeus was present. He didn't know that she had seen three ophthalmologists about the twitch, or that various lotions, salves, and drops had been tried, or that the twitch had overcome them all, persisting despite the medical industry's assaults.

In a frustrated moment, the third and final eye doctor had referred Wrasslin to a psychiatrist, who had wasted no time prescribing anti-anxiety pills and told her to give up her courtroom duties—something no elected district attorney could ever afford to do, not if she intended running for reelection based on her record. In a sense she was stuck, and Thaddeus knew that if he played his cards right that morning he would soon have the twitch fired up and the prosecutor anxious to agree to some kind of settlement just to save face—if it could be called that.

At long last the phone light blinked off on the receptionist's phone and she told Thaddeus to go right in. He picked up his own thin file, squared himself to meet the gauche attempts at debasement attempted by all prosecutors and marched in.

"So how's the newest DA in Arizona?" he asked brightly, trying to set a light tone.

"Fucked over. Defense lawyers nipping at my heels, unhappy police who think everybody belongs behind bars, secretaries with sick kids, and a nosy newspaper reporter who has requested hourly updates on the prosecution of my predecessor's killer."

"You mean my client, Angelina Steinmar. Who, it is *alleged*, is the killer."

She sighed long and hard. "See what I mean? It never ends. Now who are you here on—" she said and riffled a stack of manila files. "Yep, here we are. Next up, your girl Turquoise Begay."

"Who actually is innocent."

The prosecutor's hand, unburying the Begay file, froze in midair. "Tell me we're not going to start like that. Please tell me."

Thaddeus leaned back in his chair. He waved his hand expansively. "Then tell me what you've got that makes you think you have a case."

"I've got motive. We picked up the IHS clinic files. Evidently he was having sex with her. We're thinking it might have been consensual."

"Think again. He's been raping her since her tenth birthday."

"Maybe, maybe not."

"Even if it was consensual, Wrasslin, it would still equal stat rape."

"But you don't get to murder someone for committing stat rape. Read the rules, Counselor."

"Very ha-ha funny. So what else do you have besides records that prove statutory rape by your poor victim?"

"We've got the murder weapon. Winchester .30-.30 carbine. Fully loaded minus one. Wiped down but we're testing it for DNA."

"Meaning?"

"Someone wiped it for prints. We're testing the stock where her face rested when she was aiming. There will be body oil there that might give up the DNA that will send your girl to prison until she's at least sixty."

"So you're thinking the gun was wiped down? Isn't that *Brady* material, the lack of fingerprints? I believe I'm entitled to your lab workup."

"Not a problem. I'll give you everything I've got."

"Sure you will, madam DA. Just like you guys always do."

A look of concern came over Thaddeus' face at the mention of trace DNA. He knew that advances in DNA profiling technology sometimes allowed for the analysis of minute quantities of DNA. He knew that it was possible to obtain successful DNA results from cellular material transferred from the skin of an individual who had simply touched an object. He hoped to God Turquoise was telling him the truth. It would make the case much more complex were her DNA found on a gun that had been wiped down. Of course, she could always claim that she cleaned that room and handled that gun every Saturday when she performed her cleaning duties, but the fact the gun had been wiped was in and of itself some indicia of guilt. People don't wipe weapons down unless they're trying to hide something. Heaven forbid any DNA testing pointed to her. He knew he could easily explain it away, but it gave the DA talking points and he wanted to minimize those.

He cleared his throat. "So it looks like I'm going to have ask Judge Trautman for county money to have my own DNA testing?"

The DA laughed. "Good luck with that. He's going to tell you the cost is prohibitive, that you can use the state's testing in your defense."

"I'm sure you're right, he will, knowing that—" He wanted to use a profanity but thought better of it.

"Hey, he is what he is. Some people hate him but you have to respect him. He's damn good at judging."

"Everyone's entitled to their opinion. Ours are very different, yours and mine."

"You aren't still upset about him disbarring you, are you? You sure had it coming."

Thaddeus shook his head. "Tell the truth, I enjoyed my year off. Got to see a lot of new country, met some nice people, lost twenty pounds. A fair trade."

She paused flipping through the file. "Okay, we also have your client's statement."

"Telling you she's not guilty."

"Not exactly. She says she wanted to kill him herself and even thought of using the rifle to shoot him while he slept."

"But she didn't say she actually carried through on that."

"She didn't, no. But still, we've got her admitting she considered

113

shooting him, at the very least, *with* the murder weapon."

"Probably not even admissible in evidence."

"Probably is. Shows state of mind."

"Which would be relevant to what known fact?"

"DNA on gun."

"How about this. How about I stipulate she handled the gun. Of course her DNA's there. She cleaned the room every Saturday. It was a job her father gave her. So, what else you got? I'm sure you ran gunshot residue testing on the shirt she was wearing when the cops picked her up off the highway. The lack of GSR is exculpatory. You got that for me?"

She scowled. "We tested her shirt. Found GSR. They swabbed her hands and face, too. Nothing found. You've got me on the hands, Counsel. But I've got you on the shirt."

He had to admit he was surprised. She had said nothing about firing a gun. His pulse started to pick up. He could feel his client slip an inch away from his protective grasp.

He bluffed. "So she fired a gun at some point. She guards sheep. She might've fired off a round at some predator."

"Sure, Counsel."

"Hey, it's *Brady* material as to the hands. I want the report."

"Done. So are you ready to discuss a plea for this young lady?"

Thaddeus knew he would never plead Turquoise to anything—even with the gunshot residue. They would explain that somehow. Still, he didn't want to lay his cards on the table. Not yet.

He said, "Sure, let's talk about a plea. What's your best offer?"

"I can do second-degree murder. Fifteen to twenty-five max. She'll be out in ten years."

He was surprised. It actually wasn't a bad plea to someone facing first-degree murder charges like Turquoise. He guessed they were somewhat backing down due to the sexual abuse, which wouldn't play well with any jury. The girl would have a lot of sympathy and a jury would pull for her. If there was an out, they would probably give her a pass. Which made a plea-bargain all but impossible. Flat out, he knew the state couldn't convict his client. That was the bottom line. DNA testing might have some impact, but even that would be minimal.

"Before you answer, Counsel, let me add one more thing to the plea dynamic."

"That would be what?"

"She told us she made up the sex story about the uncle. She told us she was actually having sex with her boyfriend. That's where she got the clap."

"What? Impossible!"

"I've got it videotaped. You'll get a copy."

"Did the cops take her to the hospital for a rape kit?"

"A rape exam was done."

"Did she claim she was raped?"

Wrasslin smiled. "I just told you. She never mentioned rape, intercourse, or anything like it. It just didn't come up. They asked her, but it went nowhere. But the hospital did the swab anyhow. Standard operating procedure."

"The rape was ongoing since age ten. He had made her his wife since her tenth birthday. He raped her every night of her life."

"Nope, never mentioned it. So, rape kit came back positive for sex. Even if the DNA points at Uncle Randy and it was rape, so what? She doesn't get to kill him for rape anymore than I would get to. Murder is murder, Counselor."

"Are DNA tests being done?"

"Yes."

"And you think if it was Uncle Randy who was raping her, that that means nothing?"

"Pretty much, Counselor. In this country we don't get to shoot sleeping people."

"Ever think self-defense? She's been abused for six years. Every stinking day."

He shook his head and gave her an angry look. She picked up the nail file and acted as if she had no worries about her case.

"Tomorrow is the hearing on my motion for bail. Are you going to object to her release to the custody of a juvenile authority?"

"You betcha. She belongs in jail. You want I should agree to a shooter running around some foster home? You kidding me?"

"Shooter! Please, you have zero evidence she shot anyone. None at all. You have proximity to the scene of the crime. You have a rifle that anyone could have used and certainly does not have her fingerprints on it. You have GSR but she shot at predators that were after her sheep. You have no witness. You have no confession of shooting. You have no case!"

"Let's save the argument for H. Ivan, what do you say? We about done here?"

"What time do I get my discovery package?"

"It'll all be in your courthouse box before four. Fair enough? Now. The second degree is open until five o'clock today. After that, it's all bets off, we're going to trial and there will be no further offers."

"This is bullshit."

The DA laughed. She filed another nail and couldn't stop smiling.

"You defense attorneys are all the same. Nobody's guilty of anything. Amazing."

"I'll check my box at four o'clock. If the package isn't there I'm filing an emergency motion with the judge. We have trial in thirty days and I need that discovery."

"And have it you shall. See you tomorrow, Counselor."

Thaddeus stormed out of her office and without breaking stride marched next door to the jail. He slapped his bar card down on the counter and demanded to see Turquoise without delay. The woman behind the glass gave him a funny look and shrugged. You could read her face: just another crazy, her look said. Thaddeus turned his back on her while she paged for the inmate. He was fuming and almost losing it. Incredible as it sounded, they claimed to have Turquoise on video stating there had been no attacks by the uncle.

A thought occurred. In a way, that helped her case, the more he thought about it: without the attacks, her motive to shoot him vanished. However, there was one little problem with that: it was a lie. DNA tests would eventually prove it was untrue. So they had her in a giant lie, which would make any jury look askance at the rest of her testimony. The prosecutor would get to say, "Hey, she lied to us there, what makes you think she's not lying to you now?" And so it would go. Another client with her foot caught in the trap because she violated Criminal Law Rule 1, which was to never, ever talk to the police or the prosecutors. He was fuming when the door buzzed and the deputy told him to please pass through.

He was dismayed when he saw her. The normally black, shiny hair was flattened on her head and no longer glistened. It gave off a dull, lackluster look. Her mahogany skin looked pallid, as if she hadn't been in the sun for weeks—which was almost true. And she looked tired. New lines around her teenage eyes revealed how little sleep she had been getting inside this nuthouse where no one ever really got to sleep anyway. She was going downhill and Thaddeus felt great anxiety as he contemplated the chances of H. Ivan Trautman granting her any kind of custodial release tomorrow.

He didn't waste any time.

"You told the DA your uncle wasn't raping you?"

She looked down and away. "Yes."

"Why would you tell them that?"

"I was—it made—embarrassment. I was embarrassed by him raping me."

"You mean you felt ashamed."

"I felt like I did something wrong."

"Well, now we've got a huge lie to deal with in front of the jury."

"I'm sorry. I just felt too bad."

He touched her shoulder to give a reassuring squeeze as a big brother would to a little sister, and she pulled back.

"No, you don't need to be sorry. We all get ashamed sometimes. It's just that your history of telling the truth is going to be a big deal in front of your jury. They're going to see you lied and that makes everything you say subject to suspicion."

"I'm sorry. I really made this hard for you. But that doesn't change the main thing. I didn't shoot Uncle Randy."

"Did your boyfriend shoot him?"

"He didn't know about Uncle Randy. I never told."

"You never told anyone."

"I never told anyone. But I wrote it down."

"What? Where!"

"My diary."

"Good grief, where do you keep it?"

"In the floor of the trailer. In my bedroom, the linoleum lifts up. My diary is under there. Six of them."

"Six books?"

She nodded. "I know, how did I fill six books? Well, I started on my tenth birthday. That was my present from my aunt, a diary."

"You mean the first time Randy raped you—you wrote that down in there?"

"I did. And every time after. It's all in there."

"Oh sweet—we've got to get those books."

"Just go in my bedroom and slide the nightstand over. The linoleum curls up and there they are. But they're locked."

"Not to worry. I promise I'll get them unlocked."

"The keys are in my dresser inside the blue music box. It plays

Claire de Lune."

"I'll need all six of them."

"Just don't show them to anyone."

"Let's talk about that some other time."

"Okay.

"Now the sixty-four-dollar question. The shirt you were wearing when you were arrested. Let's talk about that."

"My Lakers shirt. What about it?"

"They found gunshot residue on it. You had fired a gun recently, according to the laboratory tests they ran on the shirt."

"I don't know. I don't remember."

"You don't remember whether you fired a gun?"

"I'm with the sheep every day. I take the gun to scare off coyotes and wild dogs."

"What about the day you were arrested? Did you shoot the gun that day?"

"Maybe. I don't—I think I did. That might have been the day I scared off a coyote."

"Do we have any way to prove that?"

"What do you mean?"

"Did you write it down in your diary?"

"I don't write that kind of stuff down. I scare off animals every day just about."

"Okay."

She nervously picked at the skin on her thumb. "What about tomorrow? Is he going to let me out?"

Thaddeus spread his hands. "I honestly don't know."

TWENTY-FIVE

Because Turquoise was a minor, H. Ivan Trautman ordered the bail hearing be heard in his office. While it should have been a public hearing because Turquoise Begay was being prosecuted as an adult, Judge Trautman had other ideas.

Ideas that soon became apparent to Thaddeus, as he sat beside his client, who was handcuffed and clothed in the orange of the CCSD inmate garb. She had found a brush and had managed to brush her hair, so it looked a hundred percent better, Thaddeus thought. But she still had that tired, thirty-year-old cocktail waitress look, as if she had suffered too many after-midnights with too much cigarette smoke in the room and too many cocktails. None of which was true, not in Turquoise's case.

The judge let it be known at exactly 2:01 p.m. why they were holding the hearing in his office. He was going off the record, he revealed, out of earshot of the general public, and he wanted privacy for what he had to say.

"Ladies and gentlemen—we're off the record," he said to the reporter, "for a minute. This is the time for the hearing on the defendant's motion for modification of conditions of release. Mr. Murfee, you're seeking to have Turquoise Begay released to Children and Family Services."

"That's correct, Your Honor."

H. Ivan Trautman leaned back in his chair, his head bookended by the shelf behind, upon which was perched his religious icons. Thaddeus studied him closely. The perverse little bastard almost looks angelic in that black robe, he thought. Or satanic. Take your pick.

Finished with his inner reflection, the judge took it up again.

"What I fail to understand"—he was talking directly to Thaddeus—"is why bail is necessary? Why don't we have a plea here? Wasn't that the goal?"

"It was," agreed Wrasslin. She was dressed in burgundy slacks and gold blazer today, festooned with gold buttons and a white pocket square edged in gold. She looked chic and fresh and ready for war.

"That was the goal, Your Honor," said Thaddeus, "from *your* standpoint. That was never the goal from *my* standpoint."

The judge shot upright. "Counsel! I made it clear to you when I appointed you that this was an open-and-shut case. You've got the niece with a motive, according to the IHS medical records. She has the clap and she killed her uncle for giving it to her."

"Actually, she recanted the uncle involvement," Thaddeus replied. "She said it was her boyfriend."

"But there's no other suspect!" the judge cried. "I expected a plea."

"And you said if there was no plea, I should be prepared for trial in thirty days. I got my discovery yesterday from the prosecutor and I'm telling the court I can be ready for trial in thirty days."

"The court reporter will put that last statement on the record. That counsel has indicated he can be ready for trial in thirty days. Now we're off the record again."

"Please, let's put everything on the record," Thaddeus responded. "My client is entitled to a record."

"This isn't about your client, Mr. Murfee. This is about you. Now listen up. You came into my court a year ago and lied to me. I can only wonder if that's what's going on right now with this demand for a trial. So here's what we're going to do. You can have your trial; your client can have her full day or two or three in court. But I'm telling you—off the record—that if your client is found guilty I *will* find some way to jerk your license permanently. I will personally take it upon myself to make sure you *never* practice law again anywhere, if you screw with me. Am I making myself clear?"

"Perfectly," said Thaddeus. He felt his skin flush and then the blood leave his face. He knew he looked pale and looked like a common liar to the judge. How would he ever come back from what happened a year ago? Would this man never believe him again about anything? Probably not, he decided, so he might as well plunge ahead.

"Defense is ready for trial," he said, and began packing his file.

"The state will be ready, Your Honor," Wrasslin was only too happy to offer. She beamed at the judge.

"On the record now. Counsel, you have filed your motion for modification of the conditions of release. Please tell the court why you believe the conditions of bail should be modified."

Thaddeus nodded. "First, Your Honor, you have set bail at one million dollars. This is a minor living in a house trailer on the Navajo reservation: The poorest per capita population of any population in the U.S., including Appalachia and West Virginia and Mississippi. The notion that somehow a child living in reservation squalor should have access to bail in that amount demonstrates that the court would have set such an amount, one, without knowing anything about the defendant's financial condition, and, two, without knowing anything about the level of proof of guilt and the presumption that could arise, and, three, with a mindset of keeping the minor in jail regardless. The law says that, in a murder case, where the proof is evident and the presumption great, bail shall be denied."

Thaddeus went on without taking a breath. "But that's for capital murder cases, which this case is not. This is an ordinary—if I can be allowed to call such a matter 'ordinary'—murder case without the heinous implications that would make it rise to the level of a capital murder case. If the shooting as charged in the indictment were proven, it would be clear there was no cruelty in the manner of death, there was no exaggerating circumstance, and there was no concomitant felony underway that would make the case fit inside the felony-murder rule. So we have a plain vanilla murder case and bail should be allowed in those cases. The question thus becomes, how much?"

The judge took on a stony look. His displeasure registered on his face. "Counsel, are you saying bail in an amount she's capable of posting should be ordered? Are you telling the court a thousand dollars might be a reasonable amount? Is that your argument?"

"Better than that, Judge. I'm telling the court she should be released without any bail at all, that, because she is a minor, she should be released to the Department of Children and Family Services and made a ward during the pendency of the case. Once I prove her innocent, the dependency should be lifted."

The judge couldn't restrain himself. He actually laughed, which caused Wrasslin to join him. Even the matron who had accompanied Turquoise into chambers couldn't help smiling.

"I don't see the humor the court evidently sees," said Thaddeus levelly. "This is a minor child who really has no business around the adult population she's exposed to in jail."

The judge's eyes grew wide. He swiped a hand across his forehead and wiped it on a tissue. "She hasn't been segregated out of the adult population? Am I hearing you right?" His voice had notched down. Jailing a minor with an adult prison population was a violation of federal law. The county was open to a huge federal lawsuit for the oversight. H. Ivan was frightened.

"That's why I asked for an expedited hearing, Your Honor. She's being locked up with adults. I've told her we can avoid the necessity of filing a federal civil rights lawsuit by simply obtaining her release from custody. Then there would be no need to sue." There. The fix was in, game on.

"Oh my sweet Jehoshaphat," the judge moaned—in what would be the closest thing to a curse that he would utter. "Miss Begay, you were never supposed to be introduced into to the adult population of our local jail. The court's sincerest apologies for that."

"That's okay," said Turquoise. "There's some nice people."

"And counsel," the judge said to the DA, "you make darn good and sure your sheriff knows this girl is a minor and belongs with other minors."

"What about my motion?" Thaddeus asked. "Will she be released to DCFS?"

"She will," said the judge. "It is so ordered. Defendant is immediately released to the custody of Children and Family Services. Placement to a proper foster home. Trial in thirty days. The clerk will put an order in your box. Anything else?"

"No, Your Honor," both attorneys said in unison.

"Then we're adjourned. Please leave my office now."

"You're free, almost," Thaddeus whispered to Turquoise.

The judge couldn't have been any nicer, in the end, Thaddeus thought. *And he couldn't shoo us out of his office fast enough. Such a tempestuous pest I can be.*

So it was done. Turquoise was sprung. Just outside the door she stopped and thanked him. She leaned up and gave him a hug even as the matron was removing handcuffs.

"Call me when you're placed," he told her. "Make an appointment to come in no later than tomorrow. We've got a lot of work to do."

Walking back downstairs in the courthouse, Thaddeus was fully lost in thought. The judge was convinced Turquoise was guilty, which would make for an unpleasant trial in and of itself. Evidentiary objections would be heavily weighted in favor of the prosecutor. The judge's demeanor toward the defendant would noticeably be one of distaste. Jury instructions—the statements of law the judge gives the jurors based on submissions by both lawyers—would wherever possible be worded in such a way as to undermine the defense theory of the case. Presumptions of innocence would be announced but downplayed.

And the evidence wasn't as clear-cut as Thaddeus had first thought. He had learned the prosecutor obtained the Lakers shirt worn by Turquoise on the day of the shooting and that the shirt contained gunshot residue and had tested positive. At some point that same day, the DA would get to argue to the jury, the defendant had fired a gun. He would get to argue it wasn't necessarily gunshot residue from that same shooting or even from that day. But that was all argument; it wasn't definitive. And there was another thing. Possibly they could tie her to the killing rifle itself if DNA testing came back with her profile. Granted these things were arguable both ways, but when they began to be added one on top of the other, as a whole they began to be more and more compelling.

The IHS medical records would be proof she had claimed her uncle gave her the STD. Which meant some form of sexual abuse, the DA could argue, which gave the young woman motive to kill.

Thaddeus walked outside the courthouse, shaking his head. He did not like the addition, the mathematics of the case, as item was stacked on top of item. He was even beginning to wonder himself about her guilt—something he seldom allowed himself to ponder

125

when defending criminal cases. The best defense attorneys remained neutral in their minds. That way they avoided personal involvement that would otherwise cloud the thinking. For this case he needed mental acuity and best judgment; he needed distance from his client, which would be difficult once Katy entered the scene and began carrying the Turquoise torch. He would need to be very careful from here on.

Later that day, when she came to his office, Thaddeus said to her, "Turquoise, I know that when women get sexually abused they might do things they wouldn't otherwise do. Maybe you became so enraged at your uncle for forcing himself on you that you finally just broke down and lost it and took the rifle in your hands for protection while he was sleeping. If that was the case—and I'm only postulating here—then I can make a good case of delayed self-defense or temporary insanity of a sort. Maybe you would like to think about this and ask yourself whether there's the possibility you shot your uncle and even now are having difficulty admitting to yourself that it happened. I mean I've seen cases like that, where people do things and later don't remember doing them at all. If it happened...I can still help you escape a jury that doesn't believe your claim of innocence."

Turquoise said in her soft voice, "I will get to tell my story at trial?"

"Yes, I mean maybe. We won't know for sure about that until we hear the state's case. Then we'll decide."

"No, I want to tell my story. I want the jury to hear the truth."

"What will you tell them?"

"I will tell them that I was angry, very angry. But that I would never kill anyone. I would tell them that I don't even try to hit the coyotes and dogs when I shoot. I would tell them that I don't even squash the big desert spiders that live in our trailer. I wouldn't kill anything. And I didn't kill my uncle."

"Got it."

"Maybe you don't believe me, Thaddeus, but the jury will listen. They will understand what happened to me. And they will know I wouldn't kill anyone because I will tell them so."

"Okay. Then we'll go with that. But I'm not saying that you'll testify. That remains to be decided."

"But I want to testify. Just so you know."

Thaddeus sighed. Criminal Law Rule 2: the defendant doesn't testify. There's too much opportunity for the kind of cross-examination by the DA that restates the state's theory of the case a pebble at a time. Questions like, "Now we know we found gunshot residue on your shirt and yet you're telling us you didn't shoot a gun that day? Yes or no?" And so it would go until the state had perfectly and indelibly told the jury its case through the defendant's own lack of opportunity to say anything other than yes or no to such closed-end questions. He shuddered inside. That day mustn't ever be allowed to come around. He would have to dissuade her from testifying at all. Which, he could now see, would be a difficult job itself.

Almost as bad as Turquoise taking the stand was the fact of H. Ivan's hatred of Thaddeus. Somehow he was now looking at permanent loss of his license to practice law if he lost the Turquoise case at trial. So he had a client with two strikes against her on one side of the equation, and a judge with two strikes against him on the other. It was no longer the defendant's guilt or non-guilt that was at stake here; it was his own future as well.

TWENTY-SIX

That night, on the drive home, Thaddeus tried to imagine what he would do with himself if he lost his law license. Money wouldn't be an issue; he had plenty of money. But his self-respect would flush straight down the toilet. He would have an incredibly hard time living with himself if he lost his license, particularly given that he had suffered and been enormously deprived even of sufficient food during his three years in law school. What, it had all come down to one trial? *Color me stupid*, he thought, *I cannot believe what this judge has suckered me into by giving me this case. Son of a*—he couldn't finish the thought. He slammed his fist hard against the dashboard and stomped the gas, angrily passing three cars at twenty over the speed limit. He was at wits' end with this Trautman guy and didn't know which way to turn.

DEFENDING TURQUOISE

◇◇◇

They drove into town that night for dinner at the Red Rainbow. They brought Sarai, who was too big for a booster chair. Sarai chatted all through dinner, spilled her milk, dropped spaghetti noodles in her lap, and devoured two scoops of rich chocolate ice cream. Thaddeus was pleased with the girl's chattiness.

The worm had definitely turned there. Whatever Katy was doing with her was definitely working.

TWENTY-SEVEN

S hep left a cryptic message with Thaddeus' office. "Tell Thad he's needed up on Coconino. Murder afoot. Shep."

Thaddeus took the pink phone slip into his office, sat at his desk, and loosened his tie. He wondered if Shep had the fifty thousand he had promised. Whatever, it was always exciting to hear from the guy, and the message was compelling. Things were *happening* in Shep's world. Always an exciting client to hear about— someone from L.A. or Tucson or Denver. Always some capital murder case moving toward trial where everything was at stake. He decided to waste no time and left on foot for Shep's office on Coconino Drive, one block north of Aspen Avenue.

The sidewalks had been bladed by a mini tractor, but the sifting snowfall was quickly covering in the machine's tracks. Thaddeus buttoned his top button and plunged ahead into the snow and wind.

DEFENDING TURQUOISE

Wendell Patterson handed him a reading file as soon as he poked his head in Shep's waiting room. Wendell—Wendy—was Shep's "touchstone," as he referred to her. She made his world make sense, keeping track of appointments, works-in-progress, client bitches and complaints, overdue accounts, judges' birthdays, anniversaries, and Suns tickets. Everything he needed to have a reasonably functional life/law practice was in her hands, and she was up to the task. "Read before you knock on his door," she said. "You can use the library. You know the way."

He nodded and accepted the file. Before heading into the library, he dusted the snow from his topcoat and stamped his boots on the rubber mat back at the door. Shep insisted: anyone caught tracking snow into his office would be banned. Reason was, Shep liked working in his stocking feet. Snow was violently unwelcome inside his environs for that reason.

Thaddeus let himself into the library, found the light switch, and removed topcoat and suit jacket. He took the seat at the far end, the head of the table, and began leafing through the file.

First thing up was a statement from Angelina Steinmar. It was recorded and transcribed by one of Shep's paralegals, a black woman Thaddeus knew only as Nony. Nony had talked with Angelina on February 4 from 10:18 a.m. to 12:22 p.m. There had been no interruptions and the tape had been changed three times. So much for the metadata, he thought to himself, and flipped up the first yellow page to the summarizing paragraphs.

Angelina was forty-three years old, married to John Steinmar, the mother of one daughter and no sons. Daughter's name was Hamilton Steinmar—"Hammy" as the family affectionately called her. Hammy had been in her first year at the University of Arizona when she hung herself. The first attempt with the pills had been a warning. However, counseling had followed that attempt plus hours of discussion. She assured them it was a mistake that wouldn't repeat. The doctor seemed genuinely satisfied, which somewhat placated the parents. The daughter insisted on returning to school.

Hammy's death was the darkest time of Angelina's life by 100 times 100, as she put it. Thaddeus made a note on his own legal pad to follow up on this. He kept reading.

Angelina was originally from Pennsylvania and was working on her Master's in Ed Psych from the University of Wisconsin— Milwaukee, when she had met John Steinmar. He was in Milwaukee for a prosecutor's conference held in a lakefront hotel.

There was a cruise the second night, aboard an enormous catamaran that nosed along the Lake Michigan shoreline. Angelina just happened to be serving cocktails as she was working her Friday night shift for the cruise line. Their meeting was literally an accident: in handing over a grasshopper to the wife of one of the prosecutors, her tray tilted with a swell on the lake and dumped a scotch down the front of John Steinmar's yellow linen shirt.

She couldn't apologize enough. But he was sporting and made light of the incident and wondered aloud if he, like the boat, had just been christened. Then he wondered aloud if Angelina would be leaving *him* a tip.

She was relieved at his sense of humor and thanked him, comping his table the rest of the evening. One thing led to another and she attended the Saturday night dinner as John Steinmar's guest in the hotel ballroom. She didn't make it back to her studio apartment that night and two weeks later he flew back into town to repeat the getting-to-know-you process.

In love and loving it, they flew to Maui and traded vows on the beach at sunset and didn't return to the mainland for two weeks. She was pregnant when she again saw the Pacific coast and suffered from morning sickness when they arrived in Flagstaff. They were never again apart.

Thaddeus took all this in and turned the page.

DEFENDING TURQUOISE

The child's name was Hamilton, obviously not a girl's name, but the name of John's father. John wanted the Hammy sobriquet passed along to his own offspring. He didn't know whether there would be a male heir, so the daughter was chosen.

Hammy was in trouble with the law her sophomore and senior years in high school, and saw a child psychologist every Tuesday after school throughout her junior year and the following summer. What they discussed wasn't revealed to the parents, Hammy's requirement. All the parents knew was that the child had become sullen and withdrawn and had zero patience for any degree of parental control or parental observation about her life. Among her friends it was known she loathed her father and resented her mother and accused them both of some form of unnamed sadism.

Thaddeus read the starred footnote at this point in the recitation, which explained there was a suicide note from the daughter included as the last page in the file. He flipped back and read:

Don't play like you don't know, mother. I'm doing it because of you. You play ignorant about his sexual abuse but any fool could see. Fuck you both. I hate you and hope this kills you. Goodbye.

Followed by a sub-text explaining the original of the note was in police custody, and that it had been found pinned by a silver brooch to her shirt. As for Hammy, the sub-text explained, she had hanged herself with a coat hanger wired to her closet door--where she was found leaning, knees buckled in death, face purple and tongue swollen and fully extruded. There was a pack of Winston's on her desk and a half-smoked one in the ashtray, lipstick on the filter end, although the daughter was never known to smoke and seldom wore lipstick and was wearing none at death. This was a conundrum that neither the detectives nor the parents had solved.

As for the truth of the note: the phrase "his sexual abuse" was ruled by the grand jury to be ambiguous and insufficient proof of anything by which anyone could be prosecuted. The mother, however, understood her daughter's message and it ignited a persistent, raging hatred for John Steinmar.

Angelina vehemently insisted on an autopsy but the vaginal swab and exam produced nothing. There was no physical evidence of sexual abuse, no evidence of trauma of any nature to any inch of her body.

Dr. Neal Gordonet, the chief medical examiner, made sure by personally performing the autopsy and personally examining every square inch of skin under magnification for even the slightest hint of trauma. Angelina believed her daughter and had no doubt the abuse had occurred, but she had no proof. Inside she raged and "wished him tortured and snuffed"—her words.

Hammy was a bright child and was majoring in chemistry at the university when she died. The suicide took place six months prior to the death of John Steinmar by gunshot from his own gun.

The next section of the file contained a half-inch of medical records surrounding the presence and treatment of bite marks on Angelina's body the morning she shot her husband. Color photographs were included, mounted inside plastic sleeves and numbering 184. They'd been taken by a children's photographer who was also certified in forensic photography and who had been summoned to the hospital by Shep the morning John Steinmar "ate the bullet"—again, Angelina's words.

She described the morning of John Steinmar's death. The digital clock's numbers were green in the pre-dawn light when she first opened her eyes. They slept in twin beds on either side of their huge bedroom. She had been awakened by his hand on her breast at 6:05 a.m. The hand was massaging her breast and toying with her nipple. She became sleepily aroused but then remembered where she was and that the man touching her was her husband, who she was ninety-nine percent certain, had been sexually abusing Hammy. Revolted, she reached and ripped his hand away and told him, "No way!"

But he persisted. He waited until she had drifted back to sleep and then began again, touching her breast and again toying her nipple erect. She awoke with a start and this time batted his hand away and swung at his crotch with her fist. He was totally nude and vulnerable, but stepped back just in time to avoid a very painful punch.

He laughed and cried, "Why not me, Angie? I'm your husband!"

He was tall, 6'3", and weighed over two-twenty, much of it muscle. He worked out most afternoons at Flagstaff Fitness Center. He could bench press 205 and chin himself twenty times. There he stood, taunting, a half-smile playing across his mouth. His white translucent skin and albino hair made him seem an apparition lowered down out of the clouds to frighten her. She was at once revolted and terrified.

She came upright in her bed and pulled the blankets around her. "Back off, fuckhead," she cursed. But he was aroused and came at her again.

He seized her shoulder and shoved her back against the headboard. With his other hand he gripped her around the throat. He squeezed hard and she couldn't cry out again. Both her hands flew up to her throat. She wrestled and tried prying his hand away. But he was stronger and she realized he was going to choke her and meant to render her unconscious. It was working; she couldn't draw a deep breath.

Finally she brought both hands overhead and slammed them down into his hand, successfully dislodging his grip on her throat. Her larynx ached and she coughed and coughed. She gagged. Tears washed through her eyes, making it difficult to see. But she could see his silhouette and again swung toward him with her balled fist. This time she connected, hitting him decisively in the "nut sack" (her words) and he crumbled to his knees. "What the fuck, Angie!" he cried several times. It gave her enough time to unwrap from the blankets and run from the bed.

She headed for the bedroom door, intent on making it downstairs to her cell phone where it was charging in the study.

She never made it.

He tackled her from behind and immediately shoved his hand up between her legs. She was wearing nothing from the waist down and he seized her genitals and forced his thumb inside her. "You will service me, bitch!" he cried. She was horrified at the assault and pleaded for him to stop. But he couldn't be deterred—tears meant nothing to him, as she put it.

He tried to rape her and the only reason he didn't was that he couldn't bring himself fully erect. "Bitch, let me taste you!" he screamed at her again and again, and rolled her over onto her back. He slid up the carpet so as to position his mouth between her legs. He chomped down hard on her labia, and then reached down to touch himself. Seeing her chance, with his hand beneath his own body, she shot up to her feet and headed for the stairs. By now she had decided she would go for his gun and warn him away. He was assaulting her and she had the marks to prove it. In fact, her crotch was on fire from the bite and she was still gasping for air from the choking. Figuring he would stop at nothing now, she pounded down the stairs.

The gun was hidden inside the roll-top desk, right top drawer. She located it, unfastened the leather safety strap from the hammer, and drew it from the holster. It was a nickel Colt .38 Detective Special, Fourth Series, loaded with six dum-dum rounds capable of dropping a charging man. She spun the cylinder and assured herself it was fully loaded.

At that exact moment he came charging into the study and saw her holding the gun pointed directly at his heart. He knew she was trained and range-qualified and he froze. "Let's talk," he said, and collapsed to the floor. His head fell forward and he began sobbing and crying their daughter's name. "Hammy, Hammy, my God, what have I done?" he repeated again and again. It was then she knew. He was expressing his guilt over what he had done to their precious child and she had to admit that at that exact moment she would gladly have blown his head off if he made the slightest move toward her. Then he moaned, "Please, Angie, let's talk."

She lowered the gun and sized up her predicament. He was cross-legged on the floor, nude and looking vulnerable and meek. She turned to replace the gun in the drawer. No sooner had she turned away than he lunged and managed to seize her right ankle. The gun flew from her hand.

She flew head first onto the floor and hit her chin hard, biting her tongue—which was corroborated by the ER records. "Laceration tongue, right anterior."

He immediately followed through with his hand, again seizing her genitals as he rocked up on his knees. She tried to get to her knees and was half-successful, managing to turn onto her back and kicking at his head. He dodged and bobbed and avoided her flailing foot.

Suddenly he drew back his right fist and slammed it against her genitals. A scream began deep in her chest and her head flew back in horrendous pain. Incapacitated, she went down on her back, whereupon he came up on her with his mouth and began biting, working inside her legs, labia, and up her body. "He was marking me as his," she told Nony. Writhing in pain, she turned and twisted but was unable to ward him off. He bit her perhaps four or five times and then crawled forward and bit her breast, breaking the skin and drawing a wide smile of blood.

She flung her hand up behind her head and patted the carpet, trying to locate the weapon. Then her hand connected, she came forward with the gun and, like she had been taught, coolly squeezed the trigger. The bullet entered the top of his head and traveled down through his cranium before exiting just below his right jawline.

The biting stopped and she managed to pull away from his dead body.

Shaking and whimpering, she climbed to her feet and blindly backed away from her dead husband. Reflexively she replaced the gun in its leather holster and carefully hid it in the drawer beneath a notebook. Later she would wonder why she did this, especially when the police asked her if she were trying to hide it. She had told them no, reminding them that it was she who had called the cops and it was she who had told them where she placed the gun when they asked.

She was acting within a cocoon of total shock.

Carefully she climbed back upstairs to their bedroom. She looked around the room and, incredibly, made her bed. She then stepped in the shower and shaved her legs and armpits. She dressed in the nice outfit she would wear to court later that morning, and returned downstairs. She made coffee.

Finally she called the police. "Oh no, he's quite dead," she calmly told the 911 operator. "Dead and turning stiff already. How do I know? I kicked his arm and it was like wood."

The police arrived and she was transported by two detectives to the ER. Two wounds were bleeding and infection was feared from the bites. Plus, they wanted the ER staff to make records of her injuries and take pictures. More than that was done: they took her blood, made her pee in a bottle, and swabbed her genitals for semen and saliva and DNA. The bite marks were likewise swabbed because DNA profiles would be attempted at any point where marks remained. Unfortunately she had bathed, the ER doc explained to the cops, and much of the transfer DNA would have been washed away. But he did what was indicated and they could only hope for helpful results.

Of course she was in shock. The ER doctor confirmed as much in the ER notes. She knew where she was but couldn't come up with the date or month. She knew Obama was the president but had no idea about the vice president and never could recall her dead husband's middle name.

Thaddeus read the account of the killing and then read it again.

This time he went much slower and made notes on his pad. Finally he had made his way to the back folder. Exhaling a long sigh, he stretched and blinked hard. He was glad that little task was done.

He then stood and went into the waiting room. He informed Wendy that he was ready to meet with Shep. She nodded without looking up from her computer screen, but reached across for the phone.

"He's ready," she said into the receiver. "Will do."

She looked at Thaddeus.

"Go on in, Thad. Big guy's ready."

Shep slumped behind his kidney-shaped desk, cut from ironwood and inlaid with mother-of-pearl. To his left was the flag of the United States; to his right the state flag of Colorado—Durango transplant that he was. Shep took off his rimless spectacles and pinched his nose between his eyes. He watched as Thaddeus took a client chair and assembled himself and legal pad. Shep twiddled his thumbs and Thaddeus noted the showy turquoise ring on his right middle. He was drinking from a Starbucks cup and puffing a Winston from a hard pack, one of four packs scattered across the ironwood. He picked up an envelope, placed it against his forehead like Johnny Carson's Carnac, and said, "What is ten times five and lots of zeroes."

Thaddeus took the bait. Carnac was able to divine unknown answers from unasked questions. Thaddeus played Ed McMahon. "What's ten times five and lots of zeroes?"

Shep tossed the envelope across the desk and said, "A check for fifty thousand dollars."

Thaddeus smiled and slipped the envelope in his shirt pocket. "Much obliged, friend."

"So you read the file?" A sly grin played at the criminal lawyer's mouth.

"I did," said Thaddeus. "Reads like a John Grisham novel."

"Naw, Grisham would be much more creative than our client

139

Angelina Steinmar. He's a great writer. She's a damn poor liar. But she'll do in a pinch."

"I don't follow."

"Hell, Thad, she's made the whole thing up. I spotted that immediately."

"What? It passed my BS-sifter test."

"That's right. We can sell it to a jury, but I'm telling you damn little of that crap actually happened. Truth be told, she capped the old boy and then bit herself."

"What?"

Shep twiddled his thumbs. "I'm going to have to spell out the entire thing for you. I'm saying once he was dead, she used his mouth."

"You're saying she bit herself with his dead mouth."

Shep's eyes narrowed to slits. "That's exactly what I'm saying."

Thaddeus shook his head. "Slow down, please. Where are you getting all this from?"

Shep pushed back from the ironwood desk. "She told me."

"She told you."

"That she did, Thaddeus, my boy. Our job is to sell the script you just read, to a jury."

"I find the script much more believable than what you say she told you."

"Thank you. Script took some doing, but it's all my creation."

"Son of a—"

"Right, son, old Shep made up every word of it."

"You know, if I didn't actually need this fifty grand I would pass this envelope back to you, Carnac, and run the hell out of here. But sad to say, I need the money."

"You're about to get schooled in how criminal cases really get won. I figured it was time for you to come to grips with how the real world of criminal defense works."

"You took pity on me."

"Hell, son, I was in court the day you got disbarred. Your mistake was telling H. Ivan that it was your own money you made the bail with. Next time type up a receipt and have your secretary's husband sign it with his left hand. Then you've got the receipt and you don't have to take a year off in North Dakota."

"So our defense is completely perjured."

"Almost. Seems like our honorable but deceased district attorney actually was raping his daughter. Way I see it, he had it coming. He was responsible for her death but the grand jury couldn't find anyone to charge. Mom was only taking him to trial and carrying out the execution. In the grand scheme of things, that's called Justice. Can you live with it?"

"I—I—"

"That's all right, Thad. You can take your time with this one. We present the defense and walk her out of there, justice is done."

"It's unethical to knowingly present perjured testimony."

"It's unethical to execute women who murder the husbands who murdered their offspring, too. Which is worse? You take your pick. I say we walk her the hell out of there and let justice have her way. It's sweet."

"Am I really hearing this?"

"Welcome aboard, Counsel."

"What's my role going to be?"

"You will be responsible for cross-examining the state's witnesses. I will put on our direct case and do closing argument. That way you're not putting on perjured testimony, as you so sanctimoniously put it. You will do opening statement. We'll share the motion practice: you write 'em, I'll argue 'em."

"Fair enough."

"So are you in or out?"

Thaddeus felt the last remnants of his naive mental constructs about justice and "doing justice" melting away. This, it seemed, was the reality of justice: you looked at the big picture, figured where your client fit into that, and carved out the facts and law to fit your best story. That was the tale of the tape: did it fit? Did it slip on easily? Did it wear well?

One thing was for sure, this was going to be one hell of a ride with Shep. He relaxed. *Might as well accept that you're going to be part of this and go along far enough to see how it feels. You can always opt out on down the road if you start wetting the bed from guilt.* He chastised himself about the last glowing vestiges of lawyering ethics and morality he harbored. Soon the chastisement was enough; those embers were doused and he was, at long last, free to be a professional gun for hire. He had killed bad guys in the real world. Maybe now it was time to do the same thing in the world of courtrooms and lesser crimes. He smiled at Shep and thumped the desk with his fist.

"I'm in."

"Put the fifty grand in your account and take Katy out on the rez for fry bread and mutton stew."

With that, they were done.

Thaddeus slipped on topcoat and gloves. He tucked the file under his arm and plunged out the door, into the snowfall and gloom of the afternoon. "As they say," he muttered as he tromped along, "lie down with dogs, get up with fleas."

TWENTY-EIGHT

At home that night he cooked steaks on the Jenn-Air for Katy and himself, a chicken leg for Sarai. Sarai had fallen in love with the Colonel's drumsticks and squealed with delight when the red-and-white bucket came home. Tonight, Thaddeus' own special drumstick would have to do. All in all she was pleased and carried the bone around, gnawing at it until bedtime.

Katy said goodnight at ten o'clock and disappeared upstairs, where she ran a hot bath and luxuriated under soap bubbles.

Thaddeus wandered aimlessly around the downstairs for the next hour, then watched Jimmy Fallon's TiVo'd monologue before heading upstairs to his office.

Sure enough, Katy had left her notes from the day's activities on his desk, as agreed. Evidently she had gone to Children and Family Services and asked that they certify her to visit Turquoise as a

143

representative of her attorney.

Her notes recited how she had met with the DCFS office manager, learned the hoops she had to jump through, and had filled out two hours worth of paperwork. She was expected to be certified in the next twenty-four hours, pending an investigation of her home and an interview with the caseworker. If that all went well, she should be able to visit Turquoise in the next couple of days. Her Action Plan was to visit with the girl's father with Turquoise present, and see what he knew about his brother's abuse of Turquoise. While there they would also retrieve the six diaries. Thaddeus inserted the pink sheet of notes into the Turquoise Begay file and undressed for bed.

He awoke at dawn to find her close by. During the night she had used the bathroom then crept into bed and pushed up beside him. Katy was asleep facing him, her lips slightly parted, black hair across her forehead, sweetly dreaming when he came awake. He stared at her for five minutes and wished they could talk about the Chicago stuff, the painful stuff. Evidently it wasn't time for that yet, and he knew better than to force it.

He quietly slid away and let himself down out of the bed, climbed to his feet, and shrugged into his ski pants and Patagonia shell, T-shirt beneath. There was a new icing of snow and he meant to put it to good use. He went into the kitchen and put the coffee on, then stepped out on the back porch and laid his backcountry skis flat in the snow. Max accompanied him as he began kicking and gliding toward the national forest, where he entered the huge stand of trees and began laying down a trail. All around him he saw a majesty that was not of man's making in the drifts and ice sculptures emplaced during the long, cold night. He was thrilled to be alone and the first one to ever lay eyes on that particular scene on that particular day. Max ran ahead and sniffed after rabbit prints from tree to tree, happily chasing down the trail.

Five minutes later Thaddeus had worked up a sweat; the

polypropylene T-shirt was wicking it away, and he remained comfortably warm and dry as he covered ground. Up the hills he would kick and herringbone, then down the other side he would race, one mile, two, and then three. Finally when he could no longer see any man-made thing he came to rest, leaning on the stout backcountry poles. Max came to a rest at his feet and sat in the snow, first scratching an ear then looking up at Thaddeus as in, "What's up?"

Thaddeus decided he was going to have to make some changes in his life. Working with Shep on the Steinmar murder case was huge and it would pay off handsomely in new work, headlines, and new notoriety not just in Arizona but around the Southwest, among other lawyers where criminal referrals might result.

But on the other hand he also had the Turquoise Begay case, where a nasty, hypercritical religious zealot of a martinet judge was after his license and after his client. She probably deserved better than what he could offer her, especially in the sense of representation by an attorney who wasn't perpetually in her judge's sights and waiting for the shot to ring out that would fell him. Definitely she deserved better than that.

So he made a decision. A preliminary decision, maybe, but he was seriously thinking of doing it. He was going to ask H. Ivan Trautman to withdraw his appointment and find another, more appropriate lawyer to defend the young girl. It wasn't fair to Turquoise and in a way it wasn't fair to Thaddeus either. Besides, with gunshot residue on her shirt and probably her DNA yet to be turned up on the gun, she was looking guiltier by the day. Maybe H. Ivan knew something or saw something that Thaddeus didn't know or see after all. Maybe it was a case where she should plea-bargain and serve her time in the Department of Corrections penal system. He kicked at the snow with his ski and Max stood up. The dog asked with his eyes, "Why are we stopped? Are we leaving yet?"

"C'mon, buddy," Thaddeus muttered to his companion. "We've

got a rough trail ahead of us. Let's get to it."

Thirty minutes later he was back home and pouring the first coffee of the day. Max was happily crunching his pellets laced with Parmesan powder.

Max had his tastes; Thaddeus was finding his own.

Getting disbarred was not among them.

TWENTY-NINE

The next day, Thaddeus crossed Aspen to the courthouse and headed upstairs to see DA Wrasslin Russell. It was time to either resolve the Turquoise Begay case or withdraw and he had decided to begin with the DA herself.

From his favorite chair in the DA's waiting room he could again look straight into her office. Again with the nails while talking on the phone. Hold up the hand, inspect the nails, talk into the phone, switch hands, and check the other nails. Something had to be noted on a pad, which stole away precious nail-gazing time, Thaddeus saw. Finally he was allowed to pass into the DA's sanctum.

"Push has come to shove," he told the DA even before he sat down. "What will you give me if Turquoise Begay pleads? Best deal?"

Wrasslin sat way back in her chair and clasped her hands behind

147

her head. She appeared thoughtful for several moments, as if the idea had never occurred to her before. Which, Thaddeus knew, was a ruse and all for show; she'd known from the first time she read the police report exactly what she wanted out of the case. Now she was just appearing to do her job as the ruminative, serious-minded prosecutor.

At last she leaned forward. "She's ready to plead?"

"I'm just saying. What if she pled?"

"At one time I suggested second-degree murder. Fifteen to twenty-five max. But you said no."

"Is it still on the table? I'm just asking here."

"Hardly. We have gunshot residue and probably DNA."

"Which is pure argument. Tell me what you really want, best offer, right now."

"Fifty years, plea to first degree. She'd be out in forty, maybe thirty-five."

"What? Get serious, Wrasslin. We're talking plea here, not worst-case scenario."

"It is best-case. Tell the truth, Mr. Murfee, I'm unwilling to trade cows. If you want less than fifty then take her to trial and prove second degree. Or manslaughter. But you asked me, so I told you."

She thinks she has me, Thaddeus realized, *and she thinks I'm afraid of the case, that's why I'm here. Maybe she even sees me down on my knees, begging.*

"She had gunshot residue on her shirt because she shot at a predator that day," he said.

"I'm sure she'd say that."

"And you don't know for certain she had Randy Begay's DNA."

"I'm betting otherwise. At the very least, I've got her in a huge lie."

He looked down at the desk. He had to admit she had him there. It definitely wasn't going to look good for Turquoise to now change her story and make the case of her life being one long sexual exploitation by Uncle Randy. *Who was going to believe she had lied? Worse yet, the prosecutor would get to say, Hey, she lied then, what makes you think she isn't lying now?* In asking the question rhetorically, the answer came to Thaddeus: the diaries. Wrasslin knew nothing about the diaries.

"Katy Murfee is picking up a half-dozen diaries today that will prove Randy Begay began raping this girl on her tenth birthday and kept committing the same crime against her every day until he was killed."

"Diaries? Where are these diaries?"

"Never mind. They're being retrieved."

"I demand the right to inspect."

"And inspect you shall."

"In fact, I want complete copies, now that you've put sexual abuse into the case."

"And complete copies you shall get. Subject to the court sealing the file."

"By Friday."

"Done. Consider this, please. Assume this monster was raping her and assume I can prove it with the diaries. What would you say to voluntary manslaughter and ten years?"

Wrasslin let out a sharp—but forced—laugh. "I'd say fifty years. Rape is no excuse. There is no claim she shot him in self-defense or she was fearful of it happening imminently. She gunned him down in cold blood near as we can tell."

"She hasn't confessed to the shooting."

"True. We don't have her admitting it. But we don't need her confession, either."

"Fifteen years and five years probation."

"Get lost, Murfee. Fifty years, bottom-line. Now, if you'll excuse me, I actually have a real job to do."

"I'm going to put her on the stand. Believe me, the jury will fall in love with this little angel."

She shrugged. "They just might. But they're still going to convict her anyway. Some of the most deadly serial killers in history were attractive, kindly men. Look at Ted Bundy. His charm swept women off their feet. Until he got them alone and then took them off their feet forever. Your girl can be attractive, which she is. And her story can be compelling, which it probably is, growing up on the reservation in all that poverty and squalor. And she may even have been the victim of serial sexual assaults by Randy Begay. That still didn't give her the right to execute him. Sorry, buddy, no dice."

"Get real, Wrasslin, give me something to take her."

"Forty years. Final offer. Take it or leave it by Friday or the deal goes away forever. We have trial in three weeks. Excuse me now, but I have to get ready and can't spend any more time with you today. Or tomorrow. Or the next day. Or—you get the picture, Mr. Murfee."

"Thad."

"Mr. Murfee. Goodbye."

Thaddeus stood in front of the DA's cluttered desk. He shrugged helplessly.

"Then you leave me no choice but to take her to trial and win her freedom. Never say I didn't give you the chance to do something reasonable here, Wrasslin."

"Roslin."

"Thad."

"Mr. Murfee."

"Wrasslin."

"Get the hell out!"

THIRTY

Two days later, early in the afternoon, Thaddeus met with Shep in his office. Shep was negotiating a Winston cigarette down to ash and waving his arms wildly as he told about his latest conquest, a tax fraud case out of San Francisco. Thaddeus listened politely, said "Ooh" and "Ahh" on cue, and waited for his employer to get down to why he had called him over.

Without breaking stride, Shep abruptly asked, "So what about our DA's widow? Was it self-defense?"

Thaddeus stiffened in his chair. He hadn't been expecting to deliver a colloquy on Arizona's self-defense laws. Still, he knew the law forward and backward.

"Self-defense flies if there's an imminent threat of great bodily harm or death. The question is, does our dearly departed DA have the chops?"

151

"Funny, funny, Thad boy. But seriously?"

"Savage biting and chasing from upstairs to downstairs, tripping and throwing down—does that equal self-defense? Put it this way, the judge has to give you a jury instruction on self-defense. Whether you can sell it to a jury is another matter."

"Oh, I can sell it to a jury. I can sell candles to General Electric."

"Then you can sell self-defense, I'm fairly confident."

"Why don't we do this? Let's task you with a brief on self-defense, something to hand to the judge when we're arguing jury instructions."

Thaddeus nodded. "Done."

"By the way, was my check good?"

He was referring to the $50,000 retainer check handed to Thaddeus last time they met.

"Good as gold. And much appreciated. I can put the cans back in the cabinet and start eating out of the refrigerator again."

"Good enough. Any other burning issues?"

Thaddeus' eyes narrowed. "One thing bothers me. If Angelina knew John was sexually abusing their daughter, why was she still with him? Why hadn't she kicked his sorry ass out in the street?"

Shep nodded in agreement. "That has been plaguing me too. Any sane woman would have immediately sued his ass for divorce and ejected him. Why did she let him hang around?"

"Unless she was planning his death all along. Maybe she set this whole thing up."

Shep smiled and stretched his arms luxuriously. "Now you're rounding third and heading for home. She *was* setting him up. I spotted that immediately. That's why I helped make up the cock and bull story about being chased downstairs and thrown to the floor."

"So why won't a jury pick up on that too?"

"Simple. We convince them he had her terrified. Battered-wife syndrome. Plus you can't forget the bite marks. Brutal attack, and all

152

that."

"You're telling me she lured him downstairs and shot him?"

"I didn't write down the details as she told them to me—never do. I wrote down the details as I told them to her."

"Don't tell me that."

"Thaddeus, I told you before. This is how it's done. If you can't live with it, you shouldn't be doing criminal law."

Thaddeus knew his face was white. He felt the blood draining away as he considered what Shep was telling him—rather, what Shep was demanding of him, that he go along with the game. Except it wasn't a game, it was making stuff up and presenting made-up stuff to a jury. The state bar would disbar someone it caught doing that. Of course, it was Shep who would be presenting the perjury, not him. He gulped a deep breath and once again decided to close his eyes and go along for the ride—if nothing else, to see where it went. He would play along and if it ever came down to a decision about him personally, he would decide then.

"I can live with it all right. If you can."

Shep sighed. "Look. The cops make shit up; I make shit up. The cops fudge, I fudge. The cops say they found her all cleaned up and tidy, I say she was in shock and acting reflexively. And on it goes until somebody wins. That's called justice."

"What about preclusion? She had a duty to shoot only as a last resort."

"Hey, he had her prone on the floor, overpowering her, biting her viciously enough to break the skin—how in the world is she supposed to retreat from that?"

"If the jury believes her story in the first place."

"They'll believe her. This is a woman who actually attends church. Twenty years taking care of other people's kids in her job at Children and Family Services. Mother of one, sadly departed."

"Sounds like somebody a jury will like."

"Which is nine-tenths of the battle. They'll be pulling for her by the time I'm done with them."

"So we tell them she tried to retreat but he grabbed her and pulled her back down."

"Which takes the duty to retreat completely out of the picture. He made retreat impossible."

"Sounds reasonable."

"Shit, boy, sounds like the truth, to me."

"If you say so, Shep."

"I do, son, I do. Not only that, why should a woman have to turn her back on a man and try to retreat from him in the first place? Turning your back on an aggressor is a good way to get killed. From behind!"

"I can't argue with that. And one more thing I've been thinking about. The gun. What if the husband went for the gun first and she got it away from him? What about that?"

"Damn, fella, now you're making sense. Were his prints on the gun?"

"Don't need to be. He went for it and she wrestled it away first. She beat him to it—which indicates he meant to kill her."

"Oh yes, I like that!"

"I'm just saying."

"You're coming through, now. I knew I thought the world of you. Now you're proving me right."

"Just trying to save our client."

Thaddeus went cold inside. *There, he was complicit. He had joined in the game and was helping concoct a story that would set their client free. Stop overthinking this,* he commanded his brain. *The DA's office is just as busy concocting their own version of the facts right now, with all their power and money and cops and experts. They'll be using everything they can to put the needle in Angelina's arm. They're out to kill her. This is no time for your damn mental*

154

games. Let it go, he told himself. *And leave it there.*

"I want you to spend some time with Angelina. Get to know her. Feed her the story in bits and pieces. See if she'll grab on and let us work our magic. Or see if she's going to fight us, which I highly doubt, but we need to nail her down."

"Hell, if she bit herself with his mouth don't we have our answer already?"

"You cannot over-prepare, Thaddeus. Now do what I say, please. I hear she likes to cross-country ski. Go skiing with her. You got skis?"

"Cross-country. Everything I need."

"Then get on it, hoss. Get on it."

THIRTY-ONE

He arrived home that night to learn that Katy had gathered and removed from the trailer all six Turquoise diaries. Thaddeus was ecstatic. Katy had retrieved the keys from the girl's nightstand. The girl said to please read them but she didn't want to be there when it happened.

They were seated at the kitchen table and in the center was Katy's fat red book bag containing the diaries. The husband and wife looked at each other. Who would go first?

"Let's make coffee," said Katy. "Then we'll open the first one."

Thaddeus nodded. He had changed into Levi's, moccasins, and a black tee. Katy was wearing the khaki pants she had worn to the reservation, with a pink tee that featured a silkscreen of Woody Woodpecker and the words "That's all, folks!" Sarai loved the shirt and was wearing one just like it. The little girl was watching a Barney video and munching corn chips in the family room. They had tried to seduce her with carrot sticks but her penchant for corn chips had won out. The carrot sticks were stacked in parallel on a small plate, a dollop of ranch dip on the side. They were all untouched.

Katy ran the Keurig and returned with steaming mugs. She placed one before Thaddeus. In serving him from the side she allowed her hand to rest momentarily on his shoulder and he felt a warmth creep into his soul from her touch. Oh wow, he thought, how he loved her touch! Then she sat beside him, casually sipping her coffee and staring with him at the book bag. What would the first diary tell them?

He opened the bag and pulled out the smallest, oldest book. It had a white, imitation leather cover with a gold-embossed title of "My Secret Diary." A frayed clasp was held in place by a small gold lock, which in part had given way to rust spots. Inserting key after key, he turned the lock clockwise. On the sixth try, the tongue slipped free and he lifted the cover. Remarkably preserved, the first item was a turquoise butterfly mounted inside a glassine cover. He would later Google and find its name: Sonoran Blue (*Philotes sonorensis*). Indigenous to the Sonoran Desert.

"The butterfly, like her name."

"Turquoise."

"Exactly. Totally charming," Katy said.

"You've gotta love this kid."

"How very touching," Katy marveled. "What's next?"

Thaddeus set the butterfly aside and turned the blank page. A paperclip held three grainy photographs of a much-younger Turquoise. The child was wearing heavy red lipstick, clumpy mascara, and rouge on her cheeks that lent a clownish look. Except the look—the photograph—was meant to be taken as a serious attempt to look the part of the attractive young woman.

"Ten years old," Katy whispered.

"I know," Thaddeus said. He shook his head. "Unbelievable. Let's read."

They turned several pages. Then came the first entry, written in blue ink, faded, and dated June 10, which, they would learn, was the girl's tenth birthday.

Four sentences into the entry and Katy's eyes moistened. Thaddeus blinked hard. For the girl told the story of her tenth birthday, how she had come awake that morning, excited to at last be in "double digits." She had quickly dressed in her customary shorts and T-shirt and Wal-Mart tennies with gold toes. She went from her bedroom in the trailer to the living room. Her father told her to look out the screen door.

There, leaned on its kickstand, was the new bike she had asked for. It was a girls' frame, red, with a silver basket and luggage rack. She had specifically asked for the basket and rack to hold the cans she found on her daily canning excursions along the highway that stretched for miles in either direction from their trailer. Soft drink cans and alcoholic beverage cans were tossed from whizzing cars and trucks and she retrieved as many as she could each morning. She recited how she daily scavenged a hundred cans and plastic bottles and earned five dollars. It was money she would spend on food. There were no savings, only can money for food when dad would disappear for several days on one of his benders. She said little about this, though the first entry in the diary covered just about every facet of her young life, as if she had been waiting to gush.

She had headed west on her new bicycle that morning and was amazed at how quickly her basket filled with cans and bottles as she worked the highway shoulders. "Crested Blue Butte," her father told her, she couldn't go beyond that.

But she wasn't the only one out to celebrate her birthday. Uncle Randy came along in his truck. He pulled in behind her, slowly following as she made her way along. She stopped several times to wave at him but he neither returned her wave nor made any effort to go around her and continue on his way. She became nervous, and then felt frightened. It "seemed like a dream," she wrote.

Finally he beeped the horn and motioned her to pull over and wait. She complied with his order. Without a word he climbed out of his truck, marched smartly up to her, and took her by the arm. He yanked her from the bicycle and it spilled onto the sandy shoulder. Pulling at her arm, he dragged her behind a Palo Verde tree and down into an arroyo. With very little description, she documented the sexual assault and her huge feeling of shame. She cried and couldn't stop. He abruptly tweaked her shoe and climbed up out of the wash. She heard his truck fire up and accelerate down the highway.

She was left with a mess in the wash. Sand had been worked up between her legs and, as she described it, she had to urinate immediately. The next portions made the tears roll down the cheeks of her readers. Thaddeus and Katy were shocked. Stunned.

The little girl described picking her bicycle up off the ground and angrily tossing all the bottles and cans, flinging them from bike basket to the desert sands. She said she was crying and turned her bike around and rode home, unable to stop crying.

Uncle Randy was waiting for her at the trailer. Her father had told him to tell her that he was gone to town for the day. Uncle Randy didn't say anything when she came inside and she went to her room. She drew the curtain across her doorway and flung herself across the bed. She buried her face in the pillow and proceeded to weep until the pillow was wet.

She cried herself to sleep and awoke to find Uncle Randy rubbing her leg. "This is for you," he told her and gave her a tube of Revlon lipstick and a small makeup case. "It's for your birthday. Put it on." She did as she was told, even though she had never been schooled in makeup magic.

He took pictures of her smeared with her makeup. The pictures were for later, he told her. But he promised he would provide her prints for her new diary. The diary was a gift from her Aunt Juana, who had dropped it by while Turquoise was canning. She had left it on the shelf below the tiny window in the girl's bedroom.

The diary entry concluded with this: "Uncle Randi wants me to come to his room. He wants more pictures. I hat him. I doan like him no more. Goodbye everyone." She had then pressed her lips against the page, leaving an ambiguous red impression of her lips that had, over time, transferred onto the facing page as well.

"That's enough for me tonight," Thaddeus announced. "Can't take anymore."

"I hear that," Katy agreed. "I'll read the rest tomorrow."

THIRTY-TWO

Thaddeus read over the CSI's résumé again. He liked everything he saw.

Lance Myer-Rothstein was available for consultation in homicide cases, including shooting scene reconstruction, crime scene evidence evaluation, bloodstain pattern analysis, and crime scene reconstruction.

Past engagements were impressive, as he had provided testimony for both the prosecution and defense in state, federal, and military courtrooms. He had been active since 1977, beginning with small police agencies as a patrolman and then working his way up in rank. He had served as patrol officer, SWAT team member, police agent, crime scene investigator, crime laboratory detective, patrol sergeant, major task force member and, finally, commander of criminal investigations in Albuquerque. He received his graduate education in forensic sciences from The George Washington University (MFS) and received advanced forensic science training from the FBI, Secret Service, Smithsonian Institution, the Armed Forces Institute of Pathology, Henry C. Lee Institute of Forensic Science and many others.

And he was available immediately. Thaddeus sent him a retainer and Myer-Rothstein caught the next flight out of Reagan National Airport.

Thaddeus met him at the Flagstaff airport and was immediately awed by the man's massive shoulders and bull neck. He looked like an O-line guard for the Cardinals. He had a round face, dark bushy eyebrows over green eyes, and black curly hair that he kept slicked back from his widow's peak. He wore tortoise-frame eyeglasses and, Thaddeus noticed as soon as they were outside, worked a cigar in and out of his mouth like a plunger. First it was lit, and then chewed until it died out, then relit, chewed again, and then relit. The cigar was plugged into a yellowish-brown filter system that looked not at all like something Thaddeus would put into his own mouth. And he talked nonstop, about the police reports he had reviewed so far, the autopsy reports and gunshot angles, and his desire to "visit the scene immediately without delay."

So Thaddeus made arrangements for them to visit the shooting scene the very next day.

THIRTY-THREE

K aty called and made an appointment for them to meet with Garcia Begay at the trailer. He was the father of Turquoise and had been "away" (on a bender) when the shooting occurred. He was withdrawn and unwilling to discuss anything by phone, but she shared with him that she was *Naabeehó Bináhásdzo*— Navajo—and he agreed to see her.

With Lance Myer-Rothstein secure in the back seat of the Escalade, the threesome drove out of Flagstaff at nine o'clock, following a quick breakfast at Little America, where the crime scene investigator spent the night. Thaddeus drove them eastbound on I-40 to 89 and then north to 160, through Tuba City, and east-northeast. All the way up, the forensic scientist worried the unlit cigar in his mouth, talking nonstop about his life and training, as if there were any doubt in anyone's mind about his superb credentials. There wasn't, of course, or he wouldn't have been there.

Later that morning, Thaddeus was parking the SUV in front of the trailer, next to Garcia's Ford F150. The man's pickup was red over white, dented and battered all along the driver's side, and was missing its tailgate. In the bed was a large roll of fencing wire, a half-dozen green and white fence posts, and a toolbox just behind the rear window. Thaddeus and Katy and Myer-Rothstein climbed the four steps and knocked on the aluminum frame of the outer door. No answer. They knocked again. No answer. Thaddeus cupped his hands against the small door window and peered inside. A man—presumably Garcia—was sleeping on the couch, his left arm across the face and mouth wide open. His boots were neatly placed side-by-side on the floor and several beer cans were strewn alongside the couch. As they listened they could hear the TV and Thaddeus thought he recognized the voice of CNN's Wolf Blitzer. He hammered his fist against the door and shouted. "Mr. Begay! Open up, please!" He hammered again. He saw the man stir and slowly sit up. He yawned, stretched, and wiped both hands across his face. He dried his mouth with his shirtsleeve, lunged upright, and came toward the door.

It slowly creaked open and the man looked out.

"I'm Katy Begay," Katy said. "We're here for the visit."

The man nodded and pushed the door open and the trio entered.

It smelled of stale cigarettes and something fried. Thaddeus would have preferred to leave the door ajar so the room could air out, but he knew it wasn't his choice, so he followed Katy to the couch.

"Hello," said the man. He appeared to be mid-thirties, maybe 5'10", and angular brown profile with sharply parted black hair that, with sleep, had fallen low across his forehead. A thin white scar ran from his left earlobe along his jawline to his chin. Some remnant from some late-night brawl, Thaddeus guessed, for the man was clearly a drinker and, as Turquoise had related, was given to three- and four-day benders where he vanished from everyone's radar, gone who-knew-where, but certainly not at home, where his own brother was having his way with his daughter. Thaddeus detested the man and made no real effort at friendliness, although he played friendly enough, knowing that the more information they could pry out of the guy about Turquoise, the better job he could do in defending her.

"You're Garcia?" Katy asked.

"Yes."

"I'm Katy Begay and this is my husband, Thaddeus Murfee. Thaddeus is the lawyer provided by the court for your daughter, Turquoise. And this is Lance, who wants to see the bedroom where your brother was shot."

"It's bad, what she did," Garcia said. He shook his head and rubbed his sad eyes. "Very bad of her."

"We don't know that," the forensics man piped up. "We don't know that she did the shooting at all."

They all three stared at him. "Well," he continued, "I have serious doubts about it, based on what I've been given to review. But we'll review the scene, take measurements and photographs, and run some field tests." He patted the bag he had brought along. "Everything we need is in here. Please show me the room and then you can leave me alone for about an hour."

Garcia took him to the rear of the trailer.

"Have you cleaned in here since the shooting?" Myer-Rothstein asked.

"She has been in jail. No one to clean," the father said.

"Got it. Okay, you can leave now."

Myer-Rothstein waited until he was alone and then bent to his bag. It contained chemical agents, string lines, two plumb bobs with lines, two cameras, one with a close-up lens, and angle-measuring devices (inclinometers, angle-finders, special protractors) and other sundry tools of the trade. Collapsible dowel rods were stacked neatly inside the bag to help establish bullet trajectory, as well as key portions of the autopsy report showing angles of entry and the like. The investigator was somewhat leery of what he had been given as assimilated by the Navajo PD CSI unit. He had never worked one of their cases before and, while he was keeping the scientist's open mind, he would be extra careful in checking and rechecking their measurements, findings, and conclusions.

He started with the doorframe and thought he saw immediately what he was expecting. He went for the chemicals and camera. If he was right, there would be no doubt about who didn't fire the gun. He glanced back down the hall. Good, he was alone and no one had sight distance. He bent to his bag and retrieved a tape measure. He measured from the floor to the dark spot on the upper doorframe. Seventy inches, he typed into his tablet. Exactly what he had hoped to find. Exactly what he thought he would find.

While the expert went about his chores, Thaddeus and Katy kept Garcia busy.

Katy went first. "We have been told by Turquoise that your brother was raping her. Were you aware of that?"

The Navajo's normally placid face was seen to tighten. His eyes darted between the husband and wife and found the far wall.

"Oh—he was going to marry her."

Katy traded looks with Thaddeus. Then she tried again. "So, did you know he was raping her?"

"As a wife. He was making her his wife."

"Mr. Begay, Turquoise was too young to be a wife. Your brother was having sex with her. Every night. Several times a night. Surely you knew about this."

"He was marrying her."

"No, he wasn't marrying her. He was raping her. Did you know about it?"

"Well—" His voice trailed off. His eyes found the front door and he focused on the far mountains twenty miles away. They were dark in the front, lighter the farther away he looked. He kept his eyes out there, as far away as possible.

"You knew, didn't you," Thaddeus said. It wasn't a question.

"I know he loved her very much. She shouldn't'a shot him."

"She didn't shoot him," Thaddeus said. "You, more than anyone, should know that. She never killed coyotes or wild dogs. She didn't even kill spiders. Tell me you didn't know that?"

The stolid face never changed expression. "I know," he agreed. "She wouldn't."

Katy came back for a turn. "Then why do you say she shouldn't have shot him? You know she didn't do it. How do we know you didn't do it?"

His eyes returned inside. They were wide and darting. "Me shoot Randy? I couldn't'a do that. He's my brudder."

Thaddeus leaned forward. "Do you know anyone who was mad at your brother?"

"No."

"Was he buying or selling drugs?"

"I—"

"Turquoise says he gave her drugs."

"Just cocaine, I think."

"Did he give you cocaine too?"

The man spread his hands and studied his long, brown fingers. "I wouldn't take the cocaine. It's too strong for me. I like whiskey."

"I'll bet you're a Wild Turkey man. You look like a Wild Turkey man."

"I like Wild Turkey."

"Sure you do. Was your brother making Turquoise use the cocaine?"

"I think. Maybe she wanted to."

"Like maybe she wanted to be married to him?"

"Mebbe."

"Mr. Begay, isn't it true you knew your brother was raping your little girl and giving her drugs and yet you did nothing to stop it?"

"I guess."

"Why didn't you stop it?"

"He was my brudder."

"But she was your daughter!" Katy cried. "I mean, what the hell?"

"I don't know. I was scared of Randy, I think."

"You were afraid he would hurt you?"

"Yes, I was."

"So you gave him ownership of your daughter."

"I don't know about ownership."

Katy was frustrated. "You basically let him do anything he wanted to Turquoise, like he owned her."

"It is our way."

"No, it's not! I'm Navajo too! She was raped because you just plain didn't give a damn. Why don't you admit that? You were just a lousy father!"

Thaddeus touched her arm. She was on the edge of the couch, ready to pounce like a wild mama lion. He pulled her back against the cushions. She resisted; he pulled even harder.

Thaddeus said, "Mr. Begay, I'm going to recommend that you allow Turquoise to come stay with Katy and me while the court is going on. She needs stability and we can give her that. Would you be able to sign papers that agreed?"

"I guess I would sign. Yes."

"We've discussed it, Mr. Begay," Katy said. "I'm not sure we would ever let her come back home to you. I know I wouldn't let her but I can't speak for a judge."

"It would be good if she could be with you, I think."

"We think so too, Mr. Begay," Thaddeus said. "Katy will be back tomorrow with papers for you to sign. We have your word, that you'll sign?"

"I give my word I will sign."

"Fair enough. Now, do you have any bottled water around here? I'm dry as a son of a bitch," Thaddeus said, the anger heavy in his voice. "Why don't you look inside that refrigerator and see what you can find?"

"Let me get you some water," the Navajo man said. He appeared relieved for the opportunity to get up and move away from these two. Katy looked at Thaddeus, who nodded at her. She nodded back. They were a team, at least for a few minutes here, and Thaddeus felt glad about that. He and his wife were united about something, about the care and feeding of one young Indian girl. It was good and made him feel better for the child.

The man returned with one bottled water, which the twosome shared.

Thaddeus wiped his mouth and swallowed hard. This was very difficult, dealing with the insanity of the child's life, but he was determined to leach out everything he could about the shooting.

He began. "Were you home the morning of the shooting?"

"I was not home."

"Where were you?"

"At Ida's house. She has four children."

"Who is Ida?"

"She's my wife."

"You're married to Ida?"

"No, but she's my wife."

"All right. Are the children yours?"

"Two young ones are mine."

"You are their father?"

"Yes. So sometimes I stay over there."

"And you leave Randy here alone with Turquoise."

"She was marrying Randy."

"Damn, man!" Thaddeus exploded. "She was not married to him! Quit saying that!"

"He wanted to marry her and I said he could marry her."

"So you gave her to him?"

"Yes."

"Did you know he gave her an STD?"

"What?"

Thaddeus sighed. The guy was all but impossible. "Did you know he gave her the clap? Gonorrhea?"

"IHS called me. I think she didn't get it from Randy. I think her boyfriend Tommy Begay."

Katy fished. "And who is Tommy Begay? Is everyone in her life named Begay?"

"Tommy is also my brother. He is ten years younger."

"Than you?"

"Than Randy."

"You're what, about thirty-five?"

"Thirty-six. Randy was twenty-six and Tommy is sixteen."

"Your mother had kids twenty years apart?"

"Thirty years apart. I have an older brudder."

"Tell me about Tommy, her boyfriend. Where does he live?"

"With my mother."

"What town?"

"Kayenta."

"What does Tommy do?"

"He goes to school and studies veterinary."

"He's studying to be a vet?"

"That's right."

"Where's that?"

"Monument Valley High School. Kayenta."

"Was Tommy having sex with Turquoise? Were *you* having sex with Turquoise?"

"I didn't have sex with her. One time mebbe. Before Randy moved here."

"You had sex with your daughter?"

"No, I was mistaken."

Again they traded looks. Thaddeus was feeling queasy. The entire ordeal was making him want to throw up. He looked at Katy. Clearly she was feeling the same way. But she was tough; she plunged ahead.

"Why do you think it was Tommy who gave the clap to Turquoise?"

"He had to take medicine for it. I think he gave it to Turquoise."

"Did Randy have the clap too?"

"Don't know about Randy and clap. He never told me nothing about that."

Katy sat back against the couch. The frustration was evident on her face. She crossed her arms across her chest. Thaddeus could see that she was exhausted from the craziness that was Turquoise's life. "She's just been treated like their receptacle," she muttered. "Whatever they wanted to put in her, they just put in her. She's been lower than a sheep."

Thaddeus nodded, his feelings exactly.

"Mr. Begay, the police have taken Turquoise and she's now in foster care. They say she shot your brother and killed him. Tell me what you know about that."

"She was a good shot. I taught her to shoot out back to care for our sheep."

"Do you know anything about who killed Randy?"

"Not her, I think."

"Why not? Why do you think it was not her?"

"She wouldn't kill nothing. I had to shoot the coyotes and dogs myself. She refused."

"So you don't think she would have killed Randy?"

"Not Turquoise."

"Even if he was raping her?"

At that moment Myer-Rothstein came back down the hall. "Okay, I'm done in there. Loaded up and ready to go."

Katy and Thaddeus stood. They told Garcia Begay that he could phone his daughter if he wanted. He answered with a stolid look that barely hid his defiance. They thanked him and left the trailer.

Pulling down the road nobody looked back.

THIRTY-FOUR

They drove up to Kayenta to talk to Tommy Begay, the boyfriend. They had no idea where to start looking. Katy said she was hungry and they stopped at the McDonald's on the west end of town. They went inside and ordered.

Except for Thaddeus and Myer-Rothstein, everyone there was Native American.

Thaddeus studied them closely, as he had many times in the past. He knew they were a people who suffered quietly. They had endured their banishment to the luckless reservation for so many generations that he was guessing it had become congenital, like depression and crossed-eyes.

All faces were forlorn, with only the occasional half-hearted smile, usually from a young girl playing eyes with some young boy. But never was there the fulsome expression of happiness or joy that would have been found in an Anglo version of the same fast food chain. There was no horseplay behind the counters, no casual meets and greets among the people, even though, Thaddeus guessed, everyone there knew everyone else. The town and region were too small not to know everyone. Kayenta was part of the Navajo Nation and was located in Navajo County in the northeastern corner of Arizona. The population of 5,500 souls was ninety-five percent Native American and had the highest per capita poverty rate of any incorporated area in the United States. Still, the local Mickey D's was jumping.

They sought out a somewhat-clean corner table, swiped over it with a handful of napkins, and plopped down with burgers, fries, and drinks. Myer-Rothstein loudly slurped his diet cola and Katy popped back up to fetch all the ketchup she would need.

Between bites of his Big Mac, Myer-Rothstein said, when Katy had returned, "Well, your client didn't fire the fatal shot and I can prove it."

Thaddeus froze, the Quarter Pounder halfway to his mouth. "Say again?"

"It'll be in my report. But she didn't fire the shot that killed him. She couldn't have."

"Because?"

"Because of her height. Relax, it will all be in my report."

"Excellent," said Thaddeus, "you just made my day. My week, my month."

"You're worth every penny of the ten thousand we sent you," Katy added. She had taken an interest in the law firm's finances, now that she was showing up on the premises every day ready to work. "You get her out of this mess and it's worth everything to us."

"We've taken a real interest in this young lady," Thaddeus said. "We're going to ask the court to let us foster-parent her."

"Is that wise?" said Myer-Rothstein. He brushed a napkin at the mayonnaise on his chin. "Excuse me," he said.

"It is important to her well-being," Katy said, "to be where she feels safe. She already trusts Thad, and I've become very close with her. We're only ten years apart—well, eleven. She could be my younger sister."

"Excellent," said the forensic expert. "She's damn lucky you feel that way. Not everyone would welcome an accused murderer into their home. Do you have kids?"

"Sarai, five. She has met Turquoise and loves her. Turquoise played Barbie's with her one afternoon and made up huge fantasy worlds for their play. She's very creative and Sarai was smitten."

"Our little girl has had some problems," Thaddeus said. "We think Turquoise will be great for her to be around."

"So it's a win-win," said Myer-Rothstein.

Twenty minutes later they were again on the road.

They located Tommy Begay at MVHS and the principal arranged for them to meet between classes. "Ten minutes, no more," they were told.

It was a small room where they met, mint walls, overhead lights, popcorn ceiling, tile floor.

The principal led Tommy Begay into the room and introduced him.

He was a handsome boy of sixteen, bright-eyed and earnest, black hair center-parted and short on the sides. He evinced a can-do attitude and love for his major, large animal veterinary assistant.

He wanted to assist vets with cattle and horse care, he said, and eventually enroll at the University of Arizona veterinary school. First he would work four years, he said, save his money by living with Turquoise and splitting costs, and then apply. His mother was a cook at Monument Valley High School and his father drove a gas delivery rig around the northern part of the state. The father was home at night, the mother was demanding of high grades and educational excellence, and Tommy appeared to be in good hands and thriving. He didn't appear, to Thaddeus, to even be related to his two older brothers, Randy and Garcia.

"As I follow it, what you're telling us is," Katy said, "you and Garcia are of the same clan but in reality you're not brothers."

"Correct," Tommy said with a smile. "We just call ourselves brothers but that's because our mothers are of the same clan."

"How close are you to Turquoise?" Thaddeus asked. "In fact, our time is limited, so let me be blunt. Have you been having sexual relations with her?"

"Good grief, no! I worship that girl!"

"Fair enough," Katy said. "Did you know about her uncle, Randy Begay, your brother?"

"Not my brother but we're of the same clan. Just like Garcia. What's to know about him?"

Katy and Thaddeus traded looks. Best to let Turquoise explain these parts to Tommy, they agreed by silence.

"I know she's in trouble. But someone should call me to be a witness. That girl wouldn't hurt anyone. She's in the CTE vet assistant program with me. She's small animals, I'm large."

"She's studying to be a veterinary assistant," said Katy, "I believe she told me that."

"Yeah, we had some courses together at first but now we're in our specializations and we don't usually get together, except at lunch. We both brown-bag and trade stuff. Like my mom makes healthy sandwiches and Turquoise usually only has Pringles and Ding-Dongs and crap food. So we trade and that way she gets a good meal every day. Plus, this year my mom even makes an extra sandwich for Turquoise."

"So you're making sure she eats well."

"Yes. Plus she doesn't get all the clothes she needs. So I help with that too."

"How do you do that?"

"I change truck tires at night at the truck stop. Ten bucks an hour. I can buy her winter coats and boots and stuff. Garcia drinks up his pay and never buys her nothing."

"So you've kind of jumped in to care for her."

"Get used to it, I say. We're going to get married as soon as we graduate. Then we're moving to Tucson so I can go to vet school."

"Fantastic," said Katy. "You sound like a great young man for her."

"I try," he said. "I do what I can to help."

Thaddeus had no more questions. Katy shrugged and looked at her husband; she had no more questions either. Myer-Rothstein was silent, lost in thought.

They thanked Tommy for coming in to talk with them, thanked the principal, and left the school property.

"Incredible kid," Katy said once on the long drive back.

"Both of them," Thaddeus said. "Turquoise and Tommy."

"Yes. Both."

THIRTY-FIVE

The Juvenile Court judge saw things Katy's way. She had appeared before him and requested temporary guardianship of Turquoise.

The judge said she had two things going for her: one, she was Navajo, like Turquoise, which would give her special insights into the girl's needs, and two, she would have an M.D. after her name in six weeks. Which gave her enormous credibility with the court, especially when Katy added that she had applied to do her residency with Indian Health Services. She wanted to study family medicine and IHS was bending over backwards to lure doctors out to the reservation. Her application for residency was approved the same day it was received. In all, the judge was impressed. He entered a finding in the sealed court records that both Thaddeus and Katy were fit and proper parties to have the temporary care, custody, and control of the minor child,

Turquoise Begay.

Turquoise left the court with Katy and they drove straight over to meet with Thaddeus. He wanted to go over the plea offer from Wrasslin Russell.

The two women sat across from him.

"I met with the DA about your case," Thaddeus explained.

Turquoise nodded. "Is it about over with?"

Thaddeus shook his head. "Hardly. We're just getting started. Anyway, in criminal cases the defense lawyer always meets with the prosecutor for plea negotiations. This is a time to talk and try to agree on the outcome for the case. Sometimes it works; sometimes it's not so great. She wants to put you in prison for forty years. She says that's her final offer."

"Did you agree?" Turquoise asked, panicky and turning pale.

"No way. I told her we would go to trial."

Turquoise leaned back in the black leather client chair. She shot a look at Katy, who reached and patted her arm. "We'll take care of you. I told you that. Now let Thad do his thing. He's very good at this stuff."

"When will the trial be?"

"One month. A little less, now. We've got lots to do to prepare."

Turquoise nodded. "Can I tell you something and have you believe me?"

"Sure. Of course I believe you."

"I didn't shoot Randy Begay. I wanted him to die, but I didn't shoot him."

"I know that."

Her eyes clouded over with tears. "And I can't go to jail. Tommy and I want to be together. We want to move to Tucson and get jobs."

"We met him," Katy said. "What a neat guy."

"I love him," Turquoise said. "He's the only man who didn't hurt me."

"We know that," Thaddeus said. "We liked him very much. Here, I got you something."

He passed her a red cell phone. "I got this for you, so you can talk in private with Tommy. You'll have the guest room at our house and you can talk to him in privacy to your heart's content."

She accepted the gift and was immediately glowing. "I always wanted my own phone."

"Now you have it. Welcome to the family," Thaddeus said.

"Thank you. I want to do good for you guys. And for Sarai. She's my best friend right now."

"Do you have any girl friends from school that you want to have visit?"

"Amendola Asi, Lupe Marquez, and Nancy Yellowman. They're my best buds. They're in small animals with me."

"Then let's wait a week or two, let you get settled in, then you can get them to come down for a sleepover. Deal?"

"Deal! What about Tommy, can he come down?"

"Sure," said Katy. "But he can't stay overnight. The judge would remove you if that happened."

"I know."

Thaddeus asked, "Did you tell the prosecution that Tommy was the one who gave you the STD?"

She looked away. "I was embarrassed to have anyone know my uncle was making me do it. I hated it for Tommy to find out. I was afraid he would turn away from me."

"Understood," said Thaddeus. "Totally." He looked at Katy, who nodded. It was beginning to make more sense, especially now that they had met Tommy and found him to be a diamond living up there in the rough.

"So do you want me to tell the DA that you reject her offer of forty years in jail?"

"Yes. I can't be in jail for something I didn't do."

"Then we'll have to get ready for trial. Katy is going to take you shopping for some clothes. The ones you have, that you brought along, are fine. But we need some clothes for court, too. Plus you might see some spring clothes on the racks. We'll help with that too."

"Am I going to school?"

"You're going to have three tutors. We've arranged with the Department of Children and Family Services for that. They're local teachers, all very good."

"So I'll have classes at home?"

"Yes, that's the best we can do right now, since it's halfway through the semester and you've already missed so much."

"I can't read so good. I need help."

"Not a problem. They will do some evaluations and take it from there. You're in excellent hands."

"I think I'm starting to see that."

"If Thad's finished, let's go swing some racks. It's dress-up time!"

For the first time, Thaddeus saw Turquoise smile. She stood and her body language said it all, for she took two steps toward Katy.

She was, she was saying, home.

THIRTY-SIX

Two days later, Thaddeus trekked across Aspen Street to attend the pre-trial status conference with H. Ivan Trautman.

The day had dawned bright and sunny but, as so often happened in the mountains, by noon the sky was swept with low-hanging snow clouds and by one it was starting to sift down in large clumpy flakes.

He shivered and buttoned the top button of his pea coat. He wanted to curse the snow; he was ready for spring. But he gave thanks instead: thanks that Katy and Sarai were with him, thanks that there was something he could do for Turquoise and her problems, and thanks for his law practice. He gave thanks the property they owned, and how well things had been going ever since Shep swooped in and gave him a hand by inviting him to join the Angelina Steinmar defense team. It had done wonders for his spirit and attitude—just to be wanted.

That day's hearing was a regularly scheduled one; the court wanted to know the status of plea negotiations in the case of *State of Arizona v. Turquoise Begay*.

Thaddeus stepped on the opposite sidewalk and hurried inside the courts building. He stamped his feet on the rubber mat and smiled at the two deputies manning the security apparatus. He walked through, set off the alarm, stepped back through and removed his belt. He tried again. No alarms went off. The guards suggested he get a different belt, one with a smaller buckle. He said he preferred the one he was wearing because of the turquoise inlay. Hand-made by Hopi craftsmen. They shrugged and watched him disappear upstairs.

Thaddeus and Wrasslin had a few minutes to duke it out while they waited to enter the judge's chambers. He announced that his client had refused the offer of forty years in the penitentiary. "Surprise!" he wanted to shout, but refrained. DA Wrasslin was visibly upset, crossed her legs, crossed her arms, and turned away from him. "Judge Trautman isn't going to like this one damn bit," she spat over her shoulder. "You have been warned."

"Come on give me something realistic. The guy was raping her."

"She said her boyfriend gave her the clap."

"So that means the uncle wasn't raping her? I don't know which in-bred-child-molesting reservation you were raised on, but on this one there's no such thing as exclusivity. Any man can have a go at any woman, blood relative or whatever. That's what we have here and you're too damn obdurate to see it."

"You can go in now," the secretary said. She was new; someone Thaddeus didn't recognize. He wanted to ask her about Judge Trautman's mood, but thought better of it. It just might get back to His Honor that Thaddeus had asked, even if it was only a joke. The little jurist could be counted on to pounce on any slight at this point, real or imagined.

Wrasslin led the way into the inner sanctum.

"Sit," said the judge. He was wearing his black robe and black frame glasses and had a look on his face that said the lynch mob was close behind. A look that said he saw nothing redeeming about the world and its creatures, especially defense lawyers named Murfee.

Or was Thaddeus simply reading too much into the guy's attitude? He wondered.

"Mr. Murfee," the judge began in a slow monotone, "tell me what plea has been entered into."

Thaddeus was quick on the uptake. "None, Judge. We're ready for trial."

Whereupon the jurist exploded, "Get the hell out of my office! No, wait! Tell me what effort you went to with your client. Does she understand the evidence against her?"

"Yes. We've been over it thoroughly."

"Who's 'we'?"

"My wife—Katy Murfee and I."

"I heard she had obtained custody of the girl in juvie. So your wife is working with her now?"

"My wife is a physician. Her specialty will be family medicine. She is totally qualified to work with this child and help her through this difficult time. Plus, like Turquoise, Katy is Navajo."

"Good grief. And where is the girl staying?"

"With us."

"No! You mean to come into my court and tell me you're housing a defendant you also represent? Didn't we do this dance once before when you made your client's bail? This is purely unethical of you to be supporting her! I'll have your license or know the reason why not!"

"Not supporting her, sir. She's a ward of the state and the state is providing all her support. We're just providing the care and attention a minor female of sixteen requires."

"So you're acting as her foster parents?"

"We are."

"Damn unethical. I'm calling the state bar as soon as we're done here. You can kiss your law license goodbye."

"I wondered the same thing, Judge, when I heard," Wrasslin volunteered. Thaddeus stared daggers at her. Great, now she was in on the crucifixion too. Here we go again.

"I'm still her counsel. We are ready for trial. You have given us a trial date and I expect you to stick with it." Then Thaddeus totally surprised himself: "And if you waver from the trial date so much as one inch I'm filing a judicial complaint against you!"

Total silence. Seething, fighting an almost overwhelming impulse to eviscerate the young lawyer, the judge reminded himself that they were on the record. Everything being said was being neatly and religiously recorded by the court reporter crouched over his machine in the corner. He took a deep breath, held it, and Thaddeus watched his lips move as he counted—slowly—to ten.

"You will have your day in court, Mr. Murfee. Your client will be given a fair trial and treated with the respect all defendants get from this court. You will represent her zealously but within the bounds of the law. Am I clear?"

"Perfectly," said Thaddeus, and he began dumping papers back into his file case. His back was bathed in sweat. He swiped a coat sleeve quickly across his forehead while the judge's eyes were downcast on his calendar. It was unbearably hot in the office and he felt out the corner of his eye the gaze of Wrasslin, who certainly was seeing him as a prisoner about to be dragged to the gas chamber. Except he wasn't. Inside, he was calm and, even more, fed up with this moron's belittlement, threats, and enmity. He'd had it and he wasn't taking any more of the guy's bullshit. Let them take his license; he'd retire to San Diego and race sailboats. Or down to Jamaica and drink rum and have more babies with Katy. Or—

"Counsel, we're twenty-three days out from trial. We will have no more meetings between now and then. Is there anything further either of you wish to bring up?"

"No."

"No."

"Fair enough. Mr. Murfee, my complaint against you will be lodged with the state bar before close of business."

Thaddeus stood and faced him head-on.

"Knock yourself out, Judge."

"Wh—"

He turned on his heel and left without being formally excused.

They could all go to hell.

It was a new day.

THIRTY-SEVEN

The symptoms were ambiguous: the right side of his face felt numb—he noticed when he absently rubbed his hand over his face. Then Madonna Sanders—a second paralegal—buzzed him and asked about the statute of limitations for homicide—something he would ordinarily spout back off the top of his head, but he suddenly couldn't remember. In fact, he wasn't even sure he'd understood the question at all. Feeling a slight panic, he stood to walk to the half-fridge for a bottle of water, and fell. His right leg didn't work. Which is when he cried out for help.

Luckily, Wendy heard his cry.

When she got to his office, he was again trying to stand and again toppling over. So she dialed 911 and brought him a bottle of water. She unscrewed the cap and held it to his mouth, but the water dribbled out the right corner of his mouth, which had formed itself into a

187

downturned scowl. In fact, the entire right side of his face was drooping at that moment, which scared her to death and she dialed 911 again. The emergency operator told her the EMTs were en route, to remain calm.

He lay on his back, studying the overhead fluorescent lights.

"Thish idn't good," he managed to say.

"Lay flat," Wendy ordered. "The EMTs are just about here. Are you cold?"

"Uh-uh."

By her watch it was four minutes later when the EMTs came charging in. They were wearing gray slacks and matching shirts, patches on their breast pockets with the serpent on the staff, stethoscopes around their necks, and lugging large boxes and telemetry equipment. They did vitals, asked him questions, and knew immediately: stroke. They gave him an aspirin, standard protocol.

He was loaded onto the transport rig and rushed out to the flashing ambulance.

At the hospital the ER staff immediately assessed.

Stroke. Wife and family were called. A t-PA was administered to dissolve clots. Aspirin was administered. Monitors were plugged in and scans made.

A day later it was very clear. A mild-to-moderate stroke had hit, the result of a blocked artery, now unblocked, and Shep was left unable to speak or think clearly. He would require months of rehab; his time at the office would cease to exist for the foreseeable future.

When word reached Thaddeus, he was stunned. He was off for the afternoon, riding Coco in the forest, when the cell phone chimed. Shep was in the hospital, said Wendy Patterson. The stroke was disabling. They were already calling clients and informing them they would need to obtain new counsel for their cases. Would Thaddeus want to hang onto the Angelina Steinmar case, assuming she wanted him? In a split second he said he wanted the case, and that he would do whatever he could to help Shep manage his practice and to hold cases together and to make upcoming court appearances. Wendy thanked him and told him she would call back when she received word from Angelina. The rest of it was covered, she explained, as most clients were simply going to move on.

Suddenly drained of all desire to see the sights and continue his ride, Thaddeus trotted Coco back to the corral. He sprayed him off and brushed him down. Fresh oats and hay, clean water in the trough, and the horse was happy. Thaddeus went inside and told Katy about Shep. She filled him in on strokes—their treatment and recovery times—and Thaddeus was left feeling very sorry for Shep. He was a great guy and good friend and one of the best trial lawyers Thaddeus had ever watched in action. He decided to drive into town and drop by the hospital, just to let him know he was there if needed.

At Flagstaff Medical Center they directed him to Shep's room, where Thaddeus found his friend hooked up to tubes and monitors. He was lying lifelessly on his back, semi-propped up, and the TV was playing *Ellen*. When he saw Thaddeus, Shep tried to smile, the smile worked only the left side of his face. His right side seemed fixed, immobile, as if the muscles were no longer attached and receiving smile signals.

"Hey," said Thaddeus. "This sucks." He indicated the hospital and devices hooked up to his Shep.

Shep nodded. "Ish dramatic, yesh?"

"Dramatic, indeed," Thaddeus grinned. Good old Shep, always ready with a laugh.

"So I'm going to get ahold of Wendy and let her know I'm available to help any way I can. I wanted you to know that, too."

"Take Angelina file. She wansh you."

"Sure? That would be great."

Shep nodded. "Wendy shez. Angie called."

"Should I call her myself?"

"Yesh. You get fee."

"No way. You keep that. I only want to help."

"Good man."

"Hey, you'd do the same for me. You gave me a hand when I was down. Just let me do what I can to help you now. That seems fair."

"Fair."

"So can I bring you anything?"

"Big Mac."

"Will do. I'll drop by tonight after work. Fries?"

"Doc shez no grease. Causes strokes. Ha!"

"Hold the fries."

"No, bring fries. Pleash."

"Done."

Thaddeus gave the lawyer's shoulder a squeeze and said his goodbyes.

THIRTY-EIGHT

After visiting Shep, Thaddeus drove back to the office and, sure enough, there was a pink phone message with Angelina Steinmar's number. "Urgent," was all it said.

"Angelina," he said when she picked up. "I just visited Shep. Looks like he'll be out of the office for a while."

"I know, isn't it just awful? Poor man. I was so counting on him, too."

"Just let me know if I can help you find a new lawyer. There are some really good ones, even around here."

"I don't want a new lawyer, Thad. I want you."

"I haven't tried that many murder cases. I don't know."

"You have what it takes, you care. That's all that really matters."

He realized then that she was crying. Her voice broke into heaving sobs over the phone.

"Listen, how about I drop by and we talk about this. That good for you?"

"C-c-c'mon by. Goodbye."

He hung up. He looked out his window, across Aspen Street, beyond the courthouse, up to the top of the San Francisco Peaks. They were snow-covered, as they were much of the year, and the very tips were buried in dark, churning clouds that were undoubtedly dropping another load of snow on the rocky mountaintops. He studied that division between trees and summit, the treeline, that exact point—that moment—where the trees surrendered to the altitude and the harsh places took over. He had the feeling that he himself had just moved from one such area to another, trees to rocks. It was going to be lonely up here, he realized, with the Attorney General and the State of Arizona bringing to bear all of their power and endless resources to send Angelina Steinmar off to her doom and the executioner's needle. The same could be said for Turquoise Begay, whom the state wished to send to the penitentiary for forty years for something he was certain she did not do. Angelina, he wasn't so sure about. Shep had told him that he'd made up her entire story, that she would be providing perjured testimony to the jury.

Which was when it struck him. He couldn't represent Angelina Steinmar; her testimony was false and he'd promised himself that he would avoid such pitfalls forevermore after his fall from grace when he posted his own money as bail for Hermano Sanchez and wound up disbarred for a year. That was the end of that kind of crapola. Not only that, if he knowingly presented her perjured testimony he was equally guilty of a very serious felony. Not one for which he was facing extinction, as was she, but a serious felony and sentence nonetheless. Knowing the local judiciary and with his past record of being less than honest with the court, he could see himself doing ten years or more for such behavior. Come on, he thought, what kind of mess had he gotten himself into now?

192

DEFENDING TURQUOISE

His hands shook as he shrugged into his topcoat. His fingers felt papery and unusually cold, as if the life were draining out of him, fingers to hands to arms to torso to—

He stopped right there. Get hold of yourself, he commanded. You can do this. You've done it before. You have Shep's file and his notes of the story given by Angelina to Nony, who wrote it all down as it was related to her. You haven't done anything wrong—you didn't make up that whopper. Revisionist history: you haven't done anything wrong...yet. But if you knowingly introduce perjured testimony, at that exact point you will cross from the trees up into the rocks. Who knows what might happen?

Then the old fight came creeping back inside. You can do this, he said. You can do this and you can make it work. One day at a time, she's entitled to a defense by law. Make it happen for her. Starting now.

He left the office and drove up San Francisco Street and turned into Angelina's subdivision. There were no cars in front of her house. He pulled into the driveway and got out. The wind was blowing, thrashing, it could be said, down off the sweep of the mountains and he felt a total chill rush through his body. He headed for the front door and it swung open just as he got there.

"Come on in, Thaddeus," she said.

She was wearing black silk pants, moccasins with heavy white socks, and a sweatshirt that said "Wildcats"—the school mascot of her daughter's college. Her dead daughter. She was wearing no rings, no jewelry, and had evidently slid into some lipstick just before he arrived, for her lips were cherry red and glossy. At her height—five-ten, five-eleven—she was always an imposing figure and carried herself almost regally, a nod to her blueblood pedigree and her family's old money from timber and ranching and mining interests across the state. Her father was wealthy and she had been imbued with the figurative and literal carriage of someone who knew his or

193

her value and lived up to it. That she was caught up in this miasma with her dead husband and the wickedness that had been going on inside her house troubled Thaddeus. Clearly, she was not the kind of woman who would suffer fools, especially fools like John Steinmar and—

He stopped the thought, realizing that he didn't know the truth about what had been going on inside this house at all. He knew only Shep's version, which was zilch. That being acknowledged, he decided to plunge ahead and see what he could turn up.

"Coffee?"

He said he would like that very much, thank you.

He looked around the living room while she was away in the kitchen. It was very formal, with two floral couches, identical, facing, and two side-by-side wingbacks at either end of the rectangle, identical covers as well. A large, oblate spheroid of ironwood with a flat bottom served as a one-of-a-kind coffee table which had been topped with a sheet of glass smooth on the edges in the shape of a huge yawn. Indian art adorned the walls, lending them a bright aura of pinks, yellows, and reds overlaying all the desert and high plains hues where the artists evidently drew inspiration. The room was attractive, native, and very expensive, thought Thaddeus. He leaned back in the couch that stretched beneath the front window and drew a deep breath. He arranged his thoughts and decided how he would broach things with his new client.

She returned with a silver tray and two cups, steaming.

"So," she said as she passed a china cup and saucer to her guest, "you're my new lawyer, eh?"

"Thank you. Yes, if that's what you want, I'm honored to serve."

"Well, Mr. Thaddeus, that's what I indeed want. Do you need more money? Or do you have a split with Shep? Just tell me how much and I'll get a check to you."

"We're fine there. Shep has already paid me for my services.

Thanks for asking."

"Hey, if you're happy, I'm happy."

"But I would like more information about the morning you shot your husband."

Her coffee cup paused just below her mouth, but she had presence of mind enough to finish the sip.

"Oh?"

"Can you tell me how it happened? I know what you told Shep and Nony, but I'd like to hear it direct from you."

"Well...I shot John. He was hurting me and I shot him. Did I mean to kill him? I suppose I did."

She balanced the saucer and cup in one hand. Thaddeus thought he might have seen a hint of a jiggle there, but wasn't sure.

"Why did you shoot him?"

She waved a hand before her eyes as if swatting gnats. "He was hurting me. He had me down and was biting me."

"I've seen the pictures."

"Well, *that's* embarrassing."

"Don't be embarrassed. No need."

"I suppose."

"Was there a struggle?"

"He was trying to sexually assault me."

"How so?"

"Good grief, didn't you read the file?"

"I did. I just want to hear how it's going to sound spoken by you."

"He was trying to insert his fingers into my vagina. He was biting my vagina. I don't know, I suppose he wanted to have intercourse. You never knew with John."

"So there was a history?"

"My God, yes. The man was a deviant. I didn't know it until after Hammy was born, of course."

"Did he ever assault your little girl?"

"Funny you should ask. Turns out he did—he had been for some time. So she killed herself. Haven't you seen her note in the file?"

"Yes. And I'm sorry."

"Me too. She hung herself from her closet door. Left that note. The grand jury said it didn't clearly implicate John. I said screw them and went after justice myself."

"As in—"

"As in I shot the bastard. Right in the head. Bang!"

She had raised both hands and demonstrated a two-handed grip that would have made the NRA instructors proud.

"Bang!" she repeated. "Now hurt a woman, you fucking deviant."

"You're still very angry at him. I'm not sure I want the jury to see you angry."

"They won't. I played Blanche DuBois in *A Streetcar Named Desire*. I can still pull it off—without the alcoholism and the delusions, of course."

"There's a relief."

"Is that sarcasm I hear?"

"Just the slightest hint, let's say. I've known a few Blanches in my time."

"Don't tell me: your mother was a Blanche!"

He suddenly felt tricked and seduced by her niceness. She had seen right through him, right through to his own alcoholic, addled mother. How good was this woman? He wondered, pulling himself together.

"Let's focus on you, why don't we? So you shot him and good riddance. Are you talking about any of this with anyone? A counselor?"

"My God no. I'm not giving up my secrets, Thaddeus. Not at this stage of the game."

"That's smart. Let's keep it that way."

"How about a refill? Coffee cold?"

"I could go for that. Please."

She returned with a Mr. Coffee carafe. Refills were poured and the half-empty carafe abandoned to the tabletop.

She tugged the sleeves of her sweatshirt and smiled at him. A nice smile, a manicured smile, he thought. Like everything in her sublime upbringing and sweet life. But he thought he saw more beneath the polished exterior. Much more.

"If I said you shot your husband because he had sexually assaulted your daughter, what would you say?"

Again the pause of cup below lips.

"I'd say you were spot-on."

"So you executed him?"

Brushing gnats again.

"He was a bad man. A very bad man."

"If you were asked that same question in court, by the attorney general, how would you answer?"

"I'd say 'John was a violent man.' I'd say 'I was only protecting myself.' I'd say 'look at the bite mark pictures.'"

"But you wouldn't say he had it coming?"

"Only to you and Shep. I played Blanche, remember?"

"I remember. And I'll keep that in mind."

They continued talking about what happened and why. She showed him into the family room where the actual shooting had taken place. The carpet had been replaced so the cutout bloodstains were nowhere to be seen. But that was okay; he'd seen the pictures; studied them in detail, in fact. She reenacted the struggle, the reach for the gun, the relative distances when the shot was fired that killed her husband. Then she stood, arms folded, staring at Thaddeus as if she were standing guard. But standing guard over what? And would her guardedness be apparent in the courtroom? Or could she pull off the role of the put-upon spouse, the battered wife, and the terrified

197

victim?

He told her he would pick up her file from Shep's office and they would talk within the next week. She thanked him for coming and thanked him for taking her case. She asked him again if he needed more money and he said he'd been paid, he was happy.

She walked him out to the car and then trotted back inside her house.

He was excited.

She was good. She was very good.

And she was Blanche. That gave him a world of talent to direct.

Out the window she watched him pull away. A pang of sadness struck her heart: there was something about him, his youth? His innocence? She remembered when she had once been young and idealistic. She remembered that from before meeting and marrying John Steinmar, but not from after. Bastard. He had taken away her naiveté with his groping hands and mouth.

Her cell phone beeped.

She read the caller ID and grabbed it.

"Hey," she said.

"He gone?"

"He's gone, Bill."

"What did you think?"

"I think he's sweet. You're sure he's the right one?"

"I've watched him try two cases in my court. One was a rape and one was an insurance bad faith case. He prevailed on both. He's smooth and more than that, he's unbelievably bright. He simply out-thinks the other side.

"Not so smart he's going to catch on to us, is he?"

"Not that. We're safe."

"Hey, you're the judge."

"And you're the defendant. It's all good, as my kids say."

"See you tonight?"

"No can do. Miriam's back from Page."

"Then SD this weekend?"

"San Diego is good. There's a judicial conference beginning Friday. I can just stay over. I'll modify your bail, check the box for out-of-state trips."

"Hotel Del?"

"I've already got our old room. We're good."

"I love you, Your Honor."

"It's mutual, old friend."

"Later."

"Later."

THIRTY-NINE

William "Bill" F. Gerhardt II was fourth-generation Flagstaff. His great-grandfather had pioneered first down on the Mogollon Rim and then moved north to Flag. His own father had served in Vietnam one tour, come out on R and R to father Bill in Honolulu, and then gone back to 'Nam and died at Di An.

Bill grew up fatherless but not without lots of male influence. His mother made certain of that. Her four brothers fought with each other to see who got to take him to Little League, who got to coach him in Pop Warner, who would buy him his first deer rifle, who would teach him to ride, to drive, and on and on.

He was a man by his sophomore year and made the varsity football squad at linebacker. He was ferocious and when, nine years later, he graduated law school in Tucson, he still retained that fighting fervor that he had inherited from his father and uncles. Three years of practice had been followed by appointment to the bench, where he had served fifteen years exactly.

He met Thaddeus for lunch at Kathy's Kafe, a common meeting place among local professionals on the south side of town. The place was well known as a pickup joint for the waitress staff, many of who were either in bad marriages or who had left bad marriages and were newly on the prowl. "You damn near gotta be a divorcée to be hired on here," Bill told Thaddeus when their iced tea arrived.

It was noontime and Judge Gerhardt had had a sparse calendar that morning. The afternoon carried the promise of twenty default divorces, during which he would fight to stay awake as the split-ups recited their agreements for marital property, custody, alimony (very rare in Bill's court), and retirement funds. He was glad for the chance to get away and have lunch with Thaddeus, who was fairly new in town but already quite successful, especially if you were willing to overlook Thaddeus' problems with H. Ivan Trautman. Bill was only too happy to do that. Frankly, he hated H. Ivan, ignored him as best you could ignore the chief judge, and socially avoided the man at all costs.

"Thanks for meeting up with me," Thaddeus said.

"Well, I am concerned about you taking on the Attorney General and his circus. I would say it's an unfair fight, except you're smarter than all of them."

"That's a nice thing to say. I'm not worried. I might be outnumbered but they can only talk one at a time."

"Attaboy. So true."

Beef and noodles arrived and the duo dug in. Heaping forkfuls of the man-food were gulped and swallowed without talk for several minutes. Then Bill paused to wipe his mouth.

"How much has Angelina—Mrs. Steinmar—told you about what happened?"

Thaddeus felt a caution sign turn yellow in his gut. Judges and attorneys were forbidden from having *ex parte* discussions about cases. Both sides had to be present to ethically discuss a case, not just one side.

"Quite a bit. I think I have a pretty good feel for what happened."

"Well, she gets my vote. Steinmar was a no-good bastard. Little albino got what he had coming."

"Well, that's good to hear. I guess," Thaddeus hesitantly added. He actually wasn't all that sure that any of it was okay to hear. *Ex parte*—if anyone found out—

"You can bet the evidence will fall her way. That's a promise."

Thaddeus nearly swallowed his fork. This definitely was over the line. He'd never heard of a judge promising a litigant's attorney that he would favor her with evidentiary rulings.

"Good to know," he mumbled.

"Just don't want you to have any more problems with Ivan the Terrible. I hear you have another case with him. Murder?"

"Sixteen-year-old Indian girl. She's innocent."

"Hell, Thaddeus, we're all innocent. We just need forgiveness."

"I hear that."

"Do you feel good about defending Angie—Mrs. Steinmar?"

Thaddeus chewed thoughtfully. He wanted to say, "I feel much better now," but didn't.

"Yes, I feel good about her case. Clear case of self-defense."

"Clear case. No doubt. You'll certainly get a self-defense instruction."

"Well—"

He wanted to say, "well thanks," but didn't. Truth was, he was speechless. He felt a discomfiture wash over him and he wanted to stand and leave before any more unethical conversation could ensue. Instead, he remained in place, calmly forking down the beef and noodles. A nod to the waitress, yes, he would like a refill on the tea.

He chewed slowly and kept his eyes off the judge.

"Nice lunch crowd," he said as tangentially as he could.

"Tell you something else, Thaddeus. Angelina wouldn't harm a fly. I mean that literally. But something snapped in her when Hammy hung herself. Changed that lady overnight. Do you know she went to bed the night before with no gray hair? Next night she had long streaks of gray. It changed her in a twinkling. Not for the better, either."

"So you've known her a long time?"

"Every Christmas Eve we're over at the Steinmars' for carols and punch. Tradition around here."

"That sounds nice."

"Here's one other tidbit. We just spent the weekend together in San Diego."

Thad dropped his fork. It hit his shoe and skittered under the table.

"Well—"

The judge beamed. "Now," he said proudly, "now you know how the cow eats the grass in this town."

"Well—"

"Don't you even think about losing this case, son. It just ain't gonna happen."

"Well—"

"Gotta get back. Mucho divorces this afternoon for old Bill. Catch you later. You can pay."

Thaddeus watched the judge bang out the door and tuck chin to chest for the walk north on the windy street. The waitress hurried over with a clean fork.

"Pie?" She smiled.

"And a shot of Jack Daniel's," he quipped.

"We don't serve alcohol."

"I wouldn't have asked if you did."

"You're losing me, Thad."

"You know my name?"

"We all know you. You're one of the cute ones."

"Are you on the jury panel next month?"

"What? What?"

"Never mind. Gotta go. Here's a twenty. Thanks again."

He studied her nametag.

"Wulanda."

"Wu—call me Wu."

"Wu."

FORTY

When he got home that night, Katy was in the driveway shoveling snow. Turquoise was at her side. The teenager was talking on her cell phone with one hand and casually sweeping a broom in the other hand. Thaddeus was warmed to see she was comfortable enough with them to talk with friends, to have her own ongoing life. Sarai was flat on her back in the early spring powder, beating arms and legs into snow angels.

He pulled his car inside the garage and hit the close button. Ducking out beneath the articulating door, he held his arms wide and Sarai happily bounced over and was encircled.

"Daddy, come see what I made in the snow."

"You've got it," he said, and allowed himself to be pulled into the yard where a covey of snow angels were in flight. "This is great," he said. "I wonder who did this?"

"Daddy, *I* did this," the little girl shouted, the beginnings of mock frustration in her voice. She was learning, he thought.

"Hey, Turquoise, what's up?" he said to their newest addition.

She held up one finger and mouthed, "It's Tommy."

He nodded and raised a finger to his lips to hush himself. Tommy couldn't be interrupted in whatever in the world he was saying. Thaddeus was glad for Turquoise; Tommy was perfect for her.

"Hey, babe," said Katy. "Want to spell me on the shovel?"

"Happy to. Hand it over."

Katy stood upright and passed him the shovel. He accepted and bent to the task. The snow was a good eight inches deep, powder, and tended to fly apart as he chunked it out of the driveway.

"What's new?" his wife asked. She was wearing hiking boots, blue jeans, and a Patagonia top. Leather work gloves completed the outfit. Her hair was braided to the shoulders and yellow ski sunglasses gave her face a warm look. She removed the gloves and beat them together as she watched him bend to the task.

"Had lunch with Bill Gerhardt this afternoon. What a twist that was."

"How so?"

"It was crazy. He all but promised me a not guilty verdict in Angelina's case."

"How could he do that?"

"Dunno. I think he said more than he meant to say. He definitely said more than he should have said."

"Like what?"

"Like, he and Angelina are a thing. They just spent the weekend together in San Diego."

"No way!"

"Way. I'm telling you. For once I was speechless."

"Well, all the better for your case. Do you feel stronger about why she shot the guy now?"

"He was raping their daughter. I probably would have shot him too."

"I would have done worse than bullets. That's too clean," Katy said darkly. "Had it coming, you ask me."

"But it also gives motive to shoot other than in self-defense. The state will try to make it look like she shot him out of rage, not in self-defense."

"That's how that works?"

"That's how that works."

"Girls, let's go in and get dinner. Okay?"

Turquoise said her goodbyes and slipped the phone into the pocket of her flannel shirt. Shirt and jeans and hiking boots courtesy of Thaddeus and Katy and he was damn happy to have been honored with the chance to help provide for her. More and more he was "falling" for the kid: she was neat, honest, polite, and worked hard with her tutors. All three had reported that she was an exceptional student and quick study, and that she had her educational sights set far beyond mere high school. She wanted to be a small animal vet and just that afternoon had enlisted Katy to drive her to the Flagstaff Humane Society, out in the pines, where she had walked several dogs, a volunteer gesture. Katy had jumped in and brought along a dog each time herself. They chatted about it as they went inside to get dinner.

Thaddeus kept his head down, shoveling and basking in the glow of family. He was extremely grateful for each and every one of them. Life was grand.

Except that one of them was charged with first-degree murder.

That night he went upstairs for bed, Max leading the way two stairs at a time. Max had a special thing for Thaddeus and it was reciprocal. Katy was in the shower, singing "Sunshine of My Life." "That you?" she shouted. He answered, and she asked him to loofah her back. She popped open the shower door and turned her back to him. Warm brown skin, soap streaming down and disappearing between the buttocks and running on down into the drain, hand circling the loofah gently but strong enough to make a difference, fighting off the urge to encircle her with his free hand and cup her breast, feeling aroused, her head turning and giving him a soapy, questioning look. "This too hard for you?" she asked.

"That's not all that's hard."

"Well, maybe tonight we can do something about that."

"I accept," he said, his breathing difficult as the old familiar swollen feeling rose up through his chest and rolled down into his abdomen and genitals.

She turned off the water and reached for her towel. He handed it in.

"Well, don't stare at me, please."

"I'm trying hard not to."

"Pervert."

"Just lonely."

"Now I don't know. All the times you came home reeking of hundred-dollar perfumes. All of a sudden I'm not feeling so friendly."

"Please don't go there."

She gave him a sharp, querulous look. "No, you went there first. I'm still bitter. You can just stay on your own side of the bed tonight."

"I'm sorry for my shortcomings. I know I hurt you."

"Come on, Thad, you killed off a part of me inside."

"Well, what about you? You had your own indiscretions."

No sooner had he said it than he wished he hadn't. More than anything he had dreaded having this conversation with her and he had made himself promise that he wouldn't point fingers. Like he had just done. Damn, he thought, damn!

"I had my flirtations at the hospital, granted. But only because I was hurt by you first."

"Now you're justifying your actions by my actions. Sorry, but that doesn't fly."

"Why not?"

"Because I was a drunk and acting out in my drunken, addled state. Your own flirtations, as you call them, were done a hundred percent sober. That's premeditation, where I work."

"Screw you and screw your premeditation. You hurt me and you're not getting off the hook by claiming drunk."

"Whatever. It's still the truth. In 1952 the World Health Organization declared alcoholism a disease. The AMA followed soon after."

"Oh, so now you're going to use the disease concept to justify getting in someone's panties? Is that where we're at? I call bullshit, Mister."

He caught himself. She was right. Disease or not, he had hurt her. It was time to call his sponsor. And time to shut the hell up.

"I'm sorry I hurt you. I can only ask forgiveness and if you're not able or willing to give it, I can live with that. Just let me keep trying, please. Don't shut me out, please. I love you and I'm sorry."

"Well."

And that's where they left it for the night. He on his side, her on her side, back turned to him, tears in her eyes.

The next morning he remembered hating on himself before drifting off to sleep.

Oh, how he hated himself sometimes. Would that never cease? And speaking of forgiveness, would he ever forgive himself?

Time to buy lunch for the sponsor. Time to work the Twelve Steps.

Max followed him to the door when he left for work.

She did not.

FORTY-ONE

Katy dressed Turquoise for trial in a pleated gray skirt, white button-down shirt, women's crossover tie, and blue blazer with gold buttons that matched her low gold and black half-heels. She looked sixteen years but no older, as the lack of makeup portrayed the glow of a very young woman who needed none. On her left wrist was a one-inch silver bracelet adorned with one inset turquoise stone. On her right wrist was a red Swatch wristwatch, as she was left-handed, which would soon become known, probably for the first time, to the DA and lead investigator. She took the seat indicated to her by Thaddeus. He was wearing an expensive navy suit with just the faintest hint of a pinstripe, plain black lace-ups, and white shirt with regimental striped tie. He handed her a yellow legal pad and pen and told her, as soon as the jury was seated, to make notes and to make sure all of them saw her writing left-handed. They had discussed all this and she whispered back that it was a done deal.

The recently enthroned district attorney, Wrasslin Russell, made her appearance flanked by a first-year ADA and an FBI agent who had headed up the investigation on the Navajo reservation. The Fibbie was a stout, capable-looking redhead named Stall Worthy. Special Agent Worthy was named in the list of witnesses both as lead investigator and as the representative of the People of the State of Arizona, which was standard operating procedure.

Thaddeus watched the procession settle in and begin unpacking *Arizona Evidence* manuals and essential *Pacific Reporters*—authority for the key legal support the DA figured she would need to call upon as the defense objected to evidence she intended to offer. Agent Worthy took a seat and flipped open his tablet and busied himself typing who knew what.

Five minutes passed. The bailiff waddled up with an icy pitcher of water and made sure the thermos pitchers at each table were full. He placed a fresh folded napkin under the pitcher on Thaddeus' table and, satisfied with this last housekeeping chore, walked over to the door leading into chambers. He softly rapped three times. The signal: all present and accounted for: the court reporter had loaded her machine with a fat new tape, the pitchers were topped off, hats were removed, books were in place, and all was ready.

Then it happened, just as Thaddeus had feared with the squirrely little judge. He was requesting—demanding—a pre-trial conference with both attorneys—without clients. The attorneys surrendered to the order and swept anxiously into the judge's chambers, leaving their partners alone at counsel table. The judge and one other person, who was introduced as Irl Kampbell, a trial monitor from the State Bar of Arizona Office of Professional Responsibility, met them.

"Mr. Kampbell is here at my request." H. Ivan smiled (for the benefit of the visitor, Thaddeus was sure). "He will monitor this trial and report back to the bar on any of Mr. Murfee's trial conduct that violates any rules of professional responsibility."

Without standing, Irl Kampbell stuck his hand out and shook hands all around. He was a wizened old man, mid-seventies, Thaddeus guessed, complete with white hair, white eyebrows, and lined bifocals, as well as a failed attempt at the vogue-ish goatee. His eyes were large and round and his smile engineered by a lifetime of dentists. "I'm a retired Court of Appeals judge," he said mildly. "You might have read my opinions if you've practiced in our wonderful state for any length of time. If you read case law, that is."

Wrasslin allowed as how she was very familiar with his rulings—an attempt to endear herself with this State Bar snitch. Thaddeus was seething inside at H. Ivan's attempt to suppress his efforts at trial to free Turquoise from the state's tentacles. He decided then and there that he would change nothing about his plans for how he would proceed, what witnesses he would produce, what arguments he would make, and what dramatic outbursts and comments he would serve up for the jury.

"I haven't read your opinions at all," said Thaddeus. "Are they still good law?"

There, the gloves were donned and he had taken the first swing.

"Why yes, Mr. Murfee, all of my opinions are still good law. If you review them and find you have differences with any, we should discuss your questions before kicking off our little trial here today."

Touché. Point made. It was going to be war and both sides had answered Ready!

"Lady and gentlemen," H. Ivan droned, "*my* question is, any last-minute problems before we begin our little inquest?"

"None," said Thaddeus. "But I'm just wondering, now that we have a State Bar trial monitor in our midst."

"Wondering?" responded the little jurist.

"I'm wondering who's going to judge the judge, just to make sure we have a fair trial? Any special guests today for that purpose?"

The judge's face froze over. "I can assure you, comments such as that are exactly the sort of insult Judge Kampbell will be noting."

"So noted," commented the Honorable Irl Kampbell. However, he didn't write anything down, not that Thaddeus could see. Which told him the retiree's presence was as much for the purpose of intimidation as it was for any useful end.

"Then let's begin, shall we?" H. Ivan said with a refresh of gusto, and he rose up out of his chair and zipped his power robe to the top.

The lawyers were allowed to file into the courtroom first, while Judge Kampbell went out the back way so he could sneak into the rear of the courtroom and ready his keen eye.

Whereupon H. Ivan Trautman swung into the courtroom and stepped quickly up to his perch, where he sat and partially unzipped the black robe about twelve inches. Underneath he was wearing a blue shirt and red tie. His hair was freshly trimmed. He surveyed the courtroom, whispered under his breath to the clerk of the court, and tapped his microphone. He nodded to the bailiff, who called court to order, and plopped back down.

"Ladies and gentlemen, please be seated. Today the court will begin the trial entitled *People of the State of Arizona versus Turquoise Begay, a minor being tried as an adult*. A jury panel of sixty registered voters from around Coconino County has been summonsed and earlier sworn to give true answers to my questions. The clerk will please draw fourteen names at random and, as your name is called, will you please come up to the jury box and take a seat in the order your name was called. The last two called will serve as alternates to the jury of twelve."

Jury selection followed, the jury was sworn, and the rest of the panel was thanked for its service and dismissed.

The judge called upon the State to present its opening statement. Wrasslin shot to her feet and looked hatefully at Turquoise. Wrasslin looked much taller than her 5'2", thanks to the spike heels and West

Point posture. A slight shake of the head. *Stride in front of the defense table, this is my territory and I'm lifting my leg and marking it.* Eating up the common ground with her presence. She edged close by the jurors, feet planted wide apart, shoulders squared, and eyes full of fire. Her look said that she was thrilled to begin, committed to her case, and that it would be a trifling task for her to convict the defendant.

She came out swinging.

"Ladies and gentlemen, this is a *circumstantial* murder case. It is circumstantial because there is no eyewitness to the murder. It is circumstantial because there is no security video like you might have in a convenience store robbery. And it is circumstantial because the connection of the defendant to the crime is not based on eyewitness or video testimony."

She allowed that to soak in. She edged closer, making certain she was cutting off Thaddeus' view of the front row jurors.

"How is this woman connected to this case? It's very simple."

Leaning yet nearer, speaking confidentially.

"The connection is based on the T-shirt she was wearing. The connection is based on the gunshot residue left behind on that T-shirt after the defendant pulled the trigger and killed Randy Begay."

She looked each juror in the eye—not a long look, just a glance and a nod. Several nodded back, as people are inclined to do.

"And the connection is based on her opportunity to kill Randy Begay, her presence at the crime scene, and her premeditation in planning his execution and death. She"—swirling and pointing hatefully at Turquoise, as all accusers since Judas had been taught— "pulled the trigger on the rifle that killed Randy Begay. She then attempted to erase evidence of her guilt. How? By wiping down the gun. She then fled the scene when she was done with her killing. And always remember, nothing says 'guilty!' as strongly as fleeing a murder scene!"

"Objection. Argumentative."

"Sustained. Proceed."

Wrasslin pulled up the whiteboard and wrote out the names of the witnesses she would call, along with their topic:

Stall Worthy - FBI lead investigator

CSI staff - crime scene

Medical Examiner - cause of death

Navajo PD - arrest of defendant

IHS nurse - defendant's gonorrhea

Clay Lattimoren - firearms expert

Cindy Petring - crime lab scientist.

"A young man in his late twenties," she began, "found dead in the defendant's bedroom. He had been shot in the head by the defendant with the Winchester rifle she left in the corner beneath a shelf of Kachina dolls. Why was he there? Because he had raped the defendant. DNA evidence will prove this. Which is why she shot him: she was angry. Worse, she was in a *blind* rage, so she did the one thing our system of laws doesn't allow: she went after justice on her own."

A few jurors looked put off. The notion of rape sat well with none of them. So Wrasslin plunged ahead to build the logic for the prosecution.

"What should she have done instead of murder? Well, she didn't call the police and report the rape. She didn't tell her father about the rape. She didn't call IHS and ask for help. No, she took matters into her own hands and murdered her aggressor. Justifiable in human affairs? Maybe so. Justifiable in the eyes of the law? Never! With premeditation and malice in her heart she murdered. Killed. A homicide. And now you're here to do the only thing our society can do in such cases. Which is find her guilty of murder. That's your only job here this week."

She looked at each juror. She made eye contact and never moved.

A minute ticked by. Thaddeus stretched languidly and made a point of exhaling loud and long. He looked around the courtroom for the clock, let his eyes tarry there, and slowly looked back to the jury. Are you as bored as I am?

"And look at the defendant. The child of an alcoholic father and an absent mother. Beset by problems of poverty and sexual abuse. That's all true. But a straight A student in school with a desire to be a veterinarian. A boyfriend, a good kid named Tommy Begay. At one point the defendant told me that it wasn't the uncle who had given her gonorrhea, that it was Tommy. Maybe this whole claim of rape by the uncle is nothing more than her attempt to justify shooting him. You'll have to make that decision. But know this: she's told it two different ways now. At least two. Which means neither story is believable. Whatever else you believe about this case, know this: you cannot believe her. She is unbelievable. So, like I said, it's a case of circumstantial evidence. The circumstances will guide your vote and when you think about the gunshot residue on her shirt, her motive and premeditation, her fleeing the scene of the crime, I'm sure you will be able to return with one verdict and one verdict only."

The pause hung in the air, chattered across the imaginary screen as if a CNN feed.

"G-U-I-L-T-Y."

Wrasslin finally said, simply, "Thank you."

And returned to her seat.

Thaddeus fiddled with his yellow pad. She had done a superb job of defusing the weak spot in her case: the rape. The ongoing rapes, plural. The hell the victim had laid on Turquoise. She had managed to make it sound like there had been no rape at all, that it was because of her boyfriend she visited Indian Health Services to report her STD.

"Six horrible years," he told the jury as he approached them. "Six horrible years he had been raping her. The DA forgot to tell you that"—turning and smiling cynically at the DA, who returned the look with a glare. He let his words work their full measure, then, "Six years of hell. But you know what the evidence is actually going to show? That in spite of the hell and hatred in her heart, she never shot the uncle at all. It wasn't her. And the state can't prove it. What the evidence will show is that the uncle was a drug smuggler. A doper and pusher. The evidence will strongly suggest that it was someone from *that* world who took his life. Not the true victim in the case, the young girl Turquoise Begay. Stand up, please"—indicating his client. "Let them see how pretty, how demure, how incapable of shooting anyone you are by your youth alone. See how her diminutive size would have been no match for the uncle's sexual abuse? And the innocence: gone from her face. Eyes bloodshot from crying. The old woman's stooped, round shoulders, courtesy of the hundred pounds of guilt and self-hate her assailant had coiled around her body and made her wear." She heard all this and she dabbed with a tissue, the tissue she was to brush over her eyes whenever the prosecutor would start to speak. And it was the left hand responsible for this tic. Always with the left hand. The strong hand.

It was a production and his troupe was ready. Coached, primed, and pushed forward to do battle.

"And let me tell you something about the actors you are going to hear from. That's right, they're all actors."

He turned and stepped to the DA's table. He pointed at FBI Agent Worthy. "Exhibit A, this fine-looking, competent, believable FBI agent. You will hear from him, what he saw at the scene and what he learned from witnesses. But remember this: neither he nor the witnesses he's talked to know anything about Turquoise shooting her uncle. Did they bother to ask her whether she had been wearing that Lakers shirt when she was watching over the family's sheep and shot the rifle at predators?"

He paused, his hand still outstretched, his finger pointed at the red-faced Worthy, who looked as if he might be fighting the urge to leap up and jam the accusing fingers back until they snapped. He looked down at the desk instead, placed his fingers on the tablet keyboard, and began typing, oblivious to the accusation.

"Uh-huh," Thaddeus said. He nodded at the agent. "Well, we'll see if he looks you in the eye when I get to cross-examine him. Please remember when the DA asks her questions and Worthy performs as the professional witness he is. That he's a paid gun, a man paid by your tax dollars to come into court and try to put your neighbors in jail."

"Objection!" cried DA Russell. "Argumentative."

"Sustained. Move along."

"Other witnesses are also paid parrots. They're going to tell you this and that about blood spatters, distances, bullet trajectories, wounds, cause of death, and the rest of the rigmarole that goes into making you believe they actually know something about Turquoise. But here's a news flash: none of them were there. None of them saw her fire a bullet into the uncle. None of them. They're going to try to make it sound like they have the goods on her, but again, just like with the chief investigator, ask yourselves, what do they have on the girl herself? And that's all she is, in the end. A girl, trapped somewhere between youth and adulthood, caught up in this unbelievable hurricane of witnesses, charts, diagrams, medical reports, firearms reports, and the rest of the storm the state is sending her way. When you see what a ruse this is, then I'm sure you'll return with the only possible verdict. A verdict of not guilty. Thank you."

He took his seat. Turquoise dabbed her eyes. He quickly assessed: he liked what he'd had to say. His sense of the moment was that Wrasslin had hit a triple. Not a home run, a triple. She was almost there but couldn't quite connect Turquoise to the actual shooting. She had motive, she had opportunity, she had fleeing the scene, and she had physical evidence in the gunshot residue. But she didn't have a confession, or a video, or an eyewitness.

Thaddeus knew that much would depend on the jury's perception of Turquoise. They would want to know whether she was capable of causing someone else's death. There would need to be some prior bad act, some black mark that would convince them they had their killer.

He drew a deep breath and released slowly. He didn't think they had that, the prior bad act. There was nothing—at least nothing he was aware of—in her history that would equal a black mark. She was as pure as the fallen snow.

Or so he thought.

A fifteen-minute break ensued. The jurors filed out, headed for restrooms and the coffeepot in the jury room, and began establishing friendships among themselves—a newly formed tribe that would try to survive the Great American Trial together.

Fifteen minutes later, the court instructed the state to call its first witness.

"Let the testimony begin," H. Ivan directed the attorneys.

The first witness was Bobby Chee, the Navajo policeman who found Randy Begay dead in the girl's bed. Thaddeus had tried to interview Bobby, but the man would never make himself available and failed to show on two different occasions after Thaddeus had twice driven out to the Navajo PD substation to meet. His supervisor each time claimed emergency. Something had come up on Bobby's shift that had required him to be out in the field and he simply wasn't available. Thaddeus thought he could make some use of the missed appointments, but he also knew juries' sympathies would fall to the cop in most cases. Everyone knew their schedules were volatile and subject to change at any moment, without notice, no explanation required.

Wrasslin took Bobby Chee through that afternoon's events and spent probably more than an hour and a half reciting everything when thirty minutes would have served their case better. At the forty-five-minute mark, two jurors were beginning to lose interest and took to studying the courtroom, the architecture, the onlookers—anything to escape the tedium of the repeated, "What happened next?" questions. By the sixty-minute mark at least half the jury had taken up the same task of counting noses and studying pictures of ancient judges mounted on the walls. By ninety minutes they were all off somewhere else in la-la land.

It had been an early afternoon of chasing speeders along the stretch of highway he and his partner were patrolling. They were hoping to tag at least three drunk drivers—their quota for the second half of that shift. They were parked at a billboard advertising "Fireworks Ahead!" in such a way that their green Toyota 4Runner was hidden from view of oncoming traffic. The speed gun was hot and they were pulling over driver after driver along the deserted highway that stretched twenty empty miles in both directions. They had one drunk driver in the bag—literally, locked in the back seat—and were preparing to head for the substation and holding cell, when the call came in. A young girl name of Turquoise Begay had been raped and was walking west on Navajo 59. They hit the gumballs and headed west, running at ninety for the better part of ten minutes. Then they spotted her, walking west on the north side of the highway, head down, arms swinging violently at her sides as she forged ahead. They pulled in behind her and whooped the siren. She stopped and turned.

"You Turquoise?" Bobby Chee called as he exited.

He closed the distance between them.

"Your name Turquoise?"

"Yes."

"Someone called Navajo PD about you. Was there a rape?"

She looked away at the one-hundred-mile wasteland. Huddled in the distance were the sandstone stumps of Monument Valley. Then she nodded. "Uh-huh."

"Are you hurt?"

"Not the first time he did it."

220

"Who did it?"

"Randy Begay."

By this time Bobby Chee's partner, Jimmy Yellowmexican, had joined.

"I know him," said Jimmy. "The one from Kayenta?"

"Yes."

"Where is he now?"

"At the trailer."

"Does he have a weapon he used on you?"

"No."

"Are there any weapons at the trailer?"

"Coyote rifle."

"Is there ammunition?"

"Uh-huh."

"Did he point it at you?"

"Uh-uh."

"Come with us, please. We need to talk to him."

She slid into the 4Runner's front seat, so she was between the two cops. The hapless drunk driver lolled in the back seat, his face pointed at the ceiling, mouth open, snoring and snorting every few minutes. Harmless, in that he wasn't going to throw up in the back seat. Security Plexiglas separated him from the cops, sound being allowed through only by a series of pencil holes grouped in the shape and size of a coffee saucer. "Go back to sleep, Mikey," Jimmy shouted through the holes. "We have a stop to make."

Mikey obliged, closing his eyes and lapsing once again into his near-coma.

They raced east, arriving at the same trailer they had passed coming west not fifteen minutes earlier. Bobby Chee quietly ascended the three metal steps and soundlessly opened the metal door. He stuck his head inside. His right hand found his holster and unsnapped the retention snap. The Glock 17's grip curled into his hand and he pushed on inside.

Jimmy Yellowmexican waited with Turquoise at the foot of the steps.

Bobby returned momentarily and spoke to Jimmy. "Call it in. Homicide. We need FBI and CSI rolling."

Jimmy returned to the SUV and Turquoise could see his mouth moving, microphone up, as he made the call. She was alone at the bottom of the steps; Bobby had disappeared back inside.

She climbed the steps and peered into her living room, which now looked strangely remote and unwelcoming to her. There was the TV in which she escaped at night with the HBO that forever came and went, depending on whether the bill was current. There was the green love seat where Randy made her sit next to him while he rubbed her thigh and watched *True Blood* or Arizona Diamondbacks baseball. She hated baseball and had little use for vampires; still, it was enough to escape from her own personal hell, so she submitted and watched the channels he chose.

Bobby Chee said that he found Randy Begay with the right half of his head blown away by the high-energy .30-.30 deer round. Randy was stiff, his brains scattered on the wall and drained down onto the pillow beneath his head. His hand was inside the waistband of his blue jeans. His fly was open and both boots were neatly arranged beside him on the floor. There was a gun in the room, he said, which he was careful not to touch. He told Turquoise to stay out, but she wasn't trying to come into her bedroom anyway.

She told Bobby she had called her caseworker Angelina Steinmar, who had told her to leave the trailer when she reported her uncle's latest assault.

Wrasslin went over this point again, evidently caught off-guard by this detail.

"You're sure she said Angelina Steinmar told her to leave?"

"That's what she said," Bobby said, nodding his head as if there was no doubt.

Wrasslin struggled with a follow-up question for several seconds. It was clear that her argument the girl had "fled the scene," was in fact itself fleeing the scene. As it turned out, she hadn't fled the scene at all, not according to Bobby Chee. As it turned out, her caseworker, a State of Arizona employee, had told her to leave and walk west on Navajo 59.

Wrasslin backed out of the problematic discussion less than gracefully, abruptly asking the officer about the gun. Did he touch it? He did not. His police academy training had taught him never to touch a weapon at the scene of a crime when there was no threat.

How had she missed such a key fact as the girl being told to leave? Thaddeus decided that Wrasslin had had the same problem with Bobby Chee as he: she hadn't been able to interview him before trial and was merely working from his written police reports. The part about the caseworker was new, not included in the reports. Obviously Stall Worthy, in sandpapering witness testimony and statements, had missed the same piece of key information. But why wouldn't they? They were certain it was Turquoise who had done the killing; of course she would flee. It was an instance of an assumption coming back to bite them in the ass. Score one for the defense. And he hadn't had to lift a finger.

"Did you ask Turquoise who shot her uncle?"

"I did. I asked her if she did it."

"What did she say?"

"She said she didn't kill anything. She said she didn't kill coyotes or wild dogs. She said she wouldn't even kill a spider."

"Was she angry at her uncle?"

"She hated him. But she didn't kill him."

"You mean, that's what she said."

"Yes."

"No further questions."

Thaddeus decided it couldn't get any better, so he declined cross-examinations.

"Defense has no questions, Your Honor."

H. Ivan Trautman cocked an eyebrow at him, but Thaddeus stood firm. Cross-examination could only serve to weaken the officer's statements. Thaddeus had no intention of doing that as parts of it favored Turquoise.

"It's eleven thirty-five," said Trautman. "We'll break for lunch. Jury back and ready to go at one p.m. Remember the admonition: do not discuss the case among yourselves or with anyone else, do not read newspaper accounts or watch TV reports of the trial or participants, report anyone who attempts to discuss the case with you. We're in recess."

Thaddeus found Katy in the hallway. She said she'd been in and out; she was too nervous to sit still for very long. They went south on San Francisco Street, ate beans and sprouts and pita at a local health food restaurant (Thaddeus begged a turkey hot dog from the waitress), and drank two iced teas while they discussed strategy.

Then back to the courthouse, where things resumed.

FORTY-TWO

With the next witness, Thaddeus knew the roof was about to cave in on Turquoise. Special Agent Stall Worthy had been through the FBI academy in Virginia and was a professional witness, both by training and the experience of testifying in thousands of trials. His office was in Flagstaff, in the Bank of America building, where he worked with seven other agents under his command. He parceled out the assignments and kept the homicides for himself as first responder.

He testified he was on the scene within hours of the call coming in. A homicide might later get passed off to another agent, but that hadn't been done in this case, mainly because Randy Begay's father was a retired Navajo PD officer—which Thaddeus hadn't known. Turquoise's own grandfather was a policeman. So what in the hell, Thaddeus mused, had happened to this worthless son, Randy, that he had become a child rapist, child molester, drug pusher/user, and total all-around drain on society and loser? They didn't come much worse than Randy Begay.

Special Agent Stall Worthy was the canvas upon which all the other testimony for the prosecution would be painted. Wrasslin got the basics out of him. He got to the scene, took control, allowed CSI and M.E. access, oversaw the collection of evidence and handling of the weapon, and ran things from the beginning up until now.

No signs of struggle, no fingerprints on the body, hands had been bagged and came back negative for DNA under fingernails and negative for evidence of scratching, which, he intoned officiously, told him Randy Begay never saw it coming. His eyes were closed at death, which didn't indicate much, except it could have meant he was asleep. Why was his hand inside his blue jeans? Actually, the hand was not only inside his blue jeans, it was also inside his JC Penney underwear and firmly gripping his penis. At the mention of hand-on-penis there was a collective inhalation of air from the jury box. By now the crowd inside the courtroom had thinned to almost nothing and there was no commotion from that part of the room. If they only knew what they were missing, Thaddeus wryly mused. It was an unimportant case; a representative from the *Coconino Examiner* had been present for the early morning session but had departed when Bobby Chee finished up. No news is good news, thought Thaddeus. The less pressure there was on the jury to "do the right thing" and convict someone, the better his case.

But then things got ugly.

Wrasslin: "Did you speak to the defendant at the scene?"

Worthy: "I did."

"Did you ask about her relationship with her uncle, the decedent?"

"I did."

"Tell the jury what she said."

Looking over at jury. "She said she seldom saw her uncle. She didn't know him that well."

"Did you ask her about rape?"

"I asked her whether she was angry with her uncle."

"What did she say?"

"She said she hadn't thought much about it either way."

"Did you ask her about the gonorrhea?"

"Later I did. After I found out about it. At the jail, when you were present."

"What did she say about the STD?"

"She said her boyfriend gave her the STD. That he had to take medicine too."

"Did she say anything about having sex with her uncle?"

"She did. She denied having sex with her uncle."

"Ever?"

"Ever."

"She never had sex with her uncle."

"I specifically asked her, 'Did you ever have sex with your uncle?' She specifically said she'd never had sex with her uncle."

"That is all. Thank you."

Thaddeus rubbed his temples and slowly looked over at the agent.

"But you wouldn't have been surprised if she'd had sex with her uncle?"

"Objection. Speculation."

"It is speculative, but harmless. He may answer."

"I wouldn't have been surprised? I wouldn't have been surprised, no. But the fact is, she said she didn't have sex with her uncle."

"Object to the commentary, ask that it be stricken and the jury told to disregard."

Judge Trautman nodded, once. "The jury is instructed to disregard the comment that she didn't have sex with her uncle. That portion of the answer is nonresponsive and should be ignored."

Wrasslin jumped up. "But Judge, the jury doesn't have to ignore that he told me the same thing on direct examination, does it?"

"Objection," said Thaddeus coolly. "If the district attorney wishes to testify why I'll be glad to call her as a witness just as soon as I'm finished with Mr. Worthy."

"Agent Worthy," said the cop.

"Yes, Agent Worthy."

"Be seated, Miss Russell. The jury will disregard counsel's question to the court. You're cautioned, Counsel. No games in my court."

Wrasslin turned her attention to her notes, neither acknowledging nor responding to the judge's admonition. Whereas he might have commented on this snub had it been Thaddeus doing the snubbing, Trautman broke off and lowered his reading glasses off his forehead. He bent again to whatever had his interest.

"Counsel, cross-examination?"

"Thank you, Your Honor. Now Mr. Worthy, isn't it true the body was examined for fingerprints?"

"Yes."

"Were Turquoise Begay's fingerprints found on the body?"

"No. But neither—"

"That's fine, you answered. Now Mr. Worthy, isn't it true the rifle found in the room was tested and found to be the one that had killed Mr. Begay?"

"Yes."

"Tell the jury whether the fingerprints of Turquoise Begay were found on the rifle."

"No they were not. There were no fingerprints on the rifle at all. It had been wiped down."

"Mr. Worthy, when you add commentary in addition to the answer to my question, are you doing that to influence the jury against

Turquoise Begay?"

"Objection!"

"He may answer. He opened the door."

"I'm doing it because—because—I don't know. I just want the jury to hear the whole story, is all."

"So you're the one who gets to decide what the jury hears?"

"No."

"Then please. Just answer my questions without embellishing. Can you do that?"

"Yes."

"Now. The crime lab reported finding gunshot residue on my client's shirt, agree?"

"Yes."

"Can you tell the jury whether that gunshot residue was from the bullet that killed Randy Begay?"

"No."

"For all you know, she might have shot that gun that day while watching over the family's sheep, correct?"

"Correct."

"Or the day before or even the week before, correct?"

"Correct."

"Because you don't know the last time the shirt was washed, do you?"

"No."

"No, you don't?"

"No, I don't."

"Truth be told, you don't even know that the gunshot residue was from that rifle, do you?"

"No."

"Was there an attempt made to match the GSR on the shirt to the GSR left by the rifle in test firing?"

"No."

"Because it's impossible to do, correct?"

"Correct."

"It's impossible to match gunshot residue to any particular firearm, correct?"

"Generally, that's correct."

"There are exceptions such as rifles that fire only black powder, correct?"

"Correct."

"And some military grade weapons, correct?"

"Correct."

"Changing the subject just slightly. Isn't it true you know of no piece of evidence that places Turquoise Begay at the scene of the crime when the shot was fired, correct?"

"Correct."

"You have nothing to connect her to the crime itself, correct?"

"Not exactly."

"Well, you don't have fingerprints, correct? And the gunshot residue isn't determinative, correct?"

"Correct."

"And there's no DNA from Turquoise found on the rifle, correct?"

"Correct."

"So what piece of evidence do you have that connects my client to the killing?"

"Opportunity. She had the opportunity to kill."

"So did the FBI, but we've ruled out the FBI as the assailant, haven't we?"

The witness looked to the judge. "Judge—"

"Answer the question, Mr. Worthy," said the judge humorlessly.

"The FBI has been ruled out, that's correct."

"So you ruled out the FBI?"

"Correct."

"But you didn't make any effort to rule out Turquoise as the killer, correct?"

"Correct."

"Your only efforts were to rule her in as the killer, correct?"

"I guess you could say that."

"I'm asking you. Is it correct that your only efforts were to try to rule her in as the killer?"

"Correct."

Thaddeus sat down. He shuffled his notes and whispered to Turquoise. Then he stood up. "I think that's all, Your Honor."

"Very well, Mr. Worthy—"

Thaddeus popped back up. "Oh, there is one more thing, I'm sorry."

"Proceed."

"Mr. Worthy, you testified that my client told you that she wasn't being forced to have sex with her uncle, correct?"

"Correct."

"Who was present when she made that statement?"

"Myself and the district attorney."

"Would that be district attorney Wrasslin—Roslin Russell?"

"Yes."

"She heard that statement?"

"I suppose so, she was right there at the table with us."

"Nothing more. Thank you."

"You may step down," said the judge. "Ladies and gentlemen, we'll take our afternoon recess now."

Again he met with Katy in the hallway. This time they were joined by Turquoise. First the girl used the restroom and then had a long drink of water from the hall fountain. She walked back up to the foster parents and pressed against Katy, laying her head on her shoulder.

"Tired?" Katy asked.

"Uh-huh. And scared."

"I would be too," said Katy.

"How are we doing?" the girl asked Thaddeus.

He took a swallow of coffee he had commandeered from the jury room, thanks to the friendly bailiff. "We're doing great," he said. "But it's nothing compared to what's about to happen."

"What's about to happen?"

"Listen and learn, little one. Listen and learn."

Turquoise looked at Katy, who only shrugged and squeezed her shoulder.

Once back inside the courtroom, the jury was seated and the judge nodded at Thaddeus. "Were you finished with Mr. Worthy, Counsel?"

"Judge, I know this would be unusual, but Mr. Worthy mentioned DA Russell as being a witness to parts of his testimony. I would like to take Ms. Russell on voir dire before I finish with the Special Agent."

The judge looked at Wrasslin, who shot to her feet. "That's absurd, Your Honor! I can't be called as a witness!"

"Judge," said Thaddeus slowly, "she was a witness and her name has been used as a person who has knowledge of statements my client allegedly made. In the defendant's case we will be denying the truth and veracity of what Mr. Worthy is saying, and part of our approach will be to use the very words he has testified to. But we don't want to have to put the defendant on the stand to do that. So we'd like to call the district attorney for voir dire on the issue."

The judge leaned back, the frustration apparent in his tight lips and red face. He rubbed his hand up and down on the side of his face. He fiddled with the reading glasses, up-down, up-down, forehead to nose, and forehead to nose. He studied his desktop.

"Ms. Russell," he finally said, "I think I have to allow it."

"Judge, it's unethical for an attorney to be a witness in a case where she's also serving as counsel. If I have to testify it would be an ethics violation."

The judge looked at Thaddeus. The disgust in his voice and anger upon his face was unmistakable. "Mr. Murfee? What authority do you rely on here?"

"Well, Judge, the district attorney is absolutely correct. It would be unethical for her to testify. I'm relying on *Arizona Rules of Professional Conduct*, ER 3.7, where it's provided a lawyer shall not act as advocate at a trial in which the lawyer is likely to be a necessary witness. There are exceptions, minor and inapplicable here. It would be unethical for her to testify, true. But the defendant's right to cross-examine the witnesses against her far supersedes the lawyer's ethical obligations. Turquoise has the right to cross-examine Ms. Russell, who has been named as a witness by the chief investigator on the case, who, we have been told, is representing the State of Arizona. In his role as representative of the State of Arizona, he clearly has the authority to name the witnesses who he knows about. He has done that, using her name as an authority to back up what he's saying, and I'm just asking for the right to take her on voir dire and see what she knows about my client's statements."

"She probably has to testify, by law," the judge said begrudgingly. His eyes were coals and they burned into Thaddeus with all the rage and fury he was struggling to control in front of the jury. But his anger wasn't lost on anyone. Everyone in the court was affected, in spite of his efforts. He cowed everyone, and he knew it. That last thing he wanted to do as a judge and an elected official was to turn off a jury box full of voters. But his scorn overrode his desires.

"Judge, I refuse to testify," said Wrasslin. "It's unethical. Besides, I don't know where it would go, where it would end. I can't take that chance."

"Then the defendant moves for a mistrial."

The judge looked from Thaddeus to Wrasslin.

"Counsel?" he asked her.

"I won't testify. If it causes a mistrial, so be it."

The judge looked at the jury.

"Mr. Bailiff, please take the jury to the jury room."

The bailiff dutifully led the jury out of the courtroom. By now there were some whispered grumblings. They considered the case belonged to them at this point and wanted to be in on everything. Slightly hostile would be good, Thaddeus thought. Good, keep them guessing. Keep them antsy to finish up and go home.

Once the jury had abandoned the courtroom, Judge Trautman turned his attention to Thaddeus.

"Counsel, what is it, exactly, that you think you can get out of the district attorney that you can't get out of our FBI agent? Why the need? Convince me, Counsel, though I doubt you can. But I'm listening, Counsel. And let's all remember the presence of State Bar Trial Monitor Judge Kampbell, shall we? Any spurious motions or arguments at this time will be reported by him, I'm confident."

Thaddeus brushed the threat aside. "Judge, the district attorney was a witness to statements allegedly made by my client. Those statements bear a disproportionate probative value on whether my client had the mental state to shoot Randy Begay in self-defense or with premeditation. That's how broad the spectrum is. It's not only what my client purportedly said that's at issue, but also how she said it, her surroundings, whether she was frightened, her own mental state—all of these are areas that I have the right to question the DA concerning."

"You have the right if I say you have the right," Trautman retorted. It was clear from his tone that he had already had his mind made up against Turquoise. Thaddeus plowed ahead.

"No, Judge, the Bill of Rights gives my client, and thus me, the right to confront her accusers. Clearly the DA is one of her accusers because it's the DA who has brought these charges in the first place.

It's not you who gives me the right of examination of the witness; it's the Bill of Rights. The Bill of Rights says in all criminal prosecutions, the accused shall enjoy the right...to be confronted with the witnesses against him—or her. Which means—"

"Counsel, I know what it means. Believe it or not I studied Constitutional Law just like you. Please don't speak down to me."

Thaddeus spread his hands. "Judge, I wasn't speaking down to you, I was merely making the point—"

"I'll decide if you're speaking down to me, Counsel."

"No, Judge, you'll get my intentions from me and it was not my intention to speak down to you!"

"I am the judge. You're just a lawyer. I will decide intention in my courtroom. Judge Kampbell, this is the kind of arrogant insulting I called you about. Here we have an attorney telling the court I don't have the power to interpret and give meaning to his intentions. Clearly I do, Judge."

"That may be, but you won't decide *my* intention. I will."

The judge showed his teeth like a rabid dog. He huffed and puffed as if entering the game on fourth-and-one with thirty seconds left. He's pumped, baby, Thaddeus thought, he's moving now. Keep after him.

"You, sir, are just about to be cited for contempt. Your attitude toward the court is contemptuous. Judge Kampbell? Are you getting this?"

The retired judge's voice was thin and unconvincing. I—I—"

"Judge, I feel contempt for this court—your court. You've belittled me and threatened me through this entire prosecution and I'm sick of it!"

"Contempt? You feel contempt for me? Is the court reporter getting all this? Judge Kampbell?"

Again the retiree's voice came from behind Thaddeus: "Noted," he said. "To be reported back to the Office of Professional

Responsibility when we're done here today."

The court reporter stretched her hands and rubbed her fingers quickly. "I am."

"And I'm asking that the court remove itself from this case and let a fair judge take over. I've come in here and made a perfectly reasonable request to call a witness who has accused my client and the court is obstructing me. I'm prepared to file a judicial complaint for obstruction of justice, Judge Trautman! And I can probably find other lawyers you've bullied and belittled to sign it with me! How about that, Judge Kampbell? Are you making notes about this judge?"

Trautman roared, "You, sir, are one sentence away from spending the weekend in jail."

"And then where does your trial go? You're going to have a trial of my client without me present? Come on, Your Honor, let me call the witness or give me time to appeal your ruling so my client isn't prejudiced!"

"Counsel—Ms. District Attorney—" Spittle was forming at the corners of his mouth and beginning to work down his chin. His face was mottled red and pale white. His eyes were full of alarm, as if he expected to be accosted by armed gunmen at any moment. His court—his sense of decorum—had fled. He was in a rage and unable to fully express it, for fear of repercussions—Judge Kampbell cut both ways. So he shifted gears.

"Yes?" said the district attorney. She was pale, afraid to interject.

"How soon can you have an assistant DA over here to take over this case so you can testify?"

"I—I—"

"Fine. I'll give you until Monday. You can re-staff this case and then prepare yourself to give testimony."

Thaddeus wasn't finished. "Judge, I begin trial in *State versus Angelina Steinmar* in two weeks. I cannot be in trial here next week and be expected to begin that trial a week later. I'm only one lawyer."

"Then take that up with the other judge."

"That would be Judge Gerhardt, Your Honor. You know he's about to be appointed to the Court of Appeals as soon as his calendar clears. The Supreme Court might not like it if you delay their appointment for your own calendar."

The judge slumped back. All in all he had to admit Thaddeus was correct in his assessment. The last thing he wanted to do was give the supremes reason to hate him any more than their rulings on his cases already indicated. He sighed deep and long. He drew a breath and bounced upright.

"Very well. We'll continue for—Madam Clerk, when is my next clear week?"

Thaddeus held up a hand. "We'll need two weeks, Judge. I have witnesses, too."

"Then *two* weeks, Madam Clerk. Where does that put us?"

The clerk clicked her tongue and sadly shook her head. "Summer. That puts us into mid-June."

H. Ivan Trautman focused again on Thaddeus. He glowered down at him and sneered in full and complete disgust. "Happy, Counsel?"

"No. Relieved for my client's sake. But I take no joy in arguing with prejudice. None."

"Noted," cried Judge Kampbell from behind. "Insulting commentary!"

"Mr. Bailiff, bring the jury back in, please."

They returned and took their seats. Several gave hard looks at the judge and the court's machinations that were eating into yet another day of their lives. They were not happy with him and their looks said so.

"Ladies and gentlemen, sometimes cases can end abruptly when one of the attorneys asks for a mistrial. Mistrials are granted where the fairness of the case is somehow tainted by something that's come up during the trial. That's our situation here. But I plan to avoid a mistrial. We have too much time invested for a mistrial, plus I know you want to decide this case, now that we're underway. We have an evidentiary problem that can't be sorted out by ordinary means, so we're going to be forced to continue trial for an extended period. I'm sorry but at this time the court is continuing this matter for a time to be decided by the clerk and communicated in writing to the jurors at their respective addresses. Counsel, in my chambers, five minutes."

Thaddeus turned to Turquoise. "Trial is over. Ride home with Katy. I'll be along later and explain it all to you."

"Did we win?" she whispered back.

"Sort of," he said. "Anytime we can stop the trial against you, that's a win. It might only be a temporary win, but still a win. We'll talk more later."

He gave her hand a quick squeeze instead of shaking it as he normally would with a client. Turquoise joined Katy at the rear of the courtroom. "Later," Katy mouthed to Thaddeus, and the twosome left.

Five minutes later the DA and Thaddeus entered the judge's office.

"Sit, both of you," the judge said in a sour voice. "Needless to say I am very unhappy. With both of you. Counsel, how long have you been a prosecutor?"

"Nine years," said Wrasslin. Thaddeus noted her hand shook as she spoke, and he realized she was frightened. Which surprised him. The wrestler Wrasslin was actually scared!

"After nine years you still don't know enough not to make yourself a witness in your cases?"

"I don't know how to answer that."

The little jurist's eyes narrowed. "Well, try the truth. The truth always works well in here."

"I—it—suddenly there were questions and she was answering."

"Hold it. Why were you even there in the jail visiting this girl?"

"I—I—"

"Prosecutors know better than to have conversations with arrestees. For this exact reason!"

"I'm sorry, Judge." She hung her head sadly. She doodled on her yellow pad. Thaddeus looked over to see what she had written. There, in all caps, was one word: SHIT.

"Judge, will the state seek to proceed, knowing that the DA is now a witness?"

Wrasslin sniffed. "We certainly will. At the next opportunity."

Judge Trautman pushed himself up to where his mid-section touched his desk. He slammed his fist against his calendar. "Counsel, my calendar is made up three months in advance. It will be at least three months before we're available."

He flung himself back and sat smoldering, eyes burning at DA Russell then shifting to Thaddeus. Back and forth they played, like a cat readying itself to pounce. Except there was no pounce left. He had made his threats and landed his blows and even succeeded in disbarring Thaddeus for a full year, but that was all past now. The young lawyer had taken him on and turned aside his best forward charge. It was at an end. Even Judge Kampbell was silent, pursuing imaginary lint on his sleeve. He was probably being paid for this nonsense, Thaddeus realized. Paid to keep tabs on me.

Which prompted Thaddeus to ask, "Judge, as appointed counsel, will I be paid for a full trial day today?"

"Out, both of you," the judge hissed. "Before I say or do something I regret."

The two attorneys clambered out of the office.

"Sorry," Thaddeus whispered to Wrasslin once they were in the hallway and heading back into the courtroom.

"Screw off, Thaddeus," she said.

"Well," he said mildly, "you just lost my vote come election time."

FORTY-THREE

That evening, he drove slowly home and studied the pine shadows in the early twilight, how they lay eastward in great, black silhouettes that reminded him of spirits in a jury box. Try as he might, he just couldn't shake the trial, the difficulties with Trautman, and whether he was going to set Turquoise free. He shook his head and punched the volume button on the stereo. REO Speedwagon came on the 'Eighties station and he abruptly turned it back off. He turned down the gravel road toward his house and slowed way down so as not to kick up dust. The neighbors appreciated as much, as did Katy.

He remembered that he had Angelina Steinmar's trial starting soon, decided he would start noodling it later tonight after everyone was in bed, then thought better of it. He would let it pass for the night, and just try to spend time with Katy, Turquoise, and Sarai.

He smiled when he thought of them and turned off at his own driveway. Coconino and Charlie were munching hay and swatting flies with their long tails. Neither bothered to look his way and, truth be told, the feeling was mutual. Ignorance is bliss, in the truest sense of "ignore." He stepped up on the huge deck that led to the front entrance and turned one last time to observe the San Francisco Peaks two miles north. He admired how steady, how grand they were, never changing but never seeking to avoid the changes nature planted on their face. He decided he would try to be more like them, steady and patient with external change.

He entered the mudroom and kicked out of his shoes. His fleecy moccasins felt good on his feet and told him he was safely home. He opened the front door and found Turquoise and Sarai watching a video. *Ice Age.* He knew the voices by heart. Who wouldn't, after the ten millionth play?

"Hey, girls," he said on his way to the kitchen.

Something smelled good and was especially welcome after the long, hard day.

Katy was cutting up onions for salad, a wooden match held between her teeth—to stop the tears, she claimed. He had tried it once before and thought it belonged in someone else's magic show, as it hadn't worked for him.

He came up behind and encircled her with his arms.

"Hey," he said in her ear.

"Hey, back," she said. She stood immobile and allowed him to embrace her. When he nibbled her ear she removed the matchstick and turned her face to kiss him. It was a long, warm kiss, lips slightly parted, a hearty welcome home.

"What's cooking? Smells fantastic."

"I made a pot roast. Just like you and Sarai like, onions, potatoes, and carrots. Plus my special gravy."

"I could eat a horse."

"How about cow instead?"

He shot a quick glance back at the door. They were still alone.

"How about you, instead?" he said.

"Maybe later."

It was said with a smile and girlish dip at the counter.

"You're a total chick."

"Glad you think so."

"You make me glad to be home."

She turned to the sink and washed onion from her hands. "You know what? You make me glad to be here. I was so proud of you today for how you stood up for Turquoise. To be honest, I didn't know you had that kind of fight in you. My bad."

"Hey, I can depend on my inner guy when the chips are down. He can come out pretty damn tough."

They were gathered together at the family room dining table, Turquoise telling Katy about her weaving hobby and Sarai mesmerized in her new "big sister," as she now referred to Turquoise.

Turquoise used her hands to talk.

"First you prepare the loom. Use the fine-spun yarn for the verticals. It has to be tightly wound so be careful on the wheel."

"Wheel?" Katy asked.

"Spinning wheel. Make a tight yarn but make it fine."

"Okay. Then what?"

"Then you thread the wefts horizontally."

"They go over and under the warp?"

"Exactly. Your weft isn't as tightly spun. It's looser. I think of it as the fluffy yarn. But it isn't really fluffy. Just fluffier."

"Got it. So what if we get a loom?"

"I'll make you a loom. Just some two-by-fours and one-by-fours.

242

Plus a batten and comb. It's pretty simple. The secret ingredient for weaving is patience. One rug takes months."

"Well, it's not like we're setting the world on fire around here with projects. Let's hit the lumberyard tomorrow and pick up some things. We'll make two looms and we can sit and weave."

"And talk."

"Yakkety-yak. Two Navajo girls with lots of catching up to do."

"I'm loving it," said Turquoise. "For a long time I've been wanting to make a rug."

"Why didn't you?"

Turquoise shot a look at Sarai and rolled her eyes that direction. "You can guess?"

Katy nodded. "Got it."

"You couldn't do *any*thing around there."

Thaddeus explained the day's events with H. Ivan the Terrible. He described the back-and-forth, the in-fighting, and the final takedown by getting the continuance. He had some new ideas about the case, he said, in case anyone was paying attention. There were no takers, so he kept the new ideas to himself.

Katy and Turquoise got lost in a conversation about relatives they might have in common on the reservation and Thaddeus had a two-way with Sarai. What letter did you learn on *Sesame Street* today? Dad, I'm five. I'm too old for that stuff. That's right, I forgot. Your bad, Dad.

After the news they went up to bed. Turquoise told them all good night and had tears in her eyes when Katy gave her a hug and said, "Welcome to the family, Biscuit."

"I'm so glad you let me stay here," the girl said. "It's been so long since I could just sleep."

"I understand what you're saying."

"He was horrible."

"Well, that's over now. Thad and I will protect you. Won't we, honey?"

"We've got it under control," Thaddeus reassured her. "I will get you out of your mess downtown and Katy will help you with everything else."

"Can Tommy come this weekend? Just for the day?"

"Sure."

"Sure."

"Oh, thank you!"

They said their goodnights and everyone disappeared for the night.

Undressing, Katy asked, "So, you had a big fight with H. Ivan?"

"Knockdown drag-out. He's such an asshole."

"From what I hear, he seems to be. He's like a demigod in court."

"Oh, make no mistake. He owns that room, not the taxpayers. It's his personal property."

"I got that distinct impression."

She turned her back to him. "Unsnap, please."

He released the bra strap. She didn't move.

He circled his hands around to her breasts and slowly played across her flesh. She came erect and he was immediately turned on. He pulled her backwards down on to his lap. He lay back and pulled her with him. His hands slid down her belly and found her labia. He toyed with her, kissing her neck, whispering in her ears, telling her how much he loved her. Then they separated while she turned over and she immediately mounted him. She rode him and they moaned softly, aware that they had an adult visitor who they didn't want to disturb with their lovemaking.

Later they cuddled and he told her how much he had missed her and how sorry he was that he'd made a mess of their lives.

She said she was sorry for her lack of patience with him and that she was mortified she had gone with other men while he was away. "Don't tell me any more than that, please," he said, and she relented.

Details weren't necessary. It was enough just to refer to the dark nights and alcohol mists and how they'd lost each other during that regrettable part of their marriage.

They renewed their vows. He promised he would never touch another woman and she returned the vow, never another man. They kissed and Katy turned her back to him and scrunched her buttocks into his mid-section. He felt himself grow tumescent and she found him with her hand. She spread herself to him and that's how they finally slept, coupled then slowly drifting apart as they tumbled through their dreams.

When he awoke it was pre-dawn and he kissed her. "Sleep," he said.

He went downstairs to his office and flipped on his computer.

Time to think about Angelina Steinmar and the amazing dead mouth of her husband, the snapping corpse.

He chased the lame attempt at humor from his mind and went into the kitchen and ran a K-cup through the coffee maker.

With a long sigh, he took up the mouse at his computer and began tracking down evidence and law.

He was back.

Fully. Back.

FORTY-FOUR

Thaddeus and Christine and Angelina rehearsed her story a dozen times in the weeks before trial.

What exactly happened?

Answer: I shot him.

Were you shooting to kill him?

Answer: I don't know. I just wanted him to stop hurting me and he wouldn't.

Why did you have the gun?

Answer: He chased me from upstairs. I went for the gun to frighten him.

So why did you shoot him with it? What changed?

Answer: I brandished the gun. That didn't even slow him. He just kept coming.

What made you finally pull the trigger? Tell us what happened at that second.

Answer: He was trying to sexually assault me. He was biting me between the legs. It was excruciating pain. I begged him to stop and he wouldn't stop.

So you pulled the trigger?

Answer: Without even thinking, I pulled the trigger.

So it was more of a reflex than a planned act?

Answer: I was hurting and suddenly it was excruciating. So I pulled the trigger out of pain.

Then what happened?

Answer: He stopped biting. The pain stopped. His head jerked and he fell face down on the carpet.

What did you do?

Answer: I remember he was partially on top of me. I scooted backwards on my rear end to get disentangled from him.

Did he moan or make any sound?

Answer: Of course not. He was shot in the head.

So there was no indication he needed an ambulance?

Answer: I immediately knew I had killed him. He stopped biting and never moved again.

So you went up and took a shower?

Answer: I was afraid of infection from his mouth so my instinct was to clean off his saliva. I don't know why. I had heard something, I guess, about the mouth and germs.

So what did you do next?

Answer: I started to use a washcloth, but that wasn't enough. So I turned on the shower and got in. I know I was in shock at this time because I really don't remember the shower or cleaning up at all.

Now, your daughter had been assaulted as well?

Answer: She committed suicide after he assaulted her.

How do you know that was why she committed suicide?

Answer: She left a note blaming him. Turns out he had been

assaulting her for some time. So she killed herself.

How did she kill herself?

Answer: She hung herself from her closet door. Left a note.

Did the death result in criminal charges?

Answer: They appointed a special prosecutor at my request. The grand jury said it didn't clearly implicate John.

If Mr. Moroney says you shot your husband because he had sexually assaulted your daughter, what would you say?"

Answer: He was a bad man. A very bad man. I was going to divorce him, that was my plan. My plan didn't involve shooting him, not at all.

Thaddeus took his measure of her testimony. It had to come across as a spur-of-the-moment act. There couldn't be even a hint of premeditation. And so far, so good. He had to admit, Shep had tutored the witness to where it sounded like self-defense. He was hurting her, she was fearful of great bodily harm or even death, so she reacted. Self-defense and then some.

The threesome continued talking about what happened and why. They returned to her house. She showed them into the family room where the shooting occurred. She reenacted the struggle, the reach for the gun, the relative distances when the shot was fired that killed her husband.

"Don't come across as defensive when you testify," they cautioned her.

"I won't. I played Blanche DuBois in *Streetcar*, remember?"

Christine looked at Thaddeus. He shrugged. "It's a play. She was in a play."

"So she's an actress?"

"What do you think?"

The meeting broke up and Thaddeus and Christine drove back to the office. They stopped along the way and bought burgers and fries to eat at the office. It was Friday and the trial began Monday with jury selection.

◇◇◇

Thaddeus met with Assistant Attorney General Jimmy Moroney in his new digs in the Bank of America building. The office was sprawled across one end of the floor two up from Thaddeus' office. Thaddeus was impressed with the setup. Receptionist, staff coming and going, a sense of great business and focus in the quiet but busy place.

The AG turned over the report from the Coconino County Medical Examiner. The doctor's name was Dr. Neal Gordonet, the CME.

The report began with some preliminary background commentary:

In criminal investigations, properly scaled photographs are indispensable in the evaluation and interpretation of bite mark impressions. The location, relative position, appearance, physical size, and depth can be illustrated using correct photographic protocols. Along with photographic preservation, the collection of properly collected blood, saliva samples, and impressions of any three-dimensional aspects of the injury may also produce additional evidence, which can result in the successful resolution of an investigation. This evidence should be collected as soon as possible.

"Which Shep Aberdeen had done at the hospital," Thaddeus said.

The AG laughed. "Problem was, she'd already showered and cleaned up. So there was no saliva, no DNA."

"But the bite marks leave no doubt according to this report. It was definitely John Steinmar's teeth that left the bite marks on her genitals and breast."

"No doubt of that, it's true."

"So what does this tell you? It tells me we've got a simple case of self-defense. The case should really be dismissed, in all fairness."

The AG spun the report on his desk. He looked out the window at the Peaks. Thaddeus knew there was little chance of any dismissal. Too political, too much public outcry, too much opportunity for a misstep at trial that just might result in a conviction.

"It's definitely not a slam-dunk for you," Thaddeus commented.

"It's not. But neither is it for you. Your client could pay the maximum price for the shooting."

"Only if you can prove premeditation and malice and lack of self-defense."

Moroney twisted in his chair. "Wrong. You have to prove the presence of self-defense. I don't have to prove the absence of self-defense. It's an affirmative defense in Arizona courts. The burden of proof is on you."

"Well, for the record, that's my defense. I think the jury will laugh this case right out of court."

"I think it was an execution of a bad man for the sexual assault of his daughter. I think the jury will see right through your self-defense claim."

"Well then how do you explain the bite marks? That was just a minor thing? Are you kidding me? He damn near chewed her labia off with that one bite. It's very clear in the photographs."

"Could be, but maybe not. Maybe the bite marks came after he was already dead. Have you thought of that?"

Thaddeus felt a cold chill race down his spine. Yes, he'd thought of that. In fact, he knew from his conversation with Shep that that was exactly what had happened. She had used his mouth to cause the bite marks after he was dead. Which brought Thaddeus back to the extremely uncomfortable role of an attorney who is about to knowingly introduce perjured testimony into the trial. He could not only lose his license if he got caught, he could also be prosecuted and sent to prison.

He forced a laugh at the prosecutor's suggestion.

"Please. Get real, Jimmy. Bit herself? Be serious, man!"

"I have proof that might be the case."

Again, the cold chill.

"What proof might that be?"

"We'll get into that at trial."

"Now hold on. Is there evidence you're not turning over to me?"

The AG's delicate hands riffled the several pages of the M.E. report. "Let's just say the evidence is in plain view but you aren't seeing it. Or you're not admitting you're seeing it. Either way, it doesn't matter to me. Welcome to the big leagues, Mr. Murfee. We've got your client dead-to-rights."

"Is there a rebuttal witness you're not telling me about?"

"Warm and getting warmer. I'm not required by law to reveal rebuttal witnesses and I'm not going to. You're stuck with that. All I can say is, you would be wise to proceed very carefully at trial. Your girl is not all that innocent as she wants everyone to believe."

Thaddeus was suddenly frightened and confused. Was the AG just bluffing, hoping for a last-minute plea? It didn't feel that way; so far, no plea offers had been made. Which was itself unusual. And he didn't feel like suggesting a plea, because he thought that a sign of weakness. He would just have to let it play out. And pray. Lots of prayer was called for.

And he wasn't a praying man.

He forced another laugh and shook it off.

"Right," he said. "You've got an eyewitness to the whole thing. Nice try."

The AG pursed his lips. "Let me just say this. This biting thing isn't the first time this has happened. You should ask your girl about this. There's a definite history there."

"What?"

The diminutive man shrugged. "That's as far as I'm willing to go. Now we'll see just how good your investigative techniques are. Good luck, Mr. Murfee. You're definitely going to need it."

Less than an hour later, Thaddeus had his client in his office, ready to grill her.

"So I met with the AG and he says the biting thing has happened before. Would you care to enlighten me?"

Angelina smiled and Thaddeus had the awful sense she had just slipped into her Blanche role. "It was awful, the biting thing, as you put it. It happened before when Hammy was in the fourth grade and we were visiting Disneyland. At the Disneyland hotel."

"Tell me exactly what happened. Christine is going to record this."

Christine flicked on the recorder. "Rolling."

"Nothing much to it. Hammy was asleep in her own room in the hotel suite. John came on too strong and bit me. It bled and I went to the ER. I was scared and told them what happened."

"So there's a record of all this."

"Yes."

Thaddeus slammed his hand flat on the desk. "Damn, woman! Why didn't you mention this before?"

She actually managed to look both surprised and off-put, attacked. "You didn't ask me!"

"You're sure it was John who did this? What kind of records were left?"

"I don't remember. A nurse and a doctor talked to me. Tetanus shot. Maybe a picture."

Thaddeus sat bolt upright. "Pictures? Of the bite marks?"

"Maybe. It's been so long I don't remember clearly."

"Oh my God. This is Friday; jury selection begins Monday. I don't have time to get the records."

"Unless we get them faxed," Christine said. "I'll get right on it. Why don't you come into my office, Mrs. Steinmar? I'll get the particulars and get right on it."

"Thanks," said Thaddeus. He waved the client off dismissively, a flick of the hand as if she were a bothersome fly flitting about. *Swatting gnats*, he thought. A bad, very bad, feeling came over him. He crossed to the floor-to-ceiling window and gazed out at the San Francisco Peaks. He wished he were anywhere but here. Two hours ago he was chomping at the bit to take the case to trial. Two hours later and he was frightened to death. It had happened before, criminal clients withholding important information. He had thought that with Angelina she was too knowledgeable, too sophisticated in the ways of the judicial process to withhold information from her attorney, but evidently not. He felt the floor shift under his feet and reached out and touched the window. For a moment he had felt like he was falling. But nothing had actually moved. Only the reality in his mind. Like a seam opening along a fault line, the truth had surfaced.

No one was more surprised at what had been revealed than Thaddeus himself.

No one.

He thumped the glass and went back to his desk. He buzzed Christine.

"Anything?"

"She's signing a medical release and I'm going to fax it over. Give me about an hour."

"Done."

FORTY-FIVE

On Monday morning, Court TV had erected a tent and commentary platform on the sidewalk outside the courthouse. CNN's TV crew was set up in the crowded hallway outside Judge Gerhardt's courtroom, along with KTVK out of Phoenix and KTLA out of Los Angeles. Halogen TV lights flooded the stark corridor, contributing a heavenly glow to the otherwise dim surroundings. Everyone who was anyone was there, including writers from *Salon, New York Magazine, The Atlantic,* and *Phoenix Magazine*. Outside the courtroom, TV personalities were confronting anyone dressed in a suit or propped up on high heels. Even sheriff's deputies were boldly confronted and asked whether they would be giving testimony.

Thaddeus arrived with Angelina at his side, Christine Sussman bringing up the rear. He was wearing a three-piece navy suit with blue button-down shirt and regimental-stripe tie. Angelina looked stunning in an expensive gray suit from Scottsdale's Fashion Square, mid-height heels, and a silver belt buckle that matched the silver pin on her left chest. Her hair had grown out and was arranged in a bun with the front pulled across her forehead and sprayed in place. She still wore her wedding ring and on her right middle finger a turquoise stone inset in highly polished sterling silver—another treasure scored in Scottsdale, and definitely not on the reservation. Christine wore a navy pantsuit and white shirt, with a red crossover tie. Her thick shoulders bulged as she moved her arms and her erect bearing bore testament to her tours of duty in the Army.

A mike was shoved in front of Thaddeus' face and CNN asked about the theory of defense. Mikes from KTLA and KTVK swung in front of his face when he paused to answer. Thaddeus smiled and said simply, "Our theory is that defendant, Mrs. Steinmar, is not guilty. Excuse me, but I'm sure the Attorney General will be much more cooperative as he tries to influence the jury panel."

Judge William Gerhardt had a rule reserving the front row of spectator seats for the press. He also allowed one camera, jury view of the courtroom, which included counsel table and judge's bench and witness stand, and he allowed one artist, no still photographs inside the courtroom doors. If one was caught filming or recording with a smartphone, it would be confiscated and destroyed.

They entered the courtroom and Angelina turned to him. "That's all you could come up with, that I'm not guilty? How about telling them that I'm innocent? What happened to innocent?"

Her voice was slightly elevated, which irritated Thaddeus and he leaned to her ear and whispered, "Not here, not now. We're going to do this my way or you're looking for another lawyer. Leave it alone!" She gave him an angry look then suddenly turned and smiled in the direction of the press. Actress, indeed, he reminded himself. It wouldn't be the last time the thought passed through his mind, either.

Thaddeus found all press seats taken and noisy conversations underway, drowning out all else in the courtroom. The courtroom TV crew was running a test picture of the Great Seal of the State of Arizona, directly behind and above the judge's heavy chair. With obvious suspicion, the bailiff was eyeing everyone coming in, while armed deputies were massed off to one side, exchanging notes about fishing for trout.

Making their way down front, Angelina again smiled at the reporters, whose conversation buckled when they spied her.

Several asked for a comment but she turned and looked up front as they made their way through the bar and on up to counsel table.

Thaddeus and Christine unloaded three CPA cases containing iPads, books, yellow pads, exhibit labels, Magic Markers, and a variety of pens, some colored, mostly black. He arranged the items on his table just as he liked, and about that time Jimmy Moroney from the AG's office swept in with two assistants and silently followed suit. Also accompanying the AG was the chief investigator on the case, Art Handelman. Art had an MS in Forensic Science and was known far and wide as the best investigator with the district attorney's office. He was actually a member of the sheriff's department but his permanent assignment was Chief, District Attorney Investigations. He was a thin man, medium height, with a brush of silvery gray hair that he had worn in a flattop since 1972 when he was two years old. He had a way of sonorously putting suspects to sleep when they were brought in for questioning and leading them through recorded statements. He would then pounce suddenly and destroy their innocence with short, staccato questions. More often than not his style resulted in admissions of guilt or incriminating statements from which they would never recover. Art was a pro and he was dressed in dark gray slacks, blue blazer, and white shirt with thin blue stripes. He was slowly munching on a stick of Juicy Fruit, as was his custom, and keeping his eyes to himself. Thaddeus knew he was a force to be reckoned with and the plan was to give him wide berth because he was known to sink many a defense from the witness stand.

At 8:55 a.m. all was in readiness and an anticipatory calm began settling over the crowd. It was only minutes now until the judge would arrive in his pomp and circumstance and they would be off and running. Billed as "The Trial of the Decade," things were ready to move.

At precisely 9 a.m., Judge Gerhardt entered in his flowing black robe and smiled at the crowd. His customary blue jeans and penny loafers could be seen protruding from the bottom of the robe, to the astute observer. "Morning," he mouthed before taking his seat. Silence fell over the room.

The bailiff called the court to order and Judge Gerhardt greeted everyone and asked the clerk to draw sixty names for the jury panel. Once that chore was completed, the judge set about asking the general questions intended to elicit problems and complaints and issues that might quickly disqualify a respondent from jury service. As a result, a half-dozen were sent packing and an hour later the clerk was told to draw fourteen names from the panel and seat the chosen in the jury box, twelve jurors and two alternates.

"This is a capital murder case," he told the jury panel, "meaning the defendant faces the execution chamber if convicted and sentenced to death. Is there anyone on the panel who, because of that fact and that fact alone cannot serve?"

Everyone traded looks but, surprisingly, no hands went up.

"Good enough," the judge said, and he continued with his questions.

Angelina leaned to Thaddeus. "Tell me I'm not being executed. Please."

He gave her a wry smile and shook his head. "Not a chance," he whispered. "You'll be heading home when the case is over."

Angelina helped the defense team make their picks. "That man in the coveralls. I think John prosecuted him for felony drunk driving. The name rings a bell. Get rid of him." Thaddeus responded that that might cut two ways, that the juror might be friendly to the woman who shot the man who prosecuted him. "I can tell by the way he glares at me," she said, her voice rising. "Get rid of him. Please! And please don't argue with me. It's all about instincts anyway and mine are highly sensitive."

Thaddeus shrugged and drew a line through the man's name. Off to the side he wrote "Defense. Peremptory."

The physician's assistant could stay as she was in general practice and knew the value of medical records such as Angelina's case would be presenting. Again Thaddeus differed with his client to the extent of explaining that the prosecution had medical records too, and maybe the PA would give too much credence to such exhibits. Angelina shook her head violently and insisted the woman stay. Thaddeus circled her name and then, fifteen minutes later, crossed her name out when the prosecutor dismissed her anyway.

Back and forth it seesawed, each side fighting to keep the jurors they wanted and dispose of the jurors they feared. Angelina was the defendant and so she was entitled to the final say-so over who stayed and who went. After the first twenty minutes, Thaddeus no longer argued with her. She was very strong-willed and some of the jurors already had given him a quizzical look when Angelina's demeanor became overly animated when arguing a juror's merits. So he backed off and gave her her head.

By Tuesday morning a jury was seated and sworn, and the judge took a break, following which opening statements would begin.

Fifteen minutes later Judge Gerhardt told Jimmy Moroney to please proceed with the state's opening statement. Thaddeus felt his heart skip. It was time; blood would be drawn, and the throw-down was underway at last.

Jimmy Moroney looked like he had aged five years over the past few months. He was forty, maybe forty-two max, thin, wire spectacles, creeping bald spot, and a reputation for spotless prosecutions. After a stint with the Department of Justice in Washington as an organized crime prosecutor, he had returned to his hometown of Phoenix and hired on with the Attorney General. He pushed back in his chair and made his way to the podium. There was no wasted motion, no wasted breath, as he launched into the state's version of the shooting.

He went over what the defendant had originally told the police about the shooting. He urged the jurors to listen for variations in her testimony from what he was telling them from the police reports. He explained those variations would be from midcourse corrections made in her story by her attorneys.

Next up, bite marks.

He launched into a discussion of forensic photography. He told the jury that bite marks are found many times in sexual assaults and can be matched back to the individual who did the biting. He laid some groundwork. The bite marks should be photographed using an ABFO No. 2 Scale with normal lighting conditions, side lighting, UV light, and alternate light sources. Color as well as black and white shots should be used. The more photographs under a variety of conditions, the better. Older bite marks, which are no longer visible on the skin, may sometimes be visualized and photographed using UV light and alternate light sources. If the bite mark has left an impression then maybe a cast can be made of it. Casts and photographs of the suspect's teeth and maybe the victim's teeth marks will be needed for comparison. One of the state's key witnesses would be a forensic odontologist, who would make sense of all this.

Then he stunned Thaddeus. "During our investigation we learned the defendant had accused John Steinmar of biting her at least once before. This was in Anaheim, California, some ten years earlier. She had gone to the ER complaining assault and biting by her husband.

Unfortunately for her, the ER was staffed by a fine young physician named Walter Joneth, who had called in a police photographer to take the kind of photos I talked about. Over thirty photos were taken. We have obtained those photos from ten years ago and we have compared them to John Steinmar's bite from the autopsy. Guess what? She had been bitten ten years ago, all right. But the bite marks weren't from John Steinmar. She was lying then. We believe the evidence will show she is lying now, as well. That will be for you to decide."

He looked over the jury then continued. Pens were flying over notepad pages. He had them in his palm, one and all.

"When you are done I have no doubt you will convict Mrs. Steinmar of first-degree murder. Her execution will follow, as it should, because her crime was coldly plotted, dramatized, and acted out by the great actress she is. We will tell you all about her dramatic skills, as well, so please don't be swayed by her histrionics. She is a cold, calculating woman who murdered her husband in cold blood and then made up a huge story, complete with forensics, to prove it. Don't believe her lies. I will prove all this to you far, far beyond a reasonable doubt. Thank you."

Judge Gerhardt immediately turned to Thaddeus. "Counsel, your turn."

Shaken from head to toe, Thaddeus slowly took to his feet. He hoped all the color hadn't drained from his face, but he wouldn't have been surprised if it had. His hand shook as he unfurled the yellow pad before him at the podium. He jammed the hand in his pocket and prayed no one had noticed.

"Ladies and gentlemen," he weakly began, and went on to describe how the defense had no burden of proof, how it was all on the state to prove guilt beyond a reasonable doubt. He made sure they understood that the defendant didn't even have to testify if she chose to remain silent.

He described the defense exhibits—consisting primarily of the photographs Shep had had made at the hospital. But even as he was talking he wasn't sure those photographs would end up freeing his client or convicting her, or what. He became angry the further he went. Angry that she hadn't told him about the incident in California. Angry that the AG had obtained the ten-year-old photographs and was now going to use them to convict her of lying ten years later. For if the state did that, nothing she could say would help her. Especially—heaven forbid—if they came through on their promise and somehow proved the current bite marks weren't from her husband. If that were the case he would have an execution to attend. By the time he sat down his head was spinning and he knew he had been faltering, disjointed, and sounded totally unconvinced himself of the lines he had delivered by reflex.

"Thank you, Counsel," Judge Gerhardt said. "Is the state ready to proceed?"

Jimmy Moroney nodded. "Ready, Your Honor."

First witness up was Dr. Kewae N. Horne, Medical Examiner. His pathological diagnosis was of gunshot wound, entrance top of head, indeterminate range. He explained the autopsy, what they were looking for, how it proceeded and what they did, and their findings and pathologic diagnoses. There was a perforation of the inferior skull base, anterior fossa, and facial skeleton. Wound was right to left and downward. Cause of death was gunshot wound, and manner was homicide. Death was immediate; there was an exit hole on the right lower jaw, portions of right jaw severely fractured and early decomposition to body. The testimony was harmless enough in that it didn't tend to implicate Angelina by its measure, so Thaddeus left him alone on cross-examination. He posited a few questions and merely went back over the approximate time of death and confirmed that the doctor had no opinion of gunshot distances and angles. All in all the witness was believable and didn't point any fingers at Angelina.

Thaddeus concluded by asking the M.E. whether he had an opinion whether John Steinmar was moving when shot.

"My opinion, he was immobile."

Thaddeus was surprised. The M.E.'s report had mentioned nothing about movement.

"You don't have evidence that he was immobile, correct?"

"Correct, no evidence. Only my interpretation."

"And your interpretation could be right or wrong, correct?"

"Correct. It's only opinion."

"Based on your experience in these cases."

"Based on my experience."

"Let's talk odds. Do you gamble when you go to Las Vegas, Doctor?"

"I might play the nickel slots for an hour. I find it boring."

"Do you ever play blackjack?"

"Maybe once a year I fill in at the physicians' Friday night game."

"Do you know the odds of drawing to an inside straight?"

"No."

"Well, let's do it this way. If I asked you on a scale of one to ten how confident you are that John Steinmar was immobile when shot, what number would you pick?"

"Eight. Maybe nine."

"So there would perhaps be two chances out of ten that you could be wrong?"

"Yes."

"And would you be wrong twenty percent of the time? In other words, what factors have a bearing on that?"

"Well, in this case I reviewed a carpet sample. No tread marks."

"That would be the carpet removed from the Steinmar residence?"

"Yes."

"And based on that carpet sample you believe your opinion that Mr. Steinmar was not moving when he was shot would be wrong two times out of ten?"

"That would be my rationale. My interpretation is probably right, however."

"Probably meaning more likely than not?"

"Yes."

"More likely than not is fifty-one percent, correct?"

"Objection," said the AG, rising slowly to his feet. "Argumentative and relevance."

"Counsel, where are you going with this?"

"Your Honor, I'm trying to understand how certain the witness is about his testimony."

"And the relevance of that?"

Thaddeus realized the judge was giving him the opportunity to make a mini closing argument.

"Judge, the relevance is that if Mr. Steinmar was moving, he was an aggressor. The doctor says there's a twenty percent chance he was moving, which would mean there's a twenty percent chance he was advancing on Mrs. Steinmar to continue his attack. Now the doctor has said the odds he was not moving is 'probably,' which, I believe, is much less than eighty percent. It could be as low as fifty-one percent or more likely than not. I'm just trying to get a percentage we can rely on."

"Objection to counsel's argument and move that it be stricken!" cried Jimmy Moroney. "That's argument, Judge, and inappropriate!"

"Well, I suppose it might be, but the court needs to understand where the questions and answers are going in order to rule on your objection or argument and relevance. Having said that, the court denies your objection. Counsel, you may proceed with your questions."

Jimmy Moroney slowly took his seat. His neck was red and all could see he was highly displeased. Frown lines furrowed his forehead and he was squinting as if taking aim. Thaddeus was pleased. First blood.

"So, Doctor"—he came back to his line of questions—"you were about to tell the jury that Mr. Steinmar was probably not moving when shot and I was asking you what percentage 'probably' is. Can you answer that?"

The doctor picked at lint on his sleeve. He drank from the witness's water glass.

"'Probably' is just that. Probably."

"Can you give us a number?"

"Sixty-five percent."

"So now you're saying your opinion of not moving is correct two times out of three?"

"Right."

"Which means your opinion is incorrect one times out of three?"

The doctor sighed. He was committed to numbers, something an expert witness never meant to do under these circumstances. "Correct."

"Now, Doctor, is being correct two times out of three equal to 'beyond a reasonable doubt'?"

"Objection!"

"Sustained."

"Thank you, Judge. I have nothing further."

Jimmy Moroney took over on redirect and tried to rehabilitate his witness, but the more he asked, the more confused and tired the doctor became. He was a man of about seventy years of age, had been to the wars for forty years or more, and in the end began coming across as detached and unsure of earlier opinions that had been given with much certitude.

The AG finally backed off and sat down.

Everyone was left wondering how the carpet sample figured in.

Its evidentiary value had never been made clear, at least not by this witness. The air in the courtroom was still. The jury had long ago set notepads aside and ceased scribbling. It had all been said and done. Thaddeus could read their faces. Maybe the district attorney had been the aggressor when he was shot, "probably" not. The witness couldn't clarify that for them, but not for lack of trying. Thaddeus had done what he set out to do: confusion reigned.

Next up was a firearms expert from the state crime lab. He had examined the decedent's skin and scalp in an effort to determine distances when the fatal shot was delivered. His opinion was that the muzzle to scalp distance was in the neighborhood of around five feet.

"But maybe closer?" Thaddeus asked on cross-examination.

"Unlikely. I would say a good five feet from gun to head."

"From muzzle to scalp."

"Correct."

"And you base this on test firing the pistol, as you described on direct examination?"

"That's correct."

"Now Mr. Adamson, what does the gunshot distance tell you about this case?"

"That the victim and the defendant were a good distance apart."

"And you told us that your opinion is based on the fact there are no powder burns or stippling on the district attorney's skin, which would place the gun muzzle farther away, correct?

"More or less, yes."

"Does that indicate to you that the shot was fired other than in self-defense?"

The witness smiled. He was a black man wearing thick glasses that kept slipping down on his nose. His head was shaved and he had been very confident on direct examination. Thaddeus knew he would be extremely experienced in the ways of court and would be all but impossible to shake in his opinions. So, he was going to get in and get out. Get what he could and leave.

"That indicates to me the shot wasn't fired in self-defense, since you ask."

Thaddeus stepped back a step from the podium, as if the answer had injured his case. It was all an act, however.

"Now, when you say self-defense, you're using a legal term, correct?"

"Correct. But I'm also talking about what was likely going on at the moment the shot was fired."

"You were there and saw what was going on?"

"Please. I wasn't there, no."

"Yet you can tell this jury what was going on when the shot was fired?"

"I can tell you that the two actors were apart far enough that the shooter wasn't in imminent fear of great bodily harm or death."

"You're not saying that John Steinmar wasn't coming for her, are you?"

"Well—"

"Let me make that easier. You have no idea what John Steinmar was doing when he was shot, do you?"

"Actually, no."

"He might have been pointing a gun at my client for all you know, correct?"

"Correct."

"And he might have been screaming that he was going to kill her, correct?"

"I wouldn't have any way of knowing."

"But he might have been screaming, correct?"

The man removed his eyeglasses and began polishing with his pocket square.

"He might have been screaming, yes."

"And he might have just finished biting her on the genitals, correct?"

"Yes."

"And he might have been coming back for more, correct?"

The little man put his eyeglasses back on. He nodded. "All I was trying to say was that he wasn't touching her at the moment he was shot. They were farther apart than that."

"But you're not saying he couldn't have closed that distance in one second and been on top of her, are you?"

"No, I'm not."

"And really, what you're telling us is merely based on the lack of gunshot residue on John's head?"

"And shirt. No burns or stippling there either."

"Head and shirt. No powder marks."

"Correct."

"Other than that, you really don't know much else about what happened that morning, do you?"

"No."

Thaddeus decided to take one more run at the guy, just to make an upcoming point.

"In fact, the best evidence about what happened that morning would be the testimony of Mrs. Steinmar herself, correct?"

"Objection!"

"Sustained. Anything else, Mr. Murfee?"

"No. We're finished here."

Chief Investigator Art Handelman was next called. He rolled back from counsel table, stood up, touched Thaddeus on the shoulder as he passed by, and climbed up on the witness stand. He pulled a white handkerchief from his breast pocket and made a washing motion of it with both hands. The jury watched this routine and a couple of them shrugged. *Unusual, but we're still open to what he has to say*, their looks said.

Jimmy Moroney asked all the right questions, the Who, What,

Why, When, and Where of being second on the scene following the shooting. First to arrive had been Dean Drake, a uniform from the Flagstaff PD. He entered the house, made sure there were no live shooters still on the premises, had the new widow sit at the kitchen table so as not to walk through the crime scene, and went back to his squad car for yellow police tape. The dispatcher had notified Art Handelman of the shooting at the same time and he made a beeline for John Steinmar's house. It was less than three miles from where Art lived and Art was just beginning his day. A second prowl car had arrived on the scene a minute before Art. Art parked across the front drive to keep gawkers off the property, and sauntered up to the front door and went inside. There was no hurry at this point, he testified, John Steinmar was dead, shot in the head, and no amount of hurry was going to change that.

Art went into the family room where the shooting had occurred. He found the district attorney lying facedown in a pool of his own blood. Actually not a pool, he then corrected himself, as the floor covering was carpet and the blood had soaked into the carpet and was spreading below on the rubber padding substrate. He went to the body, felt the carotid for a pulse (there was none) and went to join Mrs. Steinmar. Her hands were shaking and she asked if he minded if she smoked. He said it was her house and immediately she was trying to light a cigarette. They knew each other very well. He nodded at her, patted her hand, removed the Bic from her tight grasp, and held the flame up to her cigarette. She puffed, inhaled, and slapped the table with her free hand. "Damn him!" she cried. "Damn him!"

He told her he would need to record initial impressions. He Mirandized her, just to be sure, right on the recorder. First words out of his mouth, "Do you understand you have the right to remain silent..." and her responses to the standardized questions followed. He then played the recording for the jury. It was clear from her statements that John Steinmar was the aggressor and she his intended victim. It was unclear exactly what he had been trying to accomplish that morning, other than, as she put it on the recording, he, "...was trying to maul me."

Question: "He was trying to maul you. Describe that, please, Mrs. Steinmar."

Answer: "Jamming his hand between my legs and digitally penetrating me. Ravishing me with his mouth even to the point of biting me. I have bite marks between my legs and on my breast."

Comment: "We'll have the police department crime scene tech take pictures of those when we take you to the hospital."

Response: "I don't need to go to the hospital. I'm not sick, just scared."

Comment: "Still, we need to have you examined. A rape kit and photographs of your injuries will only help you on down the road."

The recording ended, the machine was put away, and AG Jimmy Moroney stood at the podium and flipped through yellow page after yellow page, ostensibly in search of some script or note to himself.

The jury stretched and yawned during this.

Thaddeus saw that Jimmy was passing a few minutes just to let it soak in, the recording, so notes could be made and interior monologues processed. The tape was inordinately helpful to the prosecution, of course, as all suspect statements almost always are. In the end it was clear that Art Handelman had left his prints all over the case in the way he had formulated his questions and obtained answers she would regret from the woman who had just shot and killed his boss, District Attorney John Steinmar. It was also clear that he wanted her. She wasn't going to just walk away from what she had done. Justice cried out for payback and reform.

Then Jimmy Moroney launched into a new page of questions.

"Please describe her demeanor as she answered your questions."

"You mean describe her emotional state?"

"Yes."

269

"Well, she was pretty well pulled together. After the first cigarette the shakes went away. We went into the kitchen, where she made us each a cup of coffee, and we talked like it was a Christmas Eve get together like we'd both attended at her house over the past several years."

"You had been her guest?"

"My wife and I had attended her Christmas Eve open house."

"Who else attended these open houses? Anyone in this courtroom today?"

"Judge Gerhardt."

Whereupon the judge nodded and continued with his own notes.

"Anyone else?"

Art looked around the room. "Not right off-hand."

"So you knew Mrs. Steinmar pretty well."

"That's hard to quantify except this way: I had been in her presence maybe thirty-forty times before that morning."

"So, a lot."

"If you say so."

"Did you have an agenda that morning, as the Chief Investigator of the Coconino County District Attorney's Office?"

"To learn what happened and preserve evidence. That was all I was there to do."

"Tell us what you learned about how the shooting occurred."

"Do you mean in addition to what she said on the tape?"

"Yes, your investigation."

"It was a .38 caliber Detective Special that killed Mr. Steinmar. A single shot to the top of his head. When the crime lab examined the carpet sample I learned that there were no hair and fiber transfers from the carpet to the body or clothing of the victim."

"The 'victim' meaning John Steinmar."

"Yes."

"Tell us what that means, no hair and fiber transfer."

"Objection, argumentative."

Judge Gerhardt: "He can tell us what hair and fiber transfer, or lack of, means generally. Just not in this case, that would be conclusory and he hasn't yet been qualified as an expert from whom I'm going to allow conclusory testimony. Mr. Handelman, just tell the jury generally what hair and fiber transfer means."

"Means he wasn't scooting across the carpet on his belly or up on his knees."

"Indicating what, to you?"

Art leaned forward, closer to the jury. "Indicating that he wasn't in pursuit."

Thaddeus' head snapped up. He hadn't been expecting that. It was an opinion reserved for the domain of an expert witness and Art Handelman hadn't been qualified as an expert witness—not in that arena, at least. They had snuck one by him. He almost objected but restrained himself. A bell once rung cannot be un-rung. The words had been said: no pursuit. And couldn't be unsaid. Damn, he thought, get into the game.

The AG didn't hesitate. "So if John wasn't in pursuit of his wife when the trigger was pulled, she wasn't in threat of great bodily harm or death?"

"Well—"

"Objection. Invades the province of the jury."

"Sustained. Mr. Moroney, he can answer questions about the physical scene and what he personally saw and observed throughout his investigation, but let's leave the interpretation of those facts to the jury. Move along, please."

"Withdrawn."

"Objection sustained before the question was withdrawn. Proceed, please."

"One thing I forgot to ask."

Here it comes, thought Thaddeus. The *coup d'état*. A mercy

killing.

"On the recording you just played, Mrs. Steinmar says Mr. Steinmar bit her that morning. Did you in fact obtain photographs of any bite marks on or about her person?"

"We did. The CSI photographer went with her to the hospital when the EMTs took her. He took lots of pictures."

"Have those pictures been analyzed?"

"They have."

"Are there bite marks in those pictures?"

"So I've been told."

"Objection, hearsay."

"Not quite, Counsel. Hearsay probably comes next."

AG Moroney continued, unflappable. "Are those bite marks made by the mouth of John Steinmar?"

"Objection! Can only be based on hearsay as he has no expertise to make that judgment."

"Sustained."

"Did you ever learn whether those were the district attorney's bite marks?"

"I did."

"What did you learn?"

Thaddeus was again on his feet. "Objection! Hearsay!"

"Let him continue," said the judge. "Mr. Handelman, first tell us how you came to that understanding."

"From the odontology report."

"This was a report commissioned by the DA's office?" asked Jimmy Moroney.

"It was. We asked the odontologist for a comparison between the photographs from Mrs. Steinmar's body and the bite mark evidence taken at the autopsy of Mr. Steinmar."

"And was a written report rendered?"

"Yes."

"Your Honor," said Jimmy Moroney, "I would like to submit through this witness that odontology report as an exception to the hearsay rule as it is a business record."

The judge eyed Thaddeus. "Defense?"

"Hearsay," said Thaddeus, although he was sure it wasn't. Business records or records of public bodies made in the ordinary course of business could come in, immune from the hearsay objection. He sat back down and waited, knowing the cat was just about out of the bag.

"Overruled. Please read the question back."

Court reporter: "No question pending."

Judge: "Mr. Attorney General?"

"Were the bites found on Mrs. Steinmar's body put there by the teeth of John Steinmar?"

"They were not. Someone else bit her."

Pandemonium erupted and several reporters beelined up the aisle for the doors. The judge decided it was a good time for a recess and took a fifteen-minute timeout.

The AG and his minions headed for the restrooms and coffee pot. They could barely suppress laughter, and grins were on all their faces. The pin was inserted through the thorax; the butterfly was affixed to the mounting board. Let the squirming begin.

Thaddeus turned on Angelina. Under his breath he whispered, "What the fuck, Angelina? What the fuck?"

She winced and glared at him. "Do we have an expert witness about this?"

His stomach fell. He had been set up. Negligence of counsel in not obtaining necessary expert testimony. He could already see the bar complaint and the appellate review of the trial.

He looked her straight in the eye. "No, we don't. You told me your husband bit you. I would have no reason to suspect otherwise. No reason to want an expert witness of my own."

She toyed with the silver bracelet on her wrist. The turquoise stone looked at him as one eye fixing him in a hard glare. Yet she avoided eye contact with him. "Maybe you should have gotten us an expert just in case."

"Maybe there's still time," Christine said. "I'll go work the phones, you want." She waited for Thaddeus to respond.

He thought for a moment. Then the answer came that he needed.

"I think I want to hear what their odontologist has to say first, before I make a record with another expert that just might go against us. One against us is enough. Two would be unacceptable and gross negligence; especially if I had paid one of them and it turned out he wasn't on our side. That would be not so pretty."

"We need to talk," said Angelina.

"Christine, please go find yourself some coffee."

"You want a cup?" she asked Thaddeus. Her question did not include their client.

"Sure. Thanks."

Christine went off in search of two cups and coffee, leaving Thaddeus alone with Angelina.

"All right. Now's a good time to tell me."

"The bites are from Bill, not John."

"Bill, not John? What the fuck are you telling me, Mrs. Steinmar?"

"Bill Gerhardt bit me."

Incredulous, Thaddeus' chin flopped down. "What? What?"

"That's right. He's my lover. He got carried away the night before. John saw the marks and it enraged him. I thought he was going to kill me. He *was* going to kill me. So I shot him."

"What? What?"

"Would you stop saying that? I'm trying to tell you the truth here."

"Are you telling me the judge bit you?"

274

"Yes."

"The judge up there, our judge?"

"Yes."

"The judge who just walked out of here."

"We're in love. And we're a little kinky. We both like it that way."

"You've go to be—"

"Grow up, Thaddeus. We're adults."

"Don't tell me! I suppose he bit you in California too?"

"Our families vacation together. He found me in the steam room."

"Ten years ago? This romance has been going on ten years?"

"Stop it, please. Pull yourself together before you lose my case!"

For a moment Thaddeus had a mental picture of him wheeling Shep Aberdeen out of the hospital in a wheelchair and making him come to court to defend his client. Shep had made it all up. Thaddeus should have known better. He trusted her. Evidently Shep did as well. They had both been wrong. She had lied to both of them and now she was caught.

So what had happened that morning when she fired off the shot? Had it just been an execution? Did she deserve the needle in her arm? He found himself shivering. He emptied his mind and forced it to stop racing. He made a conscious effort to slow his thumping heart. Get control, he demanded. Stop this shaking and quaking and get about the business of defending your client.

He decided the one thing that could save Angelina Steinmar at this point was Angelina Steinmar herself. She would have to convince the jury that her life had been threatened. Could she? Highly doubtful. They'd never believe a word she said. Face it; she was all but worm food.

He decided he would waive cross-examination of Art Handelman, subject to recall as an adverse witness during the defense case if needed. Instead, he would go for the odontologist. See what weak areas he could discover in the expert dental testimony. That was it, yes. The idea quickened inside him. Maybe this was an opening he could work. No need to surrender. Not yet. There would be weak points in the expert testimony about bite marks and he would go after the weaknesses. There were always weaknesses. It was his job to find them and make them into a headline. The odontologist had to be destroyed. Or else they might as well put her in handcuffs and haul her ass back to jail and inject her, forget any appeal.

Christine returned with coffee. Angelina traipsed off to "the ladies" room," as she put it.

"She lied to us," Christine whispered when Angelina was gone.

"No doubt," he muttered.

"So what do we do?"

"Go after the dental testimony."

Christine thought this over. "Flanking action."

"Exactly."

"Okay. Let's do it."

Five minutes later Judge Gerhardt called the court back into session. The state was finished with Art Handelman's testimony. Thaddeus surprised everyone by waiving cross but reserving recall of the witness in the defense case. So much for a directed verdict.

The state then called CSI techs that talked about the scene, preservation of the scene, measurements. Photographs and drawings were marked and admitted into evidence so the jury could take them into the jury room when that time came. By then it was 4:40 and the judge called a recess for the day.

FORTY-SIX

By the next morning, Thaddeus felt less sure of his case than ever. It had been a sleepless night, tossing and turning, and Katy had finally gone downstairs to the couch where she could sleep in peace. She offered to make him a snack in the middle of the night, but he declined. It was all he could do not to climb out of bed and go into the office at 3:30 a.m. and begin going over trial testimony, but he fought down the compulsion and made it until 5:30 a.m. before wearily calling it a night and heading for the shower.

Trial began promptly at nine o'clock.

"The state calls Dr. Zachariah Nebuling," Jimmy Moroney announced in response to the judge's nod to proceed.

The courtroom doors flapped as the next witness came striding up the aisle. Thaddeus had tried to take the man's statement but he had refused. Common enough in criminal cases were that pre-trial witness interviews were not mandated. Of all things.

Dr. Nebuling was a big-boned, ham-handed man who, one might judge, should never have his boxcar hands inside anyone's mouth. Which might explain why he had detoured past the ordinary practice of dentistry and become a forensic dental examiner. His neck was noosed inside an ill-fitting navy shirt, white tie, and blue suit that looked like it had been bought off the rack without alterations. It was tight around his shoulders and upper arms, where he was massive. His face was friendly enough and his tone was jocular, as he gave his name and educational credentials. His small mouth and rather bulbous nose were just homely enough as to make him look all innocent and trustworthy, the kind of face that would never seek to take unfair advantage. Which probably explained his success at trials around the country, Thaddeus guessed, where his fame was great among trial lawyers.

He testified that the American Association of Forensic Science certified him. To obtain that board certification he'd had to work twenty-five cases, accumulate three hundred fifty qualification points by attending meetings and other professional development programs, and pass a qualifying exam. This was all pretty basic stuff, he explained, as he had now worked over 2,500 cases, including the important airline crash cases of the past twenty years where bodies could only be identified by dental records. Enamel, he said, is the hardest substance in the human body. Enamel always survives, no matter the cause of death.

"Please call me Zach," he was telling Jimmy Moroney. "While I'm a doctor by education and practice, I am just plain Zach to everyone."

"All right, Zach. Please tell us what odontology is."

Zach unfolded his arms and dropped his hands to the desk. "Typically the forensic odontologist attends the autopsy, takes photographs, cranial measurements, dental impressions, and X-rays from the remains. These exemplars are then compared to those of known bite marks in a case like this. If a match can be made, conclusions can be drawn. If a match can't be made, other conclusions might be drawn."

"What did you do in this case?"

"Pretty much what I just described."

"You were at the autopsy?"

"I was. I took pictures, made measurements, took dental impressions."

"Who asked you to do those things?"

"You did."

"Fine, thank you. And I believe you called the work product—the pictures and impressions—I believe you called those exemplars?"

"Yes."

"What did you do with those exemplars, Zach?"

"I compared them to the photographs taken of Mrs. Steinmar's bite marks."

"Which bite marks? The California bite marks or the Flagstaff bite marks?"

"Both. You asked me to compare both."

"What conclusions did you draw from making these comparisons?"

"The bite marks were made by the same person."

"Were they made by John Steinmar?"

"The bite marks were not made by John Steinmar."

A gasp could be heard in the courtroom, coming from the spectators, press row, and even some quick inhalations from the jurors themselves.

"What's the basis of that opinion?"

The doctor leaned back against his chair, ready to recite. "John Steinmar suffered from a dental problem. It is a common disorder called hypocalcination. This is when there are pits and craters in the teeth. Because of those pits and craters, a very definite dental impression is expected. We found those pits and craters to be present in the impressions we made of John Steinmar's bite. However, and this is the key, the pits and craters were just not present in any of the two sets of Angelina Steinmar's bite mark pictures."

"Are you telling this jury John Steinmar did not bite his wife?"

All was still, the air steady, as the answer was formulated. Among the jurors, pens were poised to take down word-for-word what was about to come.

"I am saying the pictures taken of Mrs. Steinmar's body are not pictures of bite marks that would have been made by John Steinmar."

"So he didn't bite her?"

"Not in the photographs."

"Who did bite her?"

"Well, this is where it gets strange. The same person bit her in both cases."

"Ten years apart?"

"Ten years apart, yes."

"What could that mean?"

"Objection."

"Sustained."

Again Jimmy Moroney stepped back from the podium and reached to his papers. He carefully flipped through page after page while he allowed the jury time to make its notes. Thaddeus noted the room was absolutely quiet except for the sound of jurors' pens scribbling in jurors' spiral stenographer books.

At that exact moment he realized the case was lost. There was no way they could come back from this testimony. He cringed at the thought of trying to cross-examine this expert. The jury liked him, he was a good guy; he preferred his given name Zach to "Doctor." What wasn't to like? Plus, the testimony was simple and easy to follow. The jurors would take to the jury room the casts of John Steinmar's teeth with the pits and craters and they would compare them to the forensic photographs of the bite marks and the lack of any indication of pits and craters. In a word, he was done. They might as well stand up and collect their books and papers and head back to the office. It was over.

Then it was his turn to cross-examine, as Moroney said he was done with direct.

"Doctor," Thaddeus began, "is that the extent of the examination you did?"

"Except for one other item, yes."

The answer hung in the air. Everyone was waiting for him to ask the indicated follow-up, so he did.

"What one other item would that be?"

"John Steinmar ate toast with his meal the night before. I obtained a bite mark from those crusts."

"Really? What did that tell you?"

"Pits and craters. It was clearly his toast."

At that point, many jurors laid down their pens. The evidence from this witness was in and they were done. It didn't matter what Thaddeus drew out at this point, their minds were made up.

"Thank you, Doctor," said Thaddeus. "That is all."

He sat down and Angelina immediately pressed her mouth to his ear. "That's all? No searing cross-examination? What the fuck, Thaddeus!"

He turned and glowered at her. It was unprofessional, the jury saw him do it, but he just couldn't stop himself. She was done and he was done too.

A firearms expert testified about gunshot residue—or the lack of any—and the gun used in the killing. He confirmed some earlier testimony about distances, angles, and forensic probabilities.

Next came a crime lab tech that testified about blood tests and drugs found in blood, both of the decedent and the defendant. John Steinmar had suffered depression and was taking two antidepressants and he was also taking a statin for cholesterol management—both prescribed by his doctor. Angelina Steinmar was found to be chemical-free, no drugs and no alcohol when tested at the hospital.

The final witness was also crime lab, and she talked about fingerprints, DNA results (there were none), and the fact there was no evidence of a third person in the room at the time of the shooting—no prints, no hair or fiber, no shoe prints in the carpet, nothing. The testimony and cross-examination ate up the rest of the afternoon. The state ran out of witnesses then, as it was a simple case with simple forensics and very few evidentiary battles.

The prosecution rested its case and the judge sent everyone home for the day. He made the usual admonition to the jury—don't watch news accounts, don't read newspaper or magazine accounts, discuss the case with no one, and don't consider the case until you enter the jury room after jury verdicts. It was all there.

But Thaddeus knew better. He knew that nothing would stop them from thinking about what they had heard there that day and nothing would stop them from drawing conclusions. She had lied about being bitten by her husband and that colored anything else she might have to say in her defense. It was over.

Thaddeus and Christine picked their way through light traffic back across Aspen to the BOA building. While she went upstairs to shut things down, he passed through the building and out the other side to the parking lot. He drove home in a desultory fashion, taking an unusual route just so he had time to think about what had happened that day. In the end, he could come up with nothing. For once he had no idea how to defend the woman. Then he stopped. Maybe Shep could help. He pulled in at a Citgo station and made a U-turn: Back to Shep's hospital room.

Shep was just finishing a hamburger patty and applesauce when Thaddeus came into his room. Shep wiped a glaze of applesauce from his chin and profusely welcomed the young lawyer.

"Shit—shit," he said, meaning "Sit-sit," but the stroke had left his speech impaired.

Thaddeus recounted the day's events.

Shep listened intently. His right arm and hand shook loosely against the cotton bedspread. Thaddeus figured the palsy would accompany Shep for a long time and he was sorry he'd had to bother the guy. Still, the client was originally Shep's and he felt like maybe there was something he had missed. He recounted the entire trial, all key witnesses and pieces of testimony.

"So what do you think?" Thaddeus said when he was done. "What do I do?"

Shep pursed his lips—as it were, given the right side of his face was nonresponsive—and studied the air between them. Reason waited there, in that air, waiting to be defined and pronounced. But only a great legal mind like Shep's would grasp it—that was the premise between the two men. Thaddeus was counting on it.

Finally Shep drew a deep breath and said, "Like shum appleshauce?"

"What?"

"Hungry?"

"Shep—I—I was hoping—"

The old lawyer raised a palsied hand and allowed it to shake between them. "I'm jush not all there, I guesh. I'm shorry."

"Shit," Thaddeus muttered, and immediately regretted it. "I know," he said. "I understand."

"Shounds guilty, to me. Maybe plead her?"

Thaddeus beat the steering wheel of the F250 truck on the way home. "Shit!" he cried. "How could you fall for her story and not get your own workup done? How!"

FORTY-SEVEN

She arrived at the office the next morning at exactly seven o'clock, as he had demanded. She was wearing a navy suit with white piping, a small string of pearls, the turquoise bracelet, and wedding ring. A pair of glasses had appeared on her face. Her hair was up and held in place by two silver combs, each studded in turquoise stones the size of a pencil eraser. She looked studious, almost matronly, and he felt a ray of hope, for she at least looked the part of someone who was leading a normal life in a normal neighborhood in a normal job in a normal family with—wait, the normal family part? A daughter dead by her own hand and a husband now dead by her hand? Angelina was anything but normal. Her entire family was deceased and she was left behind to explain? He sighed. Might as well get on with it.

They rehearsed her testimony, starting the night before and

coming up to the time of death. They moved hour by hour in an effort to cover all the bases. She described the shooting, the struggle, the sexual assault and digital penetration, the struggle on the carpet, her momentary freedom and her hand finding the gun and pulling the trigger. There was enough doubt raised by the story that it amounted to a reasonable doubt—Thaddeus was pretty comfortable with that. But then there was the biting tale. How to deal with that? How to deal with the fact she had lied to the police about the biting and injuries recorded at the hospital?

"Who bit you?" he asked when they came to the wall.

"Bill. I thought I told you that."

"Bill Gerhardt, our judge?"

"One and the same." She took a bite of Starbucks sausage muffin and chewed thoughtfully. "We like it kinky, I told you that too."

"When did this biting occur?"

"The night before. John stayed over in Cameron on business. Bill came by and we thrashed each other and had our climaxes and broke up around ten."

"What did you do?"

"Drank a half bottle of California claret and went to bed. I remember the room spinning."

"What did you do?"

"Old sorority girl trick. I put one foot out of bed on the floor. Helps stop the spinning."

"Great," he said, weighing how this would sound to the jury. He would try to avoid these little details.

"Next morning John comes in and catches me half passed out. He pulls up my nightie and sees the marks. He goes ape-shit, chases me downstairs. I think he's going to kill me. So I shoot him."

"Give me more details."

"Oh, he tackled me in the family room, digital penetration, tried to mount me against my will, all of that stuff is true."

"Where does the gun come in?"

"I managed to buck him to the side, but he's strong and grabs my ankle when I try to stand and run. He pulls me back down; I kick free and get to the drawer with the gun. All I meant to do was scare him. I just wanted him to leave me alone. I had decided I wanted a divorce and I was going to tell him anyway. But first I had to make him listen to me."

"So what happened?"

"I had the gun and I held it up to show him. He lunged at me and I guess I shot him. Really I don't remember all that much. I know I was in shock because I replaced the gun and went upstairs and cleaned myself up. I knew there would be tests and pictures at the hospital and I didn't want Bill's DNA found on me."

"Why did you tell Art Handelman that John bit you?"

She sighed. "That was the easy part. He wasn't believing me when I told him what happened. So I embellished. I added the bite part."

"That simple?"

"Yeppers. Just threw it in to sweeten the pot. You were a gambler once, weren't you?"

Thaddeus, in spite of himself, smiled. "I once owned a casino. But I didn't gamble."

"Well, the pot needed sweetening when Handelman looked me in the eye. So I sweetened it. I tossed in the bit about John coming after me with his teeth. That was pure white lie."

"Not so white. That denigrates the whopper you told."

"Whatever."

"Yes, whatever."

FORTY-EIGHT

Two hours later she was on the witness stand and repeated almost word-for-word what she had told Thaddeus at the office. She left out the Bill Gerhardt part, of course. The jury was sitting back in their seats, arms crossed, no note-taking. None that Thaddeus could see, and he was watching them. Closely. Evidently their minds were made up and they weren't going to believe much if any of what she said at this point.

Thaddeus plowed ahead. After all, there was one critical piece of testimony that the jury couldn't ignore. Couldn't, because it had been laid down by the state's own witnesses.

"Now Angelina," Thaddeus began, taking up the new tack. "When the fatal shot was fired, where was your husband?"

"On the carpet on his knees."

"Describe his actions."

"He was about to stand up, coming upright, and coming after me."

"Did you hear the state's expert witnesses and firearms expert testify about the absence of gunshot residue, power burns or stippling on your husband's skin?"

"Yes, I heard that."

"Did you hear them testify that there was a fair amount of separation between the two of you?"

"Yes."

"Well, if there was that separation, why did you feel the need to use the gun?"

"Because of what he said."

"What was that?"

"I'm going to kill you and make it look like a suicide. Just like I did with Hammy."

"Who is Hammy?"

"Our daughter."

"Repeat that. What did John say about Hammy just before you shot him?"

"That he was going to kill me and make it look like a suicide just like he did with Hammy."

"What did that mean to you?"

"That he killed Hammy, our daughter, and made it look like a suicide."

Thaddeus went to counsel table and returned with a handwritten note.

"Mark, please," he said to the clerk, who affixed an evidence label to the exhibit and announced it was *Defendant's Exhibit 37.*

"I'm handing you this exhibit thirty-seven. What is it?"

"Hammy's handwriting. Suicide note. It was found at the time of her death."

"And it refers to her abuser?"

"Yes."

"Read the exhibit, please."

Angelina lifted the exhibit for all to see. Just like Thaddeus had coached her. "'Don't play like you don't know, mother. I'm doing it because of you. You play ignorant about his sexual abuse but any fool could see. Fuck you both. I hate you and hope this kills you. Goodbye.'"

"Where did that come from?"

"It was pinned with a brooch to my daughter when she was found dead."

"Ostensibly was dead by suicide?"

"That's what we all believed. Until John told me that he was going to kill me and make it look like a suicide just like he did with Hammy."

"That would be Hamilton Steinmar, you daughter."

"Yes. He killed her. He admitted it and all I saw was red. At that exact moment the gun went off. I don't even remember pulling the trigger. I was stunned by his confession. I was in shock. And I flew into a rage, I'm sure of it."

"Did you lose control?"

"Wouldn't you, if your spouse had been sexually abusing your child then admitted killing her?"

Thaddeus made no attempt to respond. It was rhetorical, of course, and he let it hang there in the air for the jury to consider. He looked at them out the corner of his eye. Many were making notes. He crossed back to counsel table and fiddled with his tablet. He wanted the response to soak in. It didn't mean a not guilty verdict was coming. But it could mean manslaughter. Heat-of-the-moment. A gun fired in the heat of the murder. That wasn't first-degree murder. That was manslaughter. And people weren't put to death for manslaughter. Ever.

He turned back to his client. "Describe your emotional state when you pulled the trigger."

"I didn't have an emotional state. I was a blank."

"Were you angry?"

"Of course."

"Were you enraged?"

"Of course. And shocked. I had never even suspected."

"How do you explain the note in your daughter's handwriting?"

"The note was from before. It was from the first time she tried. He told me that."

"He told you that before you shot him?"

"Uh-huh, yes. He found Hammy after she took some pills and tried suicide the first time. Evidently he found her note too and hid it. He saved it for when he would really need it."

"This sounds like something out of a movie."

"Not a very good movie, then, because I don't believe it myself. I mean, I never would have believed anyone could be so conniving. He said he saved the note. But John was sick. He was out of control."

"Objection," shouted Moroney. "She has no expertise with which to judge his mental state."

"Might be true," said Judge Gerhardt, "but she can tell what she saw. She says he was out of control, which isn't a medical opinion. It's lay testimony and I'm going to allow it. Overruled."

"You said he was out of control?"

"He was. And when he said he was going to kill me and make it look like a suicide, I had no doubt. At that very instant I believed I was in immediate danger of dying."

"You believed he was coming after the gun to kill you with it."

"Of course I did. He just said he killed my little girl. If he would kill her, he would kill me, who he was already in a rage about."

Thaddeus rattled the papers on the podium. By now everyone on the jury was making notes. And he was enervated to see that. He had just made self-defense: She was in fear for her own life, believed her own death was imminent.

At long last, he had his defense.

Jimmy Moroney wasted no time going after her on cross. With his cool reserve he stood up from counsel table and crossed to the podium. There might have been a hint of a swagger of someone holding a winning bet, but no one on the jury took note. He positioned his papers on the podium and then extended his hand, his index finger, accusingly at Angelina.

"You expect this jury of good and smart people to believe that your husband would provide a suicide note that clearly implicated him in molesting your daughter?"

"Yes."

"Why would he do that?" asked Jimmy, ignoring, in the passion of the moment, the cardinal rule of cross-examination: that the questioner never asks a "why" question to which he or she doesn't already know the answer.

"Because he knew it would go to the grand jury."

"I'm afraid I don't understand that."

Angelina sighed. She was going to have to explain to this man. *Did he really not get it?* Thought Thaddeus.

"He knew the note would go to the grand jury. Grand jury stuff is secret. He knew the note would never see the light of day."

"But he knew it implicated him. It could make the grand jury indict him," Jimmy argued.

"It was ambiguous, the note was ambiguous. It doesn't give his name. He knew that. He knew he could be viewed as a suspect, but not indicted. John was a lot of things, but he was a brilliant prosecutor and he knew how grand juries worked. They wouldn't indict him just over the note and he was sure of that. So he produced it. Understand now?"

Jimmy stared at the witness. He did, in fact, understand. But too late. Now he had allowed her to explain what would otherwise have been good argument in his closing argument. Now he had given her a club to use against him. His face said it all: crestfallen and unsmiling. He rattled the papers on the podium, evidently lost in thought as to how to proceed. His cross-examination had just had the air let out of it. Gone.

He tried a different approach. "Now, you expect this jury to believe he confessed to you that he murdered his own daughter?"

"Did you read her suicide note? My own daughter said he was molesting her. That's worse than killing her, to some of us. So if he would molest her, he would kill her, too. Don't you see that?"

"Madam, I'm asking the questions here," Jimmy responded.

"You're not asking the right questions," Angelina shot back, and Thaddeus saw three jurors smile. She had made it up to at least three of them. Fantastic, he thought, just one would be enough to get a hung jury. Now she maybe had three. Nine more and she was not guilty. Of anything. Thaddeus clasped his hands behind his head and looked up at the ceiling. It was brighter, lighter, than before.

But Jimmy wasn't going to go away easily.

"So you tell us you shot him in a rage?"

"I didn't say that. I said my mind went blank."

"Are you saying you weren't in a rage?"

"He had just told me he murdered my precious baby. I suppose there was rage. But it was like I was unconscious one second and in the next second realized he was coming for me. I had to defend myself."

"So you shot him."

"I did. I shot him."

"You meant to kill him?"

"I meant to stop him. I must admit, I was angry enough to kill him, but killing wasn't in my mind. I only wanted to keep from being killed."

Thaddeus looked back down at the table but inside he was

glowing. She had just made manslaughter with "angry enough to kill him," and then trumped her own card with "keep from being killed," because that was the language of self-defense. She had listened well around the dinner table all those years with John. She definitely knew the language of self-defense and manslaughter.

Which was the moment when he realized. She hadn't learned that around John Steinmar's table at all. Thaddeus snuck a look at the judge. Suddenly he knew where her words were coming from. Of course. Steinmar was a prosecutor; he wouldn't be using the words of self-defense and manslaughter. No, the words came from elsewhere, from a schooled resource, someone bright and intelligent. From someone who even now wouldn't look him in the eye, someone who was evidently busy with note-taking, eyes downcast to the tablet before him. Son of a bitch. He did love her. He was fighting for her. He was feeding her her lines.

"So you shot him."

"I held up the pistol to show him, warn him to stop."

"Then you shot him."

"He lunged at me. Next thing I know the gun goes off."

"Testimony from CSI indicates he was on his knees."

"Yes, and lunging at me. Did I have to wait for him to get his hands around my throat again? Is that what you're saying?"

"Madam," Moroney replied stonily, "I am asking the questions here."

"But you don't hear my answers. He was going to kill me. I know John."

"And then you told the police you had his bite marks all over you."

"I did."

"So you lied."

"I did."

"Are you lying now?"

"No."

"How do we know that?"

"How do you know I am?"

"Because you did before."

"Art Handelman was trying to put words in my mouth to make it look like I killed John because I was mad at him. And he gave me Miranda but then wouldn't shut up even when I wanted him to."

"According to the recording, you never asked him to stop asking questions."

"No, I told him that before he started recording. I told him when he first came in that I wanted to talk to a lawyer. One thing I knew from all those years with John was to never talk to the police without a lawyer."

"How do we know you asked him not to ask you questions?"

"How do you know I didn't?"

"Please answer the question."

"Your Honor," said Thaddeus, rising to his feet, "this is argument. Counsel is arguing with the witness, which is improper. Defense objects."

Judge Gerhardt nodded. "The court agrees. Move on, Counsel. Objection sustained."

"Judge," said Moroney, turning to face the judge, "I'm trying to understand how we know she's not lying now. It's a fair question."

"Counsel, I've known this witness for many years. She's come into my court hundreds of times and testified on child abuse cases. One thing I know is that she's a believable witness. She tells the truth and doesn't embellish. Your arguing with her isn't going to change that. Now move along, please."

The whole speech was improper but was delivered in the nicest way, without any indication the judge was taking sides. Moroney had sought out the confrontation and the judge had responded to him. Thaddeus saw how slick it had been handled, and he was impressed.

If not a little sorry for the prosecutor. Moroney was an all right guy but he was going to lose this case. There was too much working against him now and he was clueless. Even worse for him, the state couldn't appeal a Not Guilty verdict. The court of appeals would never read about the judge's improper comments. It was a done deal. Thaddeus never raised his eyes from his papers and notes as all this went through his mind. To anyone watching him, he appeared to be oblivious to the court's comments. They were what they were, his face said.

Moroney sallied forth again.

"How do we know you asked him not to ask you questions?"

She threw up her hands. "Ask him, why don't you?"

"Judge," began Moroney.

"Counsel, she's answered your question twice now. And I've asked you nicely to move on to something else. Now please move along."

Moroney scooped up his papers from the podium and abruptly took his seat at counsel table. His neck was red and he was whispering furiously at Art Handelman. Handelman whispered back.

Then Moroney looked up. "That's all I have, Your Honor."

"Counsel," said the judge to Thaddeus, does the defense have any other witnesses?"

"We do, Your Honor. One more."

"Please continue."

"Defense calls Art Handelman as an adverse witness."

Calling him as adverse meant Thaddeus was going to be able to lead the witness. It was an age-old tactic to be taken with non-friendly witnesses. *Non-friendly*, thought Thaddeus, *but vital*.

Art Handelman retook the stand. He brushed a hand back over his silvery gray hair and nodded when Thaddeus asked if he understood he was still under oath from the last time he testified. "I understand," he added.

"Good. Now Mrs. Steinmar testified that when you first made contact with her she asked you to allow her to get a lawyer before speaking with you?"

"Uh, her exact words were, 'Art, I've known you forever. But I know my rights and I want a lawyer before I answer any questions. A terrible thing has happened here and I want a lawyer.'"

Thaddeus was astounded. The witness had actually corroborated what Angelina had told the jury! He'd never had this happen before, where a police officer established that a witness was telling the truth.

"Did she appear to be afraid of you?"

Handelman appeared thoughtful. "She appeared to understand I wasn't there to help her. She knew I was on official police business when I went in to talk to her."

"Was she scared?"

"Like I said before, her hands were shaking so bad she couldn't light her cigarette. I had to do it for her."

"Was that before or after she said she wanted a lawyer?"

"Before. Then I asked her for a statement and she said she wanted a lawyer."

"So you of course honored her request and allowed her to get a lawyer."

"No, I didn't."

"Really. What did you do instead?"

"I took out my recorder and Mirandized her. Then I started asking her questions."

"Did you hear her testify she lied to you about the bite marks because she was scared of you?"

"I did."

"Did you hear her say, 'He wasn't believing me when I told him what happened. So I embellished. I added the bite part.' Did you hear that?"

"I did."

"Did you know she was lying to you?"

"I hadn't really formed an opinion."

"But you wouldn't have been surprised."

"No."

"Because lots of people lie to you, don't they?"

"Yes, they do."

"Why is that, do you suppose? Why do people lie to you?"

"Because they're scared. It's human nature."

"Was Angelina scared?"

"Like I said, she couldn't light her own cigarette."

"Anything else?"

"Her voice was shaky, she mentioned she might have to run in and throw up. She was terrified, you want my honest take on it."

"That's what I want. Your honest take."

"I knew she was terrified. She'd been around me for years and she knew I was very good at catching bad guys."

"So she lied. How well do you know Angelina?"

"Like I said, I've been to her house socially many times."

"Are you a good judge of character?"

"I like to think so."

"Judge her character."

He asked because he had a hunch. If he were right, the case was over.

"I think she's telling the truth in court. I know she is."

Thaddeus stopped. Now he knew. Handelman was the judge's go-to guy. He would say whatever the judge wanted him to say. Payback would come later—another case, another time, his own ass would be on the line and the judge would go to bat for him. But right now it was his turn to pay his dues. And he just had.

"But yet you're prosecuting her."

"I would prosecute anyone who shot and killed a district attorney. Goes with the job."

"So you prosecuted her even though she might have been telling the truth about what happened?"

"We never actually got that far that morning."

"Meaning?"

"At one point she held up a hand and I paused the tape. She wanted to call Shep Aberdeen. I waited while she called him. Shep told her to shut up and stop cooperating. She took his advice and I never got to hear the rest of what happened from her viewpoint. If I had I might never have prosecuted her. That simple."

Thaddeus stopped. He had nursed this thing along as far as he dared to go. Any further and it would begin to look like the Chief DA Investigator was in bed with him. Right now it looked like he was a man committed to telling the truth. But another step, especially a big step, and it was going to begin to stink. So he stopped.

"Your Honor, I believe that's all I have."

"Very well. Counsel, do you wish to examine?"

Jimmy Moroney, it would be said in the offices and taverns and restaurants around town, had never looked more morose and sad than he did just then.

He slowly lifted his eyes. The corners of his mouth were drooped sorrowfully. The earlier swagger in his voice had all but dissipated when he looked at Judge Gerhardt and said, simply, "State has no questions."

"Very well, Mr. Handelman, you may step down. Defense may call its next witness."

"Your Honor," said Thaddeus from his chair, "the defense rests."

FORTY-NINE

They broke for lunch and returned at one o'clock for closing arguments.

The state's argument was uninspired and sonorous and melancholy. Jimmy Moroney drifted somewhere between asking for the death penalty and asking for a finding of voluntary manslaughter—it was never clear exactly how he saw the facts stack up. His close took less than fifteen minutes, all told.

Thaddeus took even less time. He explained the difference between manslaughter and a justified killing, or self-defense. The jurors paid particular attention to his explanation of "imminent threat of great bodily harm or death," and made special note of how he applied that particular law to the facts of the shooting. Clearly she had been frightened for her life—if you believed her, as the judge did. Clearly she had told a whopper because the chief investigator unfairly

299

questioned her even after she had asked for a lawyer—if you believed the chief investigator himself. In other words, Thaddeus had been handed a case where both the judge and the chief investigator had vouched for the defendant. In his closing summary he was careful not to be too bold, too confident. He thanked the jury for their service and told them he expected them to return with a finding of Not Guilty of this justified homicide.

Both attorneys stared dumbly ahead while the judge read his jury instructions to the jury. Angelina fought down a smile and tried not to squirm in her chair, but her satisfaction with Thaddeus' work with the jury and presentation of her case was at its highest point. She loved, loved, loved him, as she put it to Christine during one court recess. Christine relayed all this to Thaddeus, who brushed it away. He had long ago lost control over the outcome of the case when the court had suddenly vouched for her reputation for honesty, followed by the chief investigator doing the same. It was out of his hands. A power greater than him had stepped up to the plate and ripped an in-the-park home run. It was all in the park, inside the rules, done to look fair and reasonable. Nothing went out of the park, nothing that could be traced back to anyone.

FIFTY

The jury deliberated until 4:40 p.m. before returning with its Not Guilty verdict.

Bedlam broke out among the press. Thaddeus and Christine went into the judge's chambers and a deputy led them down the back stairs of the courthouse. They went around the block and made it up to their office without being seen. Christine locked the door, Thaddeus made two cups of coffee, and they retired to his office.

Later they would hear that Angelina had answered questions from two TV crews and hung around for over an hour after the verdict. She was alternately crying and laughing. Crying, she explained, over the destruction of her family, happy that now she could begin rebuilding her life.

They talked for an hour while they waited for the crowd to clear.

The phones were ringing off the hook but going straight to voicemail. Another coffee and a cigar for each of them—a new/old routine—and they were finally out of things to say. She returned to her office and straightened her desk. He called Katy and gave her the news, and the day ended.

He drove up to the Flagstaff Medical Center to give Shep the good news, only to find he had been discharged. He had gone home, where, the nurse explained, he would probably make a full recovery. Speech therapy every day, physical therapy three times a week, and, best of all, his mind was unaffected by the stroke. He would be back in the saddle within a few months, she guessed.

He belongs in the saddle, he thought about Shep when he pulled into his own driveway that night. He tossed a look at Coco and Charlie in their corral, burning through hay and oats. He, himself, didn't belong in a saddle, not one of those saddles, anyway. He determined right then and there to get rid of the two of them but immediately reversed himself. Like him, they would die of old age on a ranch with lots of good food and shelter from the storms.

At least that was his prayer for them all as he went inside.

FIFTY-ONE

It was a circuitous route that brought Henry Landers to Thaddeus' office a week after the Angelina Steinmar victory. Henry had read about it in the newspapers. A portion of the story talked about Thaddeus and the enormous successes he had enjoyed in various courts around the country. But the interesting part came almost at the end. That's where the story focused in on the pending Turquoise Begay trial.

Henry had been astonished. He hadn't known his great-great-granddaughter was on trial. On trial for anything, much less for the murder of Henry's great-grandson, Randy Begay.

Most of all, Henry needed to discuss the case with Thaddeus. He blew through Williams at 85 MPH on his way to the lawyer's office. The two-year-old Silverado had never charged along so fast and so well.

It was a brilliant June morning when Henry pulled off I-40 into Flagstaff. He parked in the front lot of Little America and sauntered into the restaurant. Waffles, two eggs, four sausage links, and two cups of coffee later, he was ready to look up Thaddeus. He drove uptown and pulled into the BOA lot. On the directory beside the elevator he located Thaddeus' office and rode upstairs. Christine greeted him and buzzed Thaddeus, who was surprised and happy to see his old friend.

"I read about the trial," Henry said. He was 102 years old, gnarled and deeply lined about the face and eyes, but his mind was sharp as ever. Walking seven or ten miles with the sheep every day probably helped contribute to his longevity, according to the IHS workers who kept track of such things. That, Henry laughed at them, and a steady diet of beef stew and roast beef hash out of the can.

The friends caught up and traded stories and common gossip. Henry was still living in the hogan during the winter. Now that it was summer he had moved the herd back up into the Wachuska Mountains for summer pasture. Henry's granddaughter—Katy's mother—was tending the sheep while Henry was away for the day and the coming night, when he would return to the hogan, sleep there, and make the hike back into the mountains tomorrow at first light. All was well. There was plenty of money, the truck was in good shape, and he basically had no other needs. Thaddeus questioned him for several minutes about such things, making sure the old man was well cared for by the tribe and by his meager earnings from the sale of sheep and found turquoise.

"You won the case: the district attorney's wife. She was found not guilty, thanks to you."

"I'm not sure how much of it was thanks to me," said Thaddeus. "There was a good deal of help from the judge and the police."

"Really? Why would they help her if she shot the DA?"

Thaddeus spread his hands. "White man's ways, Henry. Dark and mysterious. That's all I can say about it, probably."

"I can honor that. Now, please, tell me about my great-granddaughter, Turquoise Begay."

"Turquoise was being abused by her uncle Randy."

"Randy Begay. Son of Martha Gray Mountain. My granddaughter."

"Yes, well, Randy was no damn good. He was raping Turquoise and had been since she was ten."

"Then I'm glad she shot him. I would have if she hadn't."

"That's just it. She didn't do it."

"The lady?"

"No, Turquoise."

"No, I'm talking about the lady I saw leave there. She's the one that shot him."

Thaddeus leaned forward in his chair. "Come again? What lady are you talking about?"

"The lady on the motorcycle. She shot Randy Begay. I saw her leaving. I know this because she covered up her tracks."

Thaddeus buzzed Christine. "Come on in here, please. I need you to hear this."

Christine came right inside. She blew a lock of hair from her forehead and opened the keyboard on her tablet. "What gives?"

"Listen to what Henry has to say. Henry, would you repeat that?"

"I was coming over to see about Randy Begay. This was some time ago. Weeks or a month or two. I forget. On two times I had been to Garcia Begay's trailer. Once when Kitna died and once when Garcia was sick with TB and they thought he would die. He got over that."

"So you knew where Turquoise lived. And you were going there to see about Randy Begay. See about what?"

"I heard he was bothering Turquoise. I was going to see if he should be killed."

Christine looked at Thaddeus, who only shrugged. That's just Henry, his look said.

"Okay, what happened?"

"About two or three miles off I see someone in black clothing come down off the porch and move the motorcycle onto the highway. Then this person pulls a rag from her coat pocket and begins to dust over the tracks left by her motorcycle tires."

"Her? You knew it was a her?"

"I'm coming to that. Instead of stopping at the trailer, I decide to follow her. She goes several miles and then pulls in at the New-Nav Trading Post. She goes to make a phone call and removes her helmet and gloves. That's when I see it's a woman. I don't know her. But I know she covered her tracks. So I followed her: All the way back into Flagstaff, down the alley. She put her motorcycle under the carport and covered it. She went inside the house and so I drove around front. The news people were parked in front."

"How do we prove this?" Thaddeus asked.

"Easy. I brought you my phone camera. I have pictures of her from New-Nav and from her backyard with the motorcycle. That's why I came over. If I didn't have to give it to you I just would have called."

"You could have posted online. Saved a trip," Christine commented in her matter-of-fact way.

"No online for this old Indian," Henry laughed. "Bad medicine."

"Okay, Henry, let's take a look."

The old man passed the cell phone to Thaddeus. He immediately located the pictures. Clearly it was Angelina at the New-Nav phone booth. Clearly it was Angelina on the motorcycle leaving there. Angelina in her backyard, helmet off, covering her motorcycle. Front shot of Angelina's house, news vehicles out front. All pictures were date-stamped and time-stamped. All dates fell on the same date Randy Begay was found dead in the bedroom of Turquoise Begay.

"Amazing," Thaddeus whispered to himself. "Just amazing. You caught the shooter, Henry."

"I think I did," said Henry. "She saved me a bullet."

"Did you have your rifle with you?"

"Always. In its window mount. Never leave home without it."

"My kind of guy," Christine chuckled and tapped the old man's booted foot.

"You like guns too?" Henry asked.

Christine nodded violently. "Love, love, love them."

"I shoot bad guys," said Henry. "Just ask Thaddeus."

"I do too," said Christine, not missing a beat. "So we're even. So does he," she said and inclined her head toward Thaddeus. He didn't acknowledge her.

"These pictures are going to create enough reasonable doubt for me to walk Turquoise out."

"Meaning?"

Thaddeus looked at the old man and smiled. "Meaning you've just handed me reasonable doubt, Henry. Chris, let's get these printed and blown up thirty-by-forty."

"I'm on it," she said. She took the camera and left.

"Can I give you another phone? We have a few spares around here."

"Yes, please."

Thaddeus rummaged around through his two top drawers until he found what he was looking for.

"Here we go. AT&T unlimited minutes. Don't worry about the billing, I've got it covered."

He passed the phone to the old man.

"It will tell me its number inside?"

"It will. Look under settings."

"I know that. When you get as old as me, you study things. I know everything about these cell phones."

"Then you know where to find the number."

"I know that."

"I know you do."

Henry stayed around, later having lunch with Thaddeus, until about two o'clock, when it was time to drive back west to the hogan. They shook hands in the parking lot and the old man climbed into his Chevy.

Thaddeus waved from behind as Henry pulled out of the exit driveway and disappeared south, headed for the freeway entrance.

FIFTY-TWO

They resumed trial in *State v. Turquoise Begay* on June 15.

Turquoise attended court in the uniform Katy had selected for her: gray pleated skirt, white blouse and red cross tie, navy blazer with red pocket square, gold buttons. A chic turquoise necklace was the only jewelry she wore, compliments of Thaddeus, by way of Katy, who found it in Phoenix on 24th Street and Camelback. "Your namesake," Katy told her. "Your amulet. Your protector from Earth Mother. Wear it in peace and prosperity."

Judge Trautman welcomed the jury back. He acknowledged on the record the presence of the Honorable Irl Kampbell, retired judge of the Arizona Court of Appeals. He gave the new prosecutor the opportunity to introduce himself. He was new since Wrasslin had been replaced when Thaddeus had threatened to call her as a witness at the first day of trial. The new man's name was Peter Redwash and he was fresh out of prosecutor's school and this was his first felony trial. Why had Wrasslin opted for such a young man of little experience to replace her? Thaddeus knew the answer to that as soon as he laid eyes: Navajo. The young prosecutor was Navajo and maybe ten years older than the defendant Turquoise. So they were both youthful, both of Navajo descent, and both attractive enough to pose a difficult choice for a jury's natural inclination to prefer the most attractive people in the courtroom. A good choice, thought Thaddeus.

Special Agent Stall Worthy was again seated at the prosecutor's table. He had been in charge of the investigation surrounding the murder of Randy Begay. It was his testimony that had ground the first trial to a halt when he mentioned that Turquoise had given certain statements in the presence of Roslin Russell, the DA. Thaddeus had asked to call Wrasslin at that moment for voir dire on the issue of voluntariness of the defendant's statement. Argument had erupted, the DA had refused to testify, and the court had continued the case for her to replace herself and then make herself available as a witness. Stall Worthy was dressed in the dark gray suit required of all Special Agents by FBI mandate.

The judge reminded the jury that they had gone on hiatus due to a scheduling problem for a critical witness. That witness was available now, he told them, and so trial could reconvene. He reminded counsel that Thaddeus had just asked to call Roslin Russell on *voir dire* when trial was continued last spring. Thaddeus acknowledged that and so did ADA Redwash.

"Are you ready to proceed, Counsel? Have you subpoenaed Ms. Russell for trial today?"

Thaddeus said he had, and he called Roslin Russell to the stand. She was seated and Thaddeus immediately launched into the situation and physical environment that existed when Turquoise made her statements in response to questions being asked by Special Agent Worthy.

310

"Mrs. Russell, Special Agent Worthy testified last time that my client told you that she wasn't being forced to have sex with her uncle. Do you recall him saying that?"

"Yes."

"Who was present when she made that statement?"

"I believe just me and Agent Worthy."

"You believe? Aren't you sure?"

"Counsel, I hear so many statements from so many people, it's difficult—"

"It's difficult to remember what was said?"

She shook her head. "No, I was going to say it's difficult to remember who all was present, or where, or what time of day it was, or what I was wearing, what your client had to eat for lunch that day—you get my drift."

"I do. So let me ask again. Who was present when my client supposedly made that statement?"

"My best recall is that I was there and Agent Worthy was there. No one else."

"Had she been given the Miranda warning at that time?"

"I assume so. The statement wasn't recorded, so that little detail eludes me. I know it would be our normal practice to give Miranda before ever questioning a witness. So yes, I would have to say it was given. She had been told she had the right to remain silent and have a lawyer present."

"How old was she then?"

"Fifteen. Maybe sixteen."

"Did she know what you meant when you said she had the right to have a lawyer?"

"What do you mean? I said it in English and she speaks English, so yes."

"My point is, this little girl attends reservation school and had never talked to a lawyer in her life. Probably had never seen one. So for you to be telling her she had the right to have one present, I must question whether she understood why she might want to exercise that right. My point is, her statement probably was not voluntary even though you gave Miranda to her."

She gave him a sarcastic smile. "Is there a question pending?"

"Did you ask her if she understood her rights?"

"I didn't. I assume Agent Worthy did."

"Please don't assume. Did he or didn't he, to your knowledge, ask if she understood her rights?"

"Honestly, I don't know. It's all pretty much a blur right now. Is that what you wanted to hear?"

Thaddeus nodded slowly. "If it's a blur, then yes, I needed to hear it's a blur. That's all I have, Your Honor."

Trautman peered over his glasses at ADA Redwash. "Counsel?"

"What?"

"Do you have any questions?"

"For this witness?"

"Yes, for this witness."

"I don't—I don't think so."

At which point the witness shook her head no.

"No, I don't."

At which point the jury smiled and acknowledged they had a newbie on their hands. This should be interesting, their half-smiles said.

H. Ivan Trautman told the witness she could step down, which she did, and took a seat behind the bar, in the front row, next to one of four reporters present. It wasn't a highly attended trial as the defendant was a nobody. Few spectators were there, with the exception of Katy, who was keeping a close watch over things.

The judge continued, "Counsel, you asked for *voir dire* during Agent Worthy's cross-examination by you. Did you want to conclude that cross? Or is it concluded? Why don't you tell me where we're at with that?"

"Where we are? Defendant has no other questions for Agent Worthy."

"All that just for that?" the judge remarked.

"Yes," said Thaddeus. "All that just for that. We just proved the witness didn't give that statement voluntarily so defendant moves that the last statement given by the FBI agent concerning the uncle's not sexually abusing her be stricken from the record and the jury instructed to disregard."

"I disagree. I don't think you've proven that at all, Counsel. I think you've adduced testimony that is inconclusive. The testimony will be allowed to stand. Now, are you finished in your cross-examination of Agent Worthy, yes or no?"

Thaddeus glared at the little potentate. He hated the man—no, loathed him. If there was any way he could help put Turquoise behind bars, so be it. He would help in a flash. And he had his henchman Irl Kampbell in tow just to make sure the natives didn't fight back except appropriately. Whatever the hell that meant.

"The state will call its next witness."

"State calls Dr. Kewae N. Horne, Medical Examiner of Coconino County."

Dr. Horne testified that the cause of death was gunshot wound to the head and the manner of death was homicide. There was no gunshot residue found on the decedent. Angles of entry and size of exit wound were recited. Then the doctor proved yet again that medical examiners are loathe to give precise angles of entry of bullet wounds, preferring instead, "downward angle" to "forty-five degrees," even though Thaddeus, on cross-examination tried to pin him down to an exact numerical value. Even when prodded and pushed, he refused to budge, so "downward angle," it was.

Next up came the crime scene investigator responsible for photography, scale drawing, and fingerprints/DNA. Then Thaddeus had her on cross-examination.

"Did you search the room for gunshot residue?"

"I did."

"Did you find any?"

"No."

"Did you examine the door frame?"

"Why would I do that?"

"In case the shooter used the door frame to steady his aim."

"It wasn't my impression that the shooter used the door frame to steady her aim."

"You use the pronoun 'her.' Are you sure the shooter was a woman?"

"No."

"Then why use 'her'?"

"Because a female is on trial. I believe she is guilty."

"Whoa! You believe she is guilty? Is that how you approach your job as a scientist whose job is to find scientific facts at a crime scene?"

The CSI smiled. "Are you saying I'm not allowed to have an opinion just because I'm a scientist doing a scientific job?"

"No, I'm asking whether you approached your job with a preconceived notion of guilt."

"I would never do that."

"Thank you."

Thaddeus turned and retrieved a bottle of water from counsel table before resuming. An idea had formed in his mind while he had traded barbs with the witness. He took a swig of water and swallowed hard.

"Ms. Evans, if I told you I had hired a firearms expert who did, in fact, examine the door frame for gunshot residue, would you be surprised?"

It was a setup. It didn't matter whether she was surprised or not.

He was simply laying foundation.

"No, I wouldn't be surprised. You're entitled to spend your money however you see fit."

"And if I told you my expert found gunshot residue on the door frame would that surprise you?"

"No." Less enthusiastic now.

"And if I told you that gunshot residue was found at a height of five feet ten inches, would that surprise you?"

"Maybe."

"Why would that be?"

"Because your client, according to the reports, is short. About five-two, I believe. It would be very unusual for her to have had the gun at five feet nine inches when she fired. I can only conclude that the residue was from another gunshot."

"And you can also conclude that someone much taller than my client fired the shot that killed Randy Begay, yes?"

"I could make that conclusion, yes."

"In fact, that conclusion would be just as valid as the one you mentioned, correct?"

"Correct."

"Which raises a great deal of doubt about the shooter's identity, correct?"

Thaddeus waited for the DA to explode with a very justified objection to the question.

However...there was no objection. The new ADA was busy making notes as the cross progressed. Evidently he saw nothing wrong with the argumentative and conclusory nature of the question.

"It would raise doubt, yes," said the witness, once it was clear the ADA wasn't going to jump in with an objection to save her.

"In fact, it would raise a reasonable doubt, wouldn't it?"

Again, no objection.

Then the Special Agent leaned and whispered in Mr. Redwash's ear. Whereupon the young DA jumped to his feet and shouted, "Objection!"

"Basis?" said Judge Trautman.

"Attempts to invade the province of the jury."

"Yes, something like that," said Trautman. "Sustained. Counsel, you know better."

"That is all I have for this witness," Thaddeus replied.

He took his seat, happy beyond all hope with the help this witness had been. She was just a sounding board for him to prove his points through a series of questions. Cross-examination 101.

The young DA's ears burned bright red even through his brown skin.

He had been schooled.

Another CSI testified about the evidence tagged and bagged at the scene, the chain of evidence underlying admission of the rifle, the bullet, and other items taken from the room. And again, Thaddeus went over the same gunshot residue questions and elicited pretty much the same answers as before. He was rubbing it in, making sure no one on the jury had missed a bit of it.

Recess was taken for the night.

FIFTY-THREE

Tuesday dawned dark and gloomy, heavy rain starting at six o'clock, Katy muttering for Thaddeus to make sure Sarai's window was closed and to please be quiet when he dressed. Thaddeus kissing her neck and cheek and copping a feel of a bare breast before his hand was roughly pushed away and her smiling face said No.

On the drive into town, Turquoise at his side, they discussed the business of rap music. Turquoise didn't understand how the hot rappers managed to live in mansions and drive Ferraris and jet around the world on their own private jets. She didn't understand the economics and Thaddeus tried his best to explain it to her. She asked how much money he thought they earned and he managed a wild guesstimate. She then allowed that she might like to take up rap music as an artist and be the first female Native American rap goddess—her

317

words. He laughed and pulled through Starbucks. Katy ordered a lemon bread and tea; Thaddeus had his usual venti bold and sausage muffin.

The state rested its case right out of the gate.

Thaddeus suddenly needed a witness. He had waiting in the wings Lance Myer-Rothstein.

"Dr. Myer-Rothstein," he began, "you are available for consultation in homicide cases, including shooting scene reconstruction, crime scene evidence evaluation, bloodstain pattern analysis, and crime scene reconstruction, correct?"

"That is correct."

Thaddeus proceeded to take the witness through his credentials, papers, notable trials and testimony, and his workup in the Turquoise Begay case. He testified about the characteristics of the .30-.30 caliber bullet, its impact mechanics, and what happened with the single round fired in this case. The testimony took the better part of an hour, at which time Judge Trautman sent the jury out on its first recess of the day.

They resumed fifteen minutes later.

"Now, Dr. Myer-Rothstein. You also examined the scene of the shooting, did you not?"

"I did."

"When was that?"

He gave the date, several months ago, and the jury made its notes. Thaddeus was pleased to see that they had been attentive and following right along on all of the expert's testimony. There had been no objections and the witness was easily qualified as an expert who would be allowed to give opinion testimony within his field of expertise. Which was very broad, it turned out.

"What did you do at the scene?"

"Examined the damage the bullet made to the trailer wall. Examined the carpet in the room for any gunshot residue, unburnt powder, lead riflings, things of that nature."

"How about the walls? Examine those?"

"I did. And I examined the door frame."

"Describe that, please."

"Well, the room is ten by ten with a single doorway. The frame of the door is metal and wood. It occurred to me from the angle of entry of the bullet and the distance from which the bullet had to have been fired to leave no GSR, that the shooter might very well have steadied the shot by using the door frame to press against with the gun."

"What did you learn?"

"I learned to rely on my instincts. I had learned that years ago. This was just a refresher."

"Meaning what?"

"I found gunshot residue on the door frame."

"Describe that."

"At the height of five feet nine inches, right side of door frame as one looks into the room, there was a very distinct shadow of gunshot residue some three inches by one-point-five inches. Presumably the smaller width measurement would have been as large as three inches too, but there wasn't enough doorframe depth-wise to accommodate much more than about an inch and a half. The walls are very thin in that trailer. It's a nineteen seventy-six Trailmaster Luxottica, by the way. Made in Iowa and sold out of Utah."

"You learned those facts about the house trailer itself?"

"I try to be very thorough."

"I see that. Were you able to connect the gunshot residue from the door to the rifle that fired the shot that killed Randy Begay?"

"I was."

"How so?"

"The powder characteristics were exactly the same."

"Meaning?"

"Meaning the same material found in the cartridge casing was found on the door frame. Same shot."

"How certain are you of that, one to ten?"

"Eleven."

"Fair enough. Now does the fact that the gunshot residue was found on the right side of the frame as one looks into the room—does that fact tell you anything in your role as a crime scene investigator and firearms expert?"

"Yes."

"Tell us what that tells you."

"Simple. The shooter was right-handed. Or at least shot right-handed."

"So our shooter is right-handed and his eye level is at five feet nine."

"Yes."

"Did you compare that shooter's characteristics to those of Turquoise Begay?"

"I did."

"What did you do?"

"Made her stand against the wall in your library and measured her height."

"And you found her to be?"

"Five-two."

"Five feet two inches?"

"Correct."

"Anything else?"

"Yes, I took a handwriting sample from her."

"Why handwriting sample? You're definitely not a handwriting expert."

"I wanted to see which hand she wrote with. That would tell me which hand she would shoot with."

"Which hand did she write with?"

"Left hand."

"Which told you what about how she would shoot a rifle?"

"That she would shoot left-handed. If she had shot the gun then I would have found the gunshot residue on the left side of the door frame approximately nine inches lower than actual."

"Do you have an opinion whether she shot the bullet that killed Randy Begay?"

"There's no way she could have fired that round. Unless she stood on a fairly tall stool and shot with the wrong hand. But how much sense does that make, really?"

"Thank you, Dr. Myer-Rothstein. I believe that's all I have."

Peter Redwash undertook cross-examination of the expert. Peter was a genuinely nice and polite young man, but he was clearly outmatched from the start. Dr. Myer-Rothstein was polite, charming, and never uttered an angry or defensive word. Peter kept saying, "Help me understand" this or that, and, with the open-ended question before him, Dr. Myer-Rothstein ran a learning academy for the rest of the morning. Realizing, finally, that his sole accomplishment had been to allow the expert the opportunity to restate all his opinions yet again, Peter sat down. "Nothing further," he told the judge with a flourish as if he had just shot a marauding lion. In truth, he was no nearer a conviction than he had been when the trial began.

Following the afternoon recess, Thaddeus announced that he was calling the defense's final witness.

Henry Landers entered the courtroom with no small trepidation, looked about, and saw that it was safe enough even though it was a white man's court—bane of the Native American elders. He took the witness stand and removed his Stetson almost at the same moment the bailiff was asking him to do just that. He placed the sweat-stained hat at his feet and looked curiously at the jury. Satisfied they were just people like him, he looked and fixed his gaze on Thaddeus—the man responsible for putting him in this uncomfortable setting.

"Tell us your name, please."

"Henry Begay Landers."

"And you know who I am?"

"You're Thaddeus Murfee."

"Where do you live?"

"Wachuska Mountains on the Navajo Reservation."

"Who do you live there with?"

"Two dogs and two hundred fifty-three Churro sheep."

"What is your business?"

"Sheep."

"Do you sell sheep?"

"I make wool. I sell wool."

"Do you sell sheep for food?"

"Not at all. I wouldn't do that."

"You're partial to your sheep."

"I am to them, they are to me."

"Now Mr. Landers—"

"Henry."

"Henry. You have a rather large family, I understand. Would you tell us about that?"

"I am over one hundred years old. My maternal clan is Towering House and my paternal clan is Tall Man Walking."

"And you have many offspring."

"Sons, daughters, grandchildren, great-grandchildren, great-great-grandchildren. Who can keep track?"

"So you don't know all of them?"

"Maybe. I don't know."

"Did you have a great-grandson named Randy Begay?"

"Yes."

"And is your great-great-granddaughter my client, Turquoise Begay?"

"Yes."

"Do you remember the day Randy Begay was shot?"

"I remember the day. I was there."

"You were there when he was shot?"

"I was there after. I tried to go inside but the police wouldn't let me park."

"So you never were at the scene of the shooting?"

"No. They wouldn't let me."

"Why were you in that part of the reservation?"

Henry looked at the judge. He appeared busy with other things, eyes downcast, writing.

"I went there to shoot Randy Begay."

The judge's head snapped up.

"You were there to shoot Randy Begay why?"

"He was sexually assaulting Turquoise, his niece."

"You were going to kill him?"

"Of course. Her father wouldn't do it because it was his brother. So I was coming to do it."

"Did you shoot him?"

"No, he was already shot when I came."

"Who shot him, if you know?"

"I saw a lady leaving the trailer. A lady on a motorcycle. Maybe she shot him."

"But you don't know that?"

"No."

"Tell us what you saw her do."

"She came down off the porch. She walked to her motorcycle. She rode the motorcycle onto the road and got off. She took a rag from her pocket and began dusting her motorcycle track in the sand."

"How do you know she was dusting her track?"

"Because she was dusting where her bike came from. Same thing."

"So you figured—what did you figure?"

"I figured she was hiding something. So I followed her."

"You were in your truck?"

"Yes."

"Did you have your gun with you?"

"Yes. I was going to shoot Randy with my gun."

"So you followed her. Where did you go?"

"Ten minutes up the road is New-Nav Trading Post. She turned in; I turned in and went to the gas pumps. She went to the phone."

"What was she wearing?"

"Pants, leather coat, helmet, gloves."

"What did she do at the phone?"

"Went inside, closed the door, removed her gloves, talked into the phone."

"Then what happened?"

"She came out and got back on the motorcycle and rode home."

"Home where?"

"Flagstaff. I have a picture of the motorcycle."

"Let me show you several pictures."

Thaddeus then walked Henry through the photographs he had taken with his phone. Now they were blown up with foam backs and propped up in front of the jury. One by one they went over them—Who, What, When, Where—and one by one they were admitted into evidence.

Then Thaddeus continued with the chronology.

"After she parked the motorcycle and covered it up, she went into the house?"

"Yes. Like I said, I went around front and took the pictures of the TV boys and their trucks."

"Anything else?"

"Yes. I found out her name."

"How did you do that?"

"I looked at a police report you showed me. It had her address. I matched it to her name. I went back and checked the address. It was her."

"Who?"

"Angelina Steinmar."

More loose ends were tied up. Cross-examination by the ADA was half-hearted and really could produce nothing. In the end, Henry saw what he saw and did what he did and he was unflappable. His matter-of-fact manner put the jury nearly to sleep, but it didn't matter.

Thaddeus rested the defense case.

Closing arguments could begin. First there would be a thirty-minute recess.

Thaddeus and Turquoise stood while the jury filed out. Christine had already headed downstairs for a cigarette. She had left him a single sheet of paper with the six points she would like to see him cover in closing. He looked them over and had to agree. She was spot on.

As they stood waiting for the last member of the jury to leave, Turquoise reached to her side and took Thaddeus' hand in hers. "Thank you," she whispered. He caught a glimpse of her eyes brimming with tears. It had finally hit home. The chances were very good she wasn't going to end up in jail.

"Worst part," she said, "my father didn't even come. He just didn't care."

Thaddeus could only nod. He didn't want to express what he was thinking. It was much, much worse, overall, and he would never tell the girl how he really felt about Garcia Begay. Never.

FIFTY-FOUR

Years earlier in Orbit, Illinois, Thaddeus had told a jury in closing argument that "sometimes you eat the bear and sometimes the bear eats you." Not a very original saying, he'd had to admit, but he thought it made a very valid point, meaning that sometimes bad things just happen. No one's at fault, they just happen. He had won that little trial, but it wasn't dependent on his old, homey saying about bears. Because at the moment he said, "bear eats you," the jury, as one, had looked at him with a look that said they hadn't the foggiest idea what in the hell he was talking about. Sometimes that just happens when we're talking to juries, he had told Ilene that night. Sometimes they don't get it. And when they don't get it, it's because I didn't get it either.

Turquoise was found not guilty and was placed permanently with Thaddeus and Katy, her foster parents. By now Turquoise was almost

326

seventeen years old and was ready to move on from her life with Garcia Begay, the father that had abandoned her from her tenth birthday on. So, with her new foster parents, Turquoise returned to the trailer to gather her things.

It was mid-July but cool, at least coming across Flagstaff and dropping four thousand feet to the reservation. At reservation level it was considerably warmer. Thaddeus had everyone roll up the windows and he switched on the air. After a few miles the F250 was cooled off and everyone felt much better. So Katy began singing an old Navajo lullaby and soon Turquoise had joined in. Thaddeus watched the young woman in the rearview mirror as she sang along and began wiping her eyes. The mother she had known long, long ago had sung her that song but then the music had died with her. After that there had been only silence, until now.

"I'm crying because I'm happy," she said into the mirror when she realized he was staring. He only nodded and kept driving. It was a trespass into her privacy, his staring, and he regretted it.

At the trailer, Thaddeus went to the bedroom where Turquoise had slept with Randy. Thaddeus meant to give her support while she packed the last remaining articles she had come to claim for the afterlife. Garcia was nowhere to be found, of course, and no one commented.

As they passed down the hallway into Turquoise's room, Katy ducked into the bathroom. She closed the door behind her. Turquoise and Thaddeus were emptying drawers when Turquoise suddenly paused. "Damn," she said, "there's never toilet paper in there. Garcia says it's a waste of money. He uses napkins he steals from McDonald's."

She headed for the bathroom to help and at that moment Katy opened the door. Thaddeus heard them speak briefly, and then Turquoise returned to the room.

"Funny," she mused as she resumed packing. "She knew where it was."

"Knew where what was?"

"Knew where Garcia kept the napkins."

"What do you mean?"

"He hides them in a drawer. Away from Randy. Randy wasted them so Garcia hid them. I was afraid Katy was in there without any way to—you know."

"No way to wipe."

"Exactly."

"So what happened?"

"She went right to them. She knew where they were hidden. That's all."

He thought nothing about it. She thought nothing about it.

Soon the Tide and Seagram's boxes were topped off with the last of her belongings. They loaded up the back seat, leaving room for Turquoise to fit in wearing a seatbelt.

Driving back to Flagstaff, it came to him. It was time to eat the bear.

She knew where the napkins were hidden. Without having to ask.

She had been there before? But in the bathroom?

"Katy," he said, "how did you know about the napkins in the bathroom?"

Her tone was icy. She looked angry.

"Don't ask," she ordered.

"You've been there before."

"Drive," she said, eyes straight ahead, sunglasses absorbing the glare and shielding her privacy. "Just drive."

THE END

ABOUT THE AUTHOR

John Ellsworth was born in Phoenix and practiced law in Flagstaff, surrounded by Indian reservations and Navajo, Hualapai, Havasupai, Apache, and Hopi peoples and, oftentimes, their legal cases.

For thirty years John defended criminal clients across the United States. He has defended cases ranging from shoplifting to First Degree Murder to RICO to Tax Evasion, and has gone to jury trial on hundreds. His first book, *The Defendants*, was published in January, 2014. John is presently at work on his eleventh legal thriller, which, it is hoped, will be published before Christmas 2015.

Reception to John's books has been phenomenal; more than 400,000 have been downloaded in 18 months. All are Amazon best-sellers.

John Ellsworth lives in Arizona in the mountains and in Mexico on the Pacific Ocean. He rescues guinea pigs and plays classical guitar when he's not inventing tales on his MacBook.

AFTERWORD

I make my living writing books and I'm very happy about that. The practice of law is difficult and will wear you out in a hurry. But because I make my living writing books, I would really like to ask your help. Book reviews are the lifeblood of what I do, and your review of my book would mean a lot to me. If you would take a moment or two and leave your review on Amazon that would be wonderful. I honestly thank you.

Last but not least, if you find errors in this book such as typos or inconsistencies, please email me. This will help me fix things that my editors and I might have overlooked and make for a better read for others. In return, by way of showing my gratitude, I will send you a free copy of the next book, with my sincere thanks.

—John Ellsworth

Made in the USA
Columbia, SC
24 May 2018